THE GREAT TRAIN

ROBBERY

The GREAT TRAIN ROBBERY

BY

MICHAEL CRICHTON

ALFRED A. KNOPF / NEW YORK

1975

THIS IS A BORZOI BOOK
PUBLISHED BY ALFRED A. KNOPF, INC.

Copyright © 1975 by Michael Crichton
All rights reserved under International and
Pan-American Copyright Conventions.
Published in the United States by
Alfred A. Knopf, Inc., New York, and
simultaneously in Canada by Random House
of Canada Limited, Toronto. Distributed
by Random House, Inc., New York.

Library of Congress Cataloging in Publication Data
Crichton, Michael, (date)   The great train robbery.
I. Title.
PZ4.C9178Gr   [PS3553.R48]   813'.5'4   74–25422
ISBN 0–394–49401–6

Manufactured in the United States of America

To Barbara Rose

Satan is glad—when I am bad,
And hopes that I—with him shall lie
In fire and chains—and dreadful pains

—VICTORIAN CHILD'S POEM, 1856

"I wanted the money."

—EDWARD PIERCE, 1856

CONTENTS

INTRODUCTION

It is difficult, after the passage of more than a century, to understand the extent to which the train robbery of 1855 shocked the sensibilities of Victorian England. At first glance, the crime hardly seems noteworthy. The sum of money stolen— £12,000 in gold bullion—was large, but not unprecedented; there had been a dozen more lucrative robberies in the same period. And the meticulous organization and planning of the crime, involving many people and extending over a year, was similarly not unusual. All major crimes at the mid-century called for a high degree of preparation and coordination.

Yet the Victorians always referred to this crime in capital letters, as The Great Train Robbery. Contemporary observers labeled it The Crime of the Century and The Most Sensational Exploit of the Modern Era. The adjectives applied to it were all strong: it was "unspeakable," "appalling," and "heinous." Even in an age given to moral overstatement, these terms suggest some profound impact upon everyday consciousness.

To understand why the Victorians were so shocked by the theft, one must understand something about the meaning of the railroads. Victorian England was the first urbanized, industrialized society on earth, and it evolved with stunning rapidity. At the time of Napoleon's defeat at Waterloo, Georgian England was a predominantly rural nation of thirteen million people. By the middle of the nineteenth century, the population had nearly doubled to twenty-four million, and half the people lived in urban centers. Victorian England was a nation of cities; the conversion from agrarian life seemed to have occurred almost overnight; indeed, the process was so swift that no one really understood it.

Victorian novelists, with the exception of Dickens and Gissing, did not write about the cities; Victorian painters for the most part did not portray urban subjects. There were conceptual problems as well—during much of the century, industrial production was viewed as a kind of particularly valuable harvest, and not as something new and unprecedented. Even the language fell behind. For most of the 1800s, "slum" meant a room of low repute, and "urbanize" meant to become urbane and genteel. There were no accepted terms to describe the growth of cities, or the decay of portions of them.

This is not to say that Victorians were unaware of the changes taking place in their society, or that these changes were not widely—and often fiercely—debated. But the processes were still too new to be readily understood. The Victorians were pioneers of the urban, industrial life that has since become commonplace throughout the Western world. And if we find their attitudes quaint, we must nonetheless recognize our debt to them.

The new Victorian cities that grew so fast glittered with more wealth than any society had ever known—and they stank of poverty as abject as any society had ever suffered. The inequities and glaring contrasts within urban centers provoked many calls for reform. Yet there was also widespread public complacency, for the fundamental assumption of Victorians was that progress—progress in the sense of better conditions for all mankind—was inevitable. We may find that complacency particularly risible today, but in the 1850s it was a reasonable attitude to adopt.

During the first half of the nineteenth century, the price of bread, meat, coffee, and tea had fallen; the price of coal was almost halved; the cost of cloth was reduced 80 percent;

and per-capita consumption of everything had increased. Criminal law had been reformed; personal liberties were better protected; Parliament was, at least to a degree, more representative; and one man in seven had the right to vote. Per-capita taxation had been reduced by half. The first blessings of technology were evident: gaslights glowed throughout the cities; steamships made the crossing to America in ten days instead of eight weeks; the new telegraph and postal service provided astonishing speed in communications.

Living conditions for all classes of Englishmen had improved. The reduced cost of food meant that everyone ate better. Factory working hours had been reduced from 74 to 60 hours a week for adults, and from 72 to 40 for children; the custom of working half-days on Saturday was increasingly prevalent. Average life span had increased five years.

There was, in short, plenty of reason to believe that society was "on the march," that things were getting better, and that they would continue to get better into the indefinite future. The very idea of the future seemed more solid to the Victorians than we can comprehend. It was possible to lease a box in the Albert Hall for 999 years, and many citizens did so.

But of all the proofs of progress, the most visible and striking were the railroads. In less than a quarter of a century, they had altered every aspect of English life and commerce. It is only a slight simplification to say that prior to 1830 there were no railroads in England. All transportation between cities was by horse-drawn coach, and such journeys were slow, unpleasant, dangerous, and expensive. Cities were consequently isolated from one another.

In September, 1830, the Liverpool & Manchester Railway opened and began the revolution. In the first year of operation, the number of railway passengers carried between these two cities was twice the number that had traveled the previous year by coach. By 1838, more than 600,000 people were carried annually on the line—a figure greater than the total population of either Liverpool or Manchester at that time.

The social impact was extraordinary. So was the howl of opposition. The new railroads were all privately financed, profit-oriented ventures, and they drew plenty of criticism.

There was opposition on aesthetic grounds; Ruskin's condemnation of the railway bridges over the Thames echoed a view widely held by his less refined contemporaries; the "aggregate disfigurement" of town and countryside was uniformly deplored. Landowners everywhere fought the railroads as deleterious to property values. And the tranquility of local towns was disrupted by the onslaught of thousands of rough, itinerant, camp-living "navvies," for in an era before dynamite and earthmovers, bridges were built, tracks were laid, and tunnels were cut by sheer human effort alone. It was also well recognized that in times of unemployment the navvies easily shifted to the ranks of urban criminals of the crudest sort.

Despite these reservations, the growth of the English railroads was swift and pervasive. By 1850, five thousand miles of track crisscrossed the nation, providing cheap and increasingly swift transportation for every citizen. Inevitably the railroads came to symbolize progress. According to the *Economist*, "In *locomotion by land* . . . our progress has been most stupendous—surpassing all previous steps since the creation of the human race. . . . In the days of Adam the average speed of travel, if Adam ever did such things, was four miles an hour; in the year 1828, or *4,000 years afterwards, it was still only ten miles,* and sensible and scientific men were ready to affirm and eager to prove that this rate could never be materially exceeded;—in 1850 it is habitually forty miles an hour, and *seventy* for those who like it."

Here was undeniable progress, and to the Victorian mind such progress implied moral as well as material advancement. According to Charles Kingsley, "The moral state of a city depends . . . on the physical state of that city; on the food, water, air, and lodging of its inhabitants." Progress in physical conditions led inevitably to the eradication of social evils and criminal behavior—which would be swept away much as the slums that housed these evils and criminals were, from time to time, swept away. It seemed a simple matter of eliminating the cause and, in due course, the effect.

From this comfortable perspective, it was absolutely astonishing to discover that "the criminal class" had found a way to prey upon progress—and indeed to carry out a crime aboard the very hallmark of progress, the railroad. The fact that the robbers also overcame the finest safes of the day only increased the consternation.

What was really so shocking about The Great Train Robbery was that it suggested, to the sober thinker, that the elimination of crime might not be an inevitable consequence of forward-marching progress. Crime could no longer be likened to the Plague, which had disappeared with changing social conditions to become a dimly remembered threat of the past. Crime was something else, and criminal behavior would not simply fade away.

A few daring commentators even had the temerity to suggest that crime was not linked to social conditions at all, but rather sprang from some other impulse. Such opinions were, to say the least, highly distasteful.

They remain distasteful to the present day. More than a century after The Great Train Robbery, and more than a decade after another spectacular English train robbery, the ordinary Western urban man still clings to the belief that crime results from poverty, injustice, and poor education. Our view of the criminal is that of a limited, abused, perhaps mentally disturbed individual who breaks the law out of a desperate need—the drug addict standing as a sort of modern archetype for this person. And indeed when it was recently reported that the majority of violent street crime in New York City was not committed by addicts, that finding was greeted with skepticism and dismay, mirroring the perplexity of our Victorian forebears a hundred years ago.

·   ·   ·

Crime became a legitimate focus for academic inquiry in the 1870s, and in succeeding years criminologists · have attacked all the old stereotypes, creating a new view of crime that has never found favor with the general public. Experts now agree on the following points:

First, crime is not a consequence of poverty. In the words of Barnes and Teeters (1949), "Most offenses are committed through greed, not need."

Second, criminals are not limited in intelligence, and it is probable that the reverse is true. Studies of prison populations show that inmates equal the general public in intelligence tests—and yet prisoners represent that fraction of lawbreakers who are caught.

Third, the vast majority of criminal activity goes unpunished. This is inherently a speculative question, but some authorities argue that only 3 to 5 percent of all crimes are reported; and of reported crimes, only 15 to 20 percent are ever "solved" in the usual sense of the word. This is true of even the most serious offenses, such as murder. Most police pathologists laugh at the idea that "murder will out."

Similarly, criminologists dispute the traditional view that "crime does not pay." As early as 1877, an American prison investigator, Richard Dugdale, concluded that "we must dispossess ourselves of the idea that crime does not pay. In reality, it does." Ten years later, the Italian criminologist Colajanni went a step further, arguing that on the whole crime pays better than honest labor. By 1949, Barnes and Teeters stated flatly, "It is primarily the moralist who still believes that crime does not pay."

Our moral attitudes toward crime account for a peculiar ambivalence toward criminal behavior itself. On the one hand, it is feared, despised, and vociferously condemned. Yet it is also secretly admired, and we are always eager to hear the details of some outstanding criminal exploit. This attitude was clearly prevalent in 1855, for The Great Train Robbery was not only shocking and appalling, but also "daring," "audacious," and "masterful."

We share with the Victorians another attitude—a belief in a "criminal class," by which we mean a subculture of professional criminals who make their living by breaking the laws of the society around them. Today we call this class "the Mafia," "the syndicate," or "the mob," and we are interested to know its code of ethics, its inverted value system, its peculiar language and patterns of behavior.

Without question, a definable subculture of professional criminals existed a hundred years ago in mid-Victorian England. Many of its features were brought to light in the trial of Burgess, Agar, and Pierce, the chief participants in The Great Train Robbery. They were all apprehended in 1856, nearly two years after the event. Their voluminous courtroom testimony is preserved, along with journalistic accounts of the day. It is from these sources that the following narrative is assembled.

M.C.
November, 1974

PART I

PREPARATIONS

May–October, 1854

CHAPTER 1

The Provocation

Forty minutes out of London, passing through the rolling green fields and cherry orchards of Kent, the morning train of the South Eastern Railway attained its maximum speed of fifty-four miles an hour. Riding the bright blue-painted engine, the driver in his red uniform could be seen standing upright in the open air, unshielded by any cab or windscreen, while at his feet the engineer crouched, shoveling coal into the glowing furnaces of the engine. Behind the chugging engine and tender were three yellow first-class coaches, followed by seven green second-class carriages; and at the very end, a gray, windowless luggage van.

As the train clattered down the track on its way to the coast, the sliding door of the luggage van opened suddenly, revealing a desperate struggle inside. The contest was most unevenly matched: a slender youth in tattered clothing, striking out against a burly, blue-uniformed railway guard. Although weaker, the youth made a good showing, landing one or two telling blows against his hulking opponent. Indeed, it was only by accident that the guard, having been knocked to his knees, should spring forward in such a way that the youth was caught unprepared and flung clear of the train through the open door, so that he landed tumbling and bouncing like a rag doll upon the ground.

The guard, gasping for breath, looked back at the fast-receding figure of the fallen youth. Then he closed the sliding door. The train sped on, its whistle shrieking. Soon it was gone round a gentle curve, and all that remained was the faint sound of the chugging engine, and the lingering drifting gray smoke that slowly settled over the tracks and the body of the motionless youth.

After a minute or two, the youth stirred. In great pain, he raised himself up on one elbow, and seemed about to rise to his feet. But his efforts were to no avail; he instantly collapsed back to the ground, gave a final convulsive shudder, and lay wholly still.

Half an hour later, an elegant black brougham coach with rich crimson wheels came down the dirt road that ran parallel to the railway tracks. The coach came to a hill, and the driver drew up his horse. A most singular gentleman emerged, fashionably dressed in a dark green velvet frock coat and high beaver hat. The gentleman climbed the hill, pressed binoculars to his eyes, and swept the length of the tracks. Immediately he fixed on the body of the prostrate youth. But the gentleman made no attempt to approach him, or to aid him in any way. On the contrary, he remained standing on the hill until he was certain the lad was dead. Only then did he turn aside, climb into his waiting coach, and drive back in the direction he had come, northward toward London.

CHAPTER 2

The Putter-Up

This singular gentleman was Edward Pierce, and for a man destined to become so notorious that Queen Victoria herself expressed a desire to meet him—or, barring that, to attend his hanging—he remains an oddly mysterious figure. In appearance, Pierce was a tall, handsome man in his early thirties who wore a full red beard in the fashion that had recently become popular, particularly among government employees. In his speech, manner, and dress he seemed to be a gentleman, and well-to-do; he was apparently very charming, and possessed of "a captivating address." He himself claimed to be an orphan of Midlands gentry, to have attended Winchester and then Cambridge. He was a familiar figure in many London social circles and counted among his acquaintances Ministers, Members of Parliament, foreign ambassadors, bankers, and others of substantial standing. Although a bachelor, he maintained a house at No. 12 Harrow Road, in a fashionable part of London. But he spent much of the year traveling, and was said to have visited not only the Continent but New York as well.

Contemporary observers clearly believed his aristocratic origins; journalistic accounts often referred to Pierce as a "rogue," using the term in the sense of a male animal gone bad. The very idea of a highborn gentleman adopting a life of crime was so startling and titillating that nobody really wanted to disprove it.

Yet there is no firm evidence that Pierce came from the upper classes; indeed, almost nothing of his background prior to 1850 is known with any certainty. Modern readers, accustomed to the concept of "positive identification" as an ordinary fact of life, may be puzzled by the ambiguities of Pierce's past. But in an era when birth certificates were an innovation, photography a nascent art, and fingerprinting wholly unknown, it was difficult to identify any man with certainty, and Pierce took special care to be elusive. Even his name is doubtful: during the trial, various witnesses claimed to have known him as John Simms, or Andrew Miller, or Robert Jeffers.

The source of his obviously ample income was equally

disputed. Some said he was a silent partner with Jukes in the highly successful firm that manufactured croquet equipment. Croquet—pronounced "croaky"—was the overnight rage among athletically inclined young ladies, and it was perfectly reasonable that a sharp young businessman, investing a modest inheritance in such an enterprise, should come off very well.

Others said that Pierce owned several publican houses, and a smallish fleet of cabs, headed by a particularly sinister-appearing cabby, named Barlow, with a white scar across his forehead. This was more likely true, for the ownership of pubs and cabs was an occupation where underworld connections were useful.

Of course, it is not impossible that Pierce was a wellborn man with a background of aristocratic education. One must remember that Winchester and Cambridge were in those days more often characterized by lewd and drunken behavior than serious and sober scholarship. The most profound scientific mind of the Victorian era, Charles Darwin, devoted most of his youth to gambling and horses; and the majority of wellborn young men were more interested in acquiring "a university bearing" than a university degree.

It is also true that the Victorian underworld supported many educated figures down on their luck. They were usually screevers, or writers of false letters of recommendation, or they were counterfeiters, "doing a bit of soft." Sometimes they became magsmen, or con artists. But in general these educated men were petty criminals of a pathetic sort, more deserving of public pity than condemnation.

Edward Pierce, on the other hand, was positively exuberant in his approach to crime. Whatever his sources of income, whatever the truth of his background, one thing is certain: he was a master cracksman, or burglar, who over the years had accumulated sufficient capital to finance large-scale criminal operations, thus becoming what was called "a putter-up." And toward the middle of 1854, he was already well into an elaborate plan to pull the greatest theft of his career, The Great Train Robbery.

CHAPTER 3

The Screwsman

Robert Agar—a known screwsman, or specialist in keys and safe-breaking—testified in court that when he met Edward Pierce in late May, 1854, he had not seen him for two years previously. Agar was twenty-six years old, and in fair health except for a bad cough, the legacy of his years as a child working for a match manufacturer on Wharf Road, Bethnal Green. The premises of the firm were poorly ventilated, and the white vapor of phosphorous filled the air at all times. Phosphorous was known to be poisonous, but there were plenty of people eager to work at any job, even one that might cause a person's lungs to decay, or his jaw to rot off— sometimes in a matter of months.

Agar was a matchstick dipper. He had nimble fingers, and he eventually took up his trade as screwsman, where he was immediately successful. He worked as a screwsman for six years and was never apprehended.

Agar had never had any direct dealings with Pierce in the past, but he knew of him as a master cracksman who worked other towns, thus accounting for his long absences from London. Agar had also heard that Pierce had the money to put up a lay from time to time.

Agar testified that their first meeting occurred at the Bull and Bear publican house, on Hounslow Road. Located at the periphery of the notorious criminal slum of Seven Dials, this well-known flash house was, in the words of one observer, "a gathering place for all manner of females dressed to represent ladies, as well as members of the criminal class, who could be seen at every turning."

Given the infamous nature of the place, it was almost certain that a plainclothes constable from the Metropolitan Police was lurking somewhere on the premises. But the Bull and Bear was frequented by gentlemen of quality with a taste for low life, and the conversation of two fashionably dressed young bloods lounging at the bar while they surveyed the women in the room attracted no particular attention.

The meeting was unplanned, Agar said, but he was not surprised when Pierce arrived. Agar had heard some talk about Pierce lately, and it sounded as though he might be putting up. Agar recalled that the conversation began without greetings or preliminaries.

Agar said, "I heard that Spring Heel Jack's left Westminster."

"I heard that," Pierce agreed, rapping with his silver-headed cane to draw the attention of the barman. Pierce ordered two glasses of the best whiskey, which Agar took as proof that this was to be a business discussion.

"I heard," Agar said, "that Jack was going on a south swing to dip the holiday crowd." In those days, London pickpockets left in late spring, traveling north or south to other cities. A pickpocket's stock in trade was anonymity, and one could not dip a particular locale for long without being spotted by the crusher on the beat.

"I didn't hear his plans," Pierce said.

"I also heard," Agar continued, "that he took the train."

"He might have done."

"I heard," Agar said, his eyes on Pierce's face, "that on this train he was doing some crow's peeping for a particular gent who is putting up."

"He might have done," Pierce said again.

"I also heard," Agar said with a sudden grin, "that you are putting up."

"I may," Pierce said. He sipped his whiskey, and stared at the glass. "It used to be better here," he said reflectively. "Neddy must be watering his stock. What have you heard I am putting up for?"

"A robbery," Agar said. "For a ream flash pull, if truth be told."

"If truth be told," Pierce repeated. He seemed to find the phrase amusing. He turned away from the bar and looked at the women in the room. Several returned his glances warmly. "Everybody hears the pull bigger than life," he said finally.

"Aye, that's so," Agar admitted, and sighed. (In his testimony, Agar was very clear about the histrionics involved. "Now I goes and gives a big sigh, you see, like to say my patience is wearing thin, because he's a cautious one, Pierce is, but I want to get down to it, so I gives a big sigh.")

There was a brief silence. Finally Agar said, "It's two years gone since I saw you. Been busy?"

"Traveling," Pierce said.

"The Continent?"

Pierce shrugged. He looked at the glass of whiskey in Agar's hands, and the half-finished glass of gin and water Agar had been drinking before Pierce arrived. "How's the touch?"

"Ever so nice," Agar said. To demonstrate, he held out his hands, palms flat, fingers wide: there was no tremor.

"I may have one or two little things," Pierce said.

"Spring Heel Jack held his cards close," Agar said. "I know that for a ream fact. He was all swelled mighty and important, but he kept it to his chest."

"Jack's put in lavender," Pierce said curtly.

This was, as Agar later explained it, an ambiguous phrase. It might mean that Spring Heel Jack had gone into hiding; more often it meant that he was dead; it depended. Agar didn't inquire further. "These one or two little things, could they be crib jobs?"

"They could."

"Dicey, are they?"

"Very dicey," Pierce said.

"Inside or outside?"

"I don't know. You may need a canary or two when the time comes. And you will want a tight lip. If the first lay goes right enough, there will be more."

Agar downed the rest of his whiskey, and waited. Pierce ordered him another.

"Is it keys, then?" Agar asked.

"It is."

"Wax, or straightaway haul?"

"Wax."

"On the fly, or is there time?"

"On the fly."

"Right, then," Agar said. "I'm your man. I can do a wax on the fly faster than you can light your cigar."

"I know that," Pierce said, striking a match on the counter top and holding it to the tip of his cigar. Agar gave a slight shudder; he did not himself smoke—indeed, smoking had just recently returned to fashion after eighty years—and every time he smelled the phosphorous and sulfur of a match, it gave Agar a twinge, from his days in the match factory.

He watched Pierce puff on the cigar until it caught. "What's the lay to be, then?"

Pierce looked at him coldly. "You'll know when the time comes."

"You're a tight one."

"That," Pierce said, "is why I have never been in," meaning that he had no prison record. At the trial, other witnesses disputed this claim, saying that Pierce had served three and a half years in Manchester for cracking, under the name of Arthur Wills.

Agar said that Pierce gave him a final word of caution

about keeping silent, and then moved away from the bar, crossing the smoky, noisy Bull and Bear to bend briefly and whisper into a pretty woman's ear. The woman laughed; Agar turned away, and recalls nothing further from the evening.

CHAPTER 4

The Unwitting Accomplice

Mr. Henry Fowler, forty-seven, knew Edward Pierce in rather different circumstances. Fowler admitted freely that he had little knowledge of Pierce's background: the man had said he was an orphan, and he was clearly educated, and well-to-do, keeping a most excellent house, which was always fitted out with the latest appurtenances, some of them exceedingly clever.

Mr. Fowler remembered particularly an ingenious hallway stove for warming the entrance to the house. This stove was in the shape of a suit of armor, and functioned admirably. Mr. Fowler also recalled seeing a pair of beautifully constructed aluminum field glasses covered in Moroccan leather; these had so intrigued Mr. Fowler that he had sought a pair of his own and was astounded to discover that they were eighty shillings, an exorbitant price. Clearly, Pierce was well-heeled, and Henry Fowler found him amusing for an occasional dinner.

He recalled, with difficulty, an episode at Pierce's home in late May, 1854. It had been a dinner of eight gentlemen; the conversation chiefly concerned a new proposal for an underground railway within London itself. Fowler found the idea tedious, and he was disappointed when it was still discussed over brandy in the smoking room.

Then the topic of conversation turned to cholera, of late an epidemic in certain parts of London, where the disease was snatching up one person in a hundred. The dispute over the proposals of Mr. Edwin Chadwick, one of the Sanitary Commissioners, for new sewer systems in the city and for a cleaning-up of the polluted Thames, was profoundly boring to Mr. Fowler. Besides, Mr. Fowler had it on good authority that old "Drain Brain" Chadwick was soon to be discharged, but he was sworn not to divulge this information. He drank his coffee with a growing sense of fatigue. Indeed, he was thinking of taking his leave when the host, Mr. Pierce, asked him about a recent attempt to rob a gold shipment from a train.

It was only natural that Pierce should ask Fowler, for Henry Fowler was the brother-in-law of Sir Edgar Huddleston, of the banking firm of Huddleston & Bradford, Westminster. Mr. Fowler was the general manager of that prosperous enterprise, which had specialized in dealings in foreign currency since its founding in 1833.

This was a time of extraordinary English domination of world commerce. England mined more than half the world's coal, and her output of pig iron was greater than that of the rest of the world combined. She produced three-quarters of the world's cotton cloth. Her foreign trade was valued at £700,000,000 annually, twice that of her leading competitors, the United States and Germany. Her overseas empire was the greatest in world history and still expanding, until ultimately it accounted for almost a quarter of the earth's surface and a third of her population.

Thus it was only natural that foreign business concerns of all sorts made London their financial center, and the London banks thrived. Henry Fowler and his bank profited from the general economic trends, but their emphasis on foreign-currency transactions brought them additional business as well. Thus, when England and France had declared war on Russia two months previously, in March, 1854, the firm of Huddleston & Bradford was designated to arrange for the payment of British troops fighting the Crimean campaign. It was precisely such a consignment of gold for troop payments that had been the object of a recent attempted theft.

"A trivial endeavor," Fowler declared, conscious he was speaking on behalf of the bank. The other men in the room, smoking cigars and drinking brandy, were substantial gentlemen who knew other substantial gentlemen. Mr. Fowler felt obliged to put down any suspicion of the bank's inadequacy in the strongest possible terms. "Yes, indeed," he said, "trivial and amateurish. There was not the slightest chance of success."

"The villain expired?" asked Mr. Pierce, seated opposite him, puffing his cigar.

"Quite," Mr. Fowler said. "The railroad guard threw him from the train at a goodly speed. The shock must have killed him instantly." And he added, "Poor devil."

"Has he been identified?"

"Oh, I shouldn't think so," Fowler said. "The manner of his departure was such that his features were considerably— ah, disarrayed. At one time it was said he was named Jack Perkins, but one doesn't know. The police have taken no great interest in the matter, as is, I think, only wise. The whole manner of the robbery speaks of the rankest amateurism. It could never have succeeded."

"I suppose," Pierce said, "that the bank must take considerable precautions."

"My dear fellow," Fowler said, "considerable precautions indeed! I assure you, one doesn't transport twelve thousand pounds in bullion to France each month without the most extensive safeguards."

"So the blackguard was after the Crimean payments?" asked another gentleman, Mr. Harrison Bendix. Bendix was a well-known opponent of the Crimean campaign, and Fowler had no wish to engage in political disputes at this late hour.

"Apparently so," he said shortly, and was relieved when Pierce spoke again.

"We should all be curious to know the nature of your precautions," he said. "Or is that a secret of the firm?"

"No secret at all," Fowler said, taking the opportunity to withdraw his gold watch from the pocket of his waistcoat, flick open the cover, and glance at the dial. It was past eleven; he should retire; only the necessity to uphold the bank's reputation kept him there. "In point of fact, the precautions are of my own devising. And if I may say so, I invite you to point out any weakness in the established plan." He glanced from one face to the next as he talked.

"Each gold bullion shipment is loaded within the confines of the bank itself, which I hardly need mention is wholly impregnable. The bullion is placed in a number of ironbound strongboxes, which are then sealed. A sensible man might regard this as protection enough, but of course we go much further." He paused to sip his brandy.

"Now, then. The sealed strongboxes are taken by armed guard to the railway station. The convoy follows no established route, nor any established timetable; it keeps to populous thoroughfares, and thus there is no chance that it may be waylaid on the road to the station. Never do we employ fewer than ten guards, all trusted and longstanding servants of the firm, and all heavily armed.

"Now, then. At the station, the strongboxes are loaded into the luggage van of the Folkestone railway, where we place them into two of the latest Chubb safes."

"Indeed, Chubb safes?" Pierce said, raising an eyebrow. Chubb manufactured the finest safes in the world, and was universally recognized for skill and workmanship.

"Nor are these the ordinary line of Chubb safes," Fowler continued, "for they have been specially built to the bank's specifications. Gentlemen, they are on all sides constructed of one-quarter-inch tempered steel, and the doors are hung with interior hinges which offer no external purchase for tampering. Why, the very weight of these safes is an impediment to theft, for they each weigh in excess of two hundred and fifty pounds."

"Most impressive," Pierce said.

"So much so," Fowler said, "that one might in good conscience consider this to be adequate safeguard for the bullion shipment. And yet we have added still further refinements. Each of the safes is fitted with not one but two locks, requiring two keys."

"Two keys? How ingenious."

"Not only that," Fowler said, "but each of the four keys— two to each safe—is individually protected. Two are stored in the railway office itself. A third is in the custody of the bank's president, Mr. Trent, whom some of you may know to be a most reliable gentleman. I confess I do not know precisely where Mr. Trent has sequestered his key. But I know of the fourth key, for I myself am entrusted with guarding it."

"How extraordinary," Pierce said. "A considerable responsibility, I should think."

"I must admit I felt a certain need for invention in the matter," Fowler admitted, and then he lapsed into a dramatic pause.

It was Mr. Wyndham, a bit stiff with drink, who finally spoke up. "Well, damn it all, Henry, will you tell us where you have hidden your bloody key?"

Mr. Fowler took no offense, but smiled benignly. He was not a serious drinking man himself, and he viewed the foibles of those who overindulged with a certain modest satisfaction. "I keep it," he said, "about my neck." And he patted his starched shirt front with a flat hand. "I wear it at all times, even while bathing—indeed, even in my sleep. It is never off my person." He smiled broadly. "So, gentlemen, you see that the crude attempt of a mere child from the dangerous classes can hardly be of concern to Huddleston & Bradford, for the little ruffian had no more chance of stealing that bullion than I have of—well, of flying to the moon."

Here Mr. Fowler allowed himself a chuckle at the absurdity of it all. "Now, then," he said, "can you discern any flaw in our arrangements?"

"None whatsoever," said Mr. Bendix coldly.

But Mr. Pierce was warmer. "I must congratulate you, Henry," he said. "It is really quite the most ingenious strategy I have ever heard for protecting a consignment of valuables."

"I rather think so myself," Mr. Fowler said.

Soon thereafter, Mr. Fowler took his leave, arising with the comment that if he were not soon home to his wife, she should think him dallying with a judy—"and I should hate to suffer the pains of chastisement without the antecedent reward." His comment drew laughter from the assembled gentlemen; it was, he thought, just the right note on which to depart. Gentlemen wanted their bankers prudent but not prudish; it was a fine line.

"I shall see you out," Pierce said, also rising.

CHAPTER 5

The Railway Office

England's railroads grew at such a phenomenal rate that the city of London was overwhelmed, and never managed to build a central station. Instead, each of the lines, built by private firms, ran their tracks as far into London as they could manage, and then erected a terminus. But in the mid-century this pattern was coming under attack. The dislocation of poor people, whose dwellings were demolished to make way for the incoming lines, was one argument; another focused on the inconvenience to travelers forced to cross London by coach to make connections from one station to another in order to continue their journey.

In 1846, Charles Pearson proposed, and drew plans for, an enormous Central Railway Terminus to be located at Ludgate Hill, but the idea was never adopted. Instead, after the construction of several stations—the most recent being Victoria Station and King's Cross, in 1851—there was a moratorium on further construction because of the fury of public debate.

Eventually, the concept of a central London terminus was completely abandoned, and new outlying stations were built. When the last, Marylebone Station, was finished in 1899, London had fifteen railroad terminals, more than twice that of any other major city in Europe; and the bewildering array of lines and schedules was apparently never mastered by any Londoner except Sherlock Holmes, who knew it all by heart.

The mid-century halt in construction left several of the new lines at a disadvantage, and one of these was the South Eastern Railway, which ran from London to the coastal town of Folkestone, some eighty miles away. The South Eastern had no access to central London until 1851, when the London Bridge Terminus was rebuilt.

Located on the south shore of the Thames River near its namesake, London Bridge was the oldest railway station in the city. It was originally constructed in 1836 by the London & Greenwich Railway. Never popular, the station was attacked as "inferior in design and conception" to such later stations as Paddington and King's Cross. Yet when the station was rebuilt in 1851, the *Illustrated London News* recalled that the old station had been "remarkable for the neatness, artistic character, and reality of its *façade*. We regret, therefore, that this has disappeared, to make room, apparently, for one of less merit."

This is precisely the kind of critical turnabout that has

always frustrated and infuriated architects. No less a figure than Sir Christopher Wren, writing two hundred years earlier, complained that "the peoples of London may despise some eyesore until it is demolished, whereupon by magick the replacement is deemed inferior to the former edifice, now eulogized in high and glowing reference."

Yet one must admit that the new London Bridge Terminus was most unsatisfactory. Victorians regarded the train stations as the "cathedrals of the age"; they expected them to blend the highest principles of aesthetics and technological achievement, and many stations fulfill that expectation with their high, arching, elegant glass vaults. But the new London Bridge Station was depressing in every way. An L-shaped two-story structure, it had a flat and utilitarian appearance, with a row of dreary shops under an arcade to the left, and the main station straight ahead, unadorned except for a clock mounted on the roof. Most serious, its interior floor plan— the focus of most earlier criticism—remained wholly unaltered.

It was during the reconstruction of the station that the South Eastern Railway arranged to use the London Bridge Terminus as the starting point for its routes to the coast. This was done on a leasing arrangement; South Eastern leased tracks, platforms, and office space from the London & Greenwich line, whose owners were not disposed to give South Eastern any better facilities than necessary.

The traffic supervisor's offices consisted of four rooms in a remote section of the terminal—two rooms for clerks, one storage area for valuable checked items, and a larger office for the supervisor himself. All the rooms had glass frontings. The whole suite was located on the second floor of the terminus and accessible only by an ironwork staircase leading up from the station platform. Anyone climbing or descending the stairs would be in plain view of the office workers, as well as all the passengers, porters, and guards on the platforms below.

The traffic supervisor was named McPherson. He was an elderly Scotsman who kept a close eye on his clerks, seeing to it that they did no daydreaming out the window. Thus no one in the office noticed when, in early July, 1854, two travelers took up a position on a bench on the platform, and remained there the entire day, frequently consulting their watches, as if impatient for their journey to begin. Nor did anyone notice when the same two gentlemen returned the following week, and again spent a day on the same bench, watching the activity in the station while they awaited their train, and frequently checking their pocketwatches.

In fact, Pierce and Agar were not employing pocket-watches, but rather stopwatches. Pierce had an elegant one, a chronograph with two stopwatch faces, with a case of 18-karat gold. It was considered a marvel of the latest engineering, sold for racing and other purposes. But he held it cupped in his hand, and it attracted no notice.

After the second day of watching the routine of the office clerks, the changes of the railway guards, the arrival and departure of visitors to the office, and other matters of importance to them, Agar finally looked up the iron staircase to the office and announced, "It's bloody murder. She's too wide open. What's your pogue up there, anyway?"

"Two keys."

"What two keys is that?"

"Two keys I happen to want," Pierce said.

Agar squinted up at the offices. If he was disappointed in Pierce's answer he gave no indication. "Well," he said, in a professional tone, "if it's two bettys you want, I reckon they are in that storage room"—he nodded, not daring to point a finger—"just past the space for the clerks. You see the cupboard?"

Pierce nodded. Through the glass fronting, he could see all the office. In the storage area was a shallow, wall-mounted lime green cupboard. It looked like the sort of place keys might be stored. "I see it."

"There's my money, on that cupboard. Now you'll cool she has a lock on her, but that will give us no great trouble. Cheap lock."

"What about the front door?" Pierce said, shifting his gaze. Not only was the cupboard inside locked, but the door to the suite of offices—a frosted door, with SER stenciled on it, and underneath, TRAFFIC SUPERVISOR DIVISION—had a large brass lock above the knob.

"Appearances," Agar snorted. "She'll crack open with any cheap twirl to tickle her innards. I could open her with a ragged fingernail. We've no problems there. The problem is the bloody crowds."

Pierce nodded, but said nothing. This was essentially Agar's operation, and he would have to figure it out. "The pogue is two keys, you say?"

"Yes," Pierce said. "Two keys."

"Two keys is four waxes. Four waxes is nigh on a minute, to do it proper. But that doesn't count cracking the outside, or the inside cabinet. That's more time again." Agar looked around at the crowded platform, and the clerks in the office. "Bloody flummut to try and crack her by day," he said. "Too many people about."

"Night?"

"Aye, at night, when she's empty, and a proper deadlurk. I think the night is best."

"At night, the crushers make rounds," Pierce reminded him. They had already learned that during the evening, when the station was deserted, the policemen patrolled it at four- or five-minute intervals throughout the night. "Will you have time?"

Agar frowned, and squinted up at the office. "No," he said finally. "Unless . . ."

"Yes?"

"Unless the offices were already open. Then I can make my entrance neat as you please, and I do the waxes quick-like, and I'm gone in less than two minutes flat."

"But the offices will be locked," Pierce said.

"I'm thinking of a snakesman," Agar said, and he nodded to the supervisor's office.

Pierce looked up. The supervisor's office had a broad glass window; through it, he could see Mr. McPherson, in his shirtsleeves, with white hair and a green shade over his forehead. And behind McPherson was a window for ventilation, a window approximately a foot square. "I see it," Pierce said. And he added, "Damn small."

"A proper snakesman can make it through," Agar said. A snakesman was a child adept at wriggling through small spaces. Usually he was a former chimney sweep's apprentice. "And once he's in the office, he unlocks the cupboard, and he unlocks the door from the inside, and he sets it all up proper for me. That will make this job a bone lay, and no mistake," he said, nodding in satisfaction.

"If there's a snakesman."

"Aye."

"And he must be the devil's own," Pierce said, looking again at the window, "if we are to break that drum. Who's the best?"

"The best?" Agar said, looking surprised. "The best is Clean Willy, but he's in."

"Where's he in?"

"Newgate Prison, and there's no escaping that. He'll do his days on the cockchafer, and be a good lad, and wait for his ticket-of-leave if it comes. But there's no escape. Not from Newgate."

"Perhaps Clean Willy can find a way."

"Nobody can find a way," Agar said heavily. "It's been tried before."

"I'll get a word to Willy," Pierce said, "and we shall see."

Agar nodded. "I'll hope," he said, "but not too excessive."

The two men resumed watching the offices. Pierce stared at the storage room of the offices, at the little cupboard mounted on the wall. It occurred to him that he had never seen it opened. He had a thought: what if there were more keys—perhaps dozens of keys—in that little closet? How would Agar know which ones to copy?

"Here comes the escop," Agar said.

Pierce looked, and saw that the police constable was making his rounds. He flicked his chronometer: seven minutes forty-seven seconds since the last circuit. But the constable's routine would be more rapid at night.

"You see a lurk?" Pierce said.

Agar nodded to a baggage stand in a corner, not more than a dozen paces from the staircase. "There'd do."

"Well enough," Pierce said.

The two men remained seated until seven o'clock, when the clerks left the office to return home. At seven-twenty, the supervisor departed, locking the outside door after him. Agar had a look at the key, from a distance.

"What kind of a key?" Pierce asked.

"Cheap twirl will manage," Agar said.

The two men remained another hour, until it became inconvenient for them to stay in the station. The last train had departed, and they were now too conspicuous. They remained just long enough to clock the constable on night duty as he made his rounds of the station. The constable passed the traffic manager's office once every five minutes and three seconds.

Pierce snapped the button on his chronometer and glanced at the second hand. "Five and three," he said.

"Dub lay," Agar said.

"Can you do it?"

"Of course I can do it," Agar said. "I can get a judy preggers in less—a dub lay is all I said. Five and three?"

"I can light a cigar faster," Pierce reminded him.

"I can do it," Agar said firmly, "if I have a snakesman such like Clean Willy."

The two men left the railway station. As they stepped into the fading twilight, Pierce signaled his cab. The cabby with a scar across his forehead whipped up his horse and clattered toward the station entrance.

"When do we knock it over?" Agar said.

Pierce gave him a gold guinea. "When I inform you," he said. And then he got into the cab and rode off into the deepening night darkness.

CHAPTER 6

The Problem and the Solution

By the middle of July, 1854, Edward Pierce knew the location of three of the four keys he needed to rob the safes. Two keys were in the green cupboard of the traffic supervisor's office of the South Eastern Railway. A third hung around the neck of Henry Fowler. To Pierce, these three keys presented no major problem.

There was, of course, the question of opportune timing in making a clandestine break to obtain a wax impression. There was also the problem of finding a good snakesman to aid in the break at the railway offices. But these were all easily surmountable obstacles.

The real difficulty centered around the fourth key. Pierce knew that the fourth key was in the possession of the bank's president, Mr. Trent, but he did not know *where*—and this lack of knowledge represented a formidable challenge indeed, and one that occupied his attention for the next four months.

A few words of explanation may be useful here. In 1854, Alfred Nobel was just beginning his career; the Swedish chemist would not discover dynamite for another decade, and the availability of nitroglycerin "soup" lay still further in the future. Thus, in the mid-nineteenth century, any decently constructed metal safe represented a genuine barrier to theft.

This truth was so widely acknowledged that safe manufacturers devoted most of their energies to the problem of making safes fireproof, since loss of money and documents through incineration was a much more serious hazard than loss through theft. During this period, a variety of patents were issued for ferromanganese, clay, marble dust, and plaster of Paris as fireproof linings for safes.

A thief confronted with a safe had three options. The first was to steal the whole safe outright, carrying it off to break open at his leisure. This was impossible if the safe was of any size or weight, and manufacturers were careful to employ the heaviest and most unwieldy construction materials to discourage this maneuver.

Alternatively, a thief could employ a "petter-cutter," a drill that clamped to the keyhole of the safe and permitted a hole to be bored over the lock. Through this hole, the lock mechanism could be manipulated and the lock opened. But the petter-cutter was a specialist's tool; it was noisy, slow, and uncertain; and it was expensive to purchase and bulky to carry on a job.

The third choice was to look at the safe and give up. This was the most common outcome of events. In another twenty years, the safe would be transformed from an impregnable obstacle to a mere irritant in the minds of burglars, but for the moment it was virtually unbeatable.

Unless, that is, one had a key to the safe. Combination locks had not yet been invented; all locks were operated by key, and the most reliable way to break a safe was to come prepared with a previously obtained key. This truth lies behind the nineteenth-century criminal's preoccupation with keys. Victorian crime literature, official and popular, often seems obsessed with keys, as if nothing else mattered. But in those days, as the master safe-cracker Neddy Sykes said in his trial in 1848, "The key is everything in the lay, the problem and the solution."

Thus it was Edward Pierce's unquestioned assumption in planning the train robbery that he must first obtain copies of all the necessary keys. And he must do this by gaining access to the keys themselves, for although there was a new method of using wax "blanks" and inserting them into the locks of the actual safes, this technique was undependable. Safes of the period were usually left unguarded for this reason.

The true criminal focus was upon the keys to the safe, wherever they might be. The copying process presented no difficulty: wax impressions of the key could be made in a few moments. And any premises containing a key could be cracked with relative ease.

But, if one stops to think of it, a key is really rather small. It can be concealed in the most unlikely places; it can be hidden almost anywhere on a person's body, or in a room. Particularly a Victorian room, where even so ordinary an item of furniture as a wastebasket was likely to be covered in cloth, layers of fringes, and decorative rings of tassels.

We forget how extraordinarily cluttered Victorian rooms were. Innumerable hiding places were provided by the prevailing décor of the period. Furthermore, the Victorians themselves adored secret compartments and concealed spaces; a mid-century writing desk was advertised as "containing 110 compartments, including many most artfully concealed from detection." Even the ornate hearths, found in every room of a house, offered dozens of places to hide an object as small as a key.

Thus, in the mid-Victorian period, information about the location of a key was almost as useful as an actual copy of the key itself. A thief seeking a wax impression might break into a house if he knew exactly where the key was hidden, or even if he knew in which room it was hidden. But if he did not know where in the house it was, the difficulty of making a thorough search—silently, in a house full of residents and servants, using a single shaded lantern that threw only a "bull's-eye" spot of light—was so great as to be not worth the attempt in the first instance.

Therefore, Pierce directed his attention to discovering where Mr. Edgar Trent, president of the firm of Huddleston & Bradford, kept his key.

The first question was whether Mr. Trent kept his key in the bank. Junior clerks of Huddleston & Bradford took their dinner at one o'clock at a pub called the Horse and Rider, across the street from the firm. This was a smallish establishment, crowded and warm at the noon dinner hour. Pierce struck up an acquaintance with one of the clerks, a young man named Rivers.

Normally, the servants and junior clerks of the bank were wary of casual acquaintances, for one never knew when one was talking to a criminal out of twig; but Rivers was relaxed, in the knowledge that the bank was impregnable to burglary —and recognizing, perhaps, that he had a deal of resentment toward the source of his employment.

In this regard, one may profitably record the revised "Rules for Office Staff" posted by Mr. Trent in early 1854. These were as follows:

1. Godliness, cleanliness and punctuality are the necessities of a good business.
2. The firm has reduced the working day to the hours from 8:30 a.m. to 7 p.m.
3. Daily prayers will be held each morning in the main office. The clerical staff will be present.
4. Clothing will be of a sober nature. The clerical staff will not disport themselves in raiment of bright color.
5. A stove is provided for the benefit of the clerical staff. It is recommended that each member of the clerical

staff bring 4 lbs. of coal each day during cold weather.
6. No member of the clerical staff may leave the room without permission from Mr. Roberts. The calls of nature are permitted and clerical staff may use the garden beyond the second gate. This area must be kept clean in good order.
7. No talking is allowed during business hours.
8. The craving of tobacco, wines or spirits is a human weakness, and as such is forbidden to the clerical staff.
9. Members of the clerical staff will provide their own pens.
10. The managers of the firm will expect a great rise in the output of work to compensate for these near Utopian conditions.

However Utopian, the working conditions of Huddleston & Bradford led the clerk Rivers to speak freely about Mr. Trent. And with less enthusiasm than one might expect for a Utopian employer.

"Bit of a stiff, he is," Rivers said. "Snapping his watch at eight-thirty sharp, and checking all to see they are at their places, no excuses. God help the man whose omnibus is late in the traffic of the rush."

"Demands his routine, does he?"

"With a vengeance, he does. He's a stiff one—the job must be done, and that's all he cares for. He's getting on in years," Rivers said. "And vain, too: grew whiskers longer than yours, he did, on account of the fact he's losing the hair up top."

During this period, there was considerable debate about the propriety of whiskers on gentlemen. It was a new fashion, and opinion was divided on its benefits. Similarly, there was a new fashion in smoking, called cigarettes, just introduced, but the most conservative men did not smoke—certainly not in public, or even at home. And the most conservative men were clean-shaven.

"He has this brush, I hear," Rivers went on. "Dr. Scott's electric hairbrush, comes from Paris. You know how dear it is? Twelve shillings sixpence, that's what it is."

Rivers would find this expensive: he was paid twelve shillings a week.

"What's it do?" Pierce inquired.

"Cures headaches, dandruff, and baldness, too," Rivers said, "or so it's claimed. Queer little brush. He locks himself into his office and brushes once an hour, punctual." Here Rivers laughed at the foibles of his employer.

"He must have a large office."

"Aye, large and comfortable, too. He's an important man, Mr. Trent is."

"Keeps it tidy?"

"Aye, the sweeper's in every night, dusting and arranging just so, and every night as he leaves, Mr. Trent says to the sweeper, 'A place for everything, and everything in its place,' and then he leaves, seven o'clock punctual."

Pierce did not recall the rest of the conversation, for it was of no interest to him. He already knew what he wanted— that Trent did not keep the key in his office. If he did, he would never leave the place to be cleaned in his absence, for sweepers were notoriously easy to bribe, and to the casual eye there was little difference between a thorough cleaning and a thorough search.

But even if the key was not in the office, it might still be kept in the bank. Mr. Trent might choose to lock it in one of the vaults. To determine if this was so, Pierce could strike up a conversation with a different clerk, but he was anxious to avoid this. Instead, he chose another method.

CHAPTER 7

The Swell

Teddy Burke, twenty-four, was working the Strand at two in the afternoon, the most fashionable hour. Like the other gentlemen, Teddy Burke was decked out, wearing a high hat, a dark frock coat, narrow trousers, and a dark silk choker. This outfit had cost him a pretty, but it was essential to his business, for Teddy Burke was one of the swellest of the swell mobsmen.

In the throng of gentlemen and ladies who browsed among the elegant shops of this thoroughfare, which Disraeli called "the first street in Europe," no one would notice that Teddy Burke was not alone. In fact, he was working his usual operation, with himself as dipper, a stickman at his side, and two stalls front and back—altogether, four men, each as well-dressed as the next. These four slipped through the crowd, attracting no attention. There was plenty of diversion.

On this fine early summer day, the air was warm and redolent of horse dung, despite the busy working of a dozen street-urchin sweepers. There was heavy traffic of carts, drays, brightly lettered rattling omnibuses, four-wheel and hansom cabs, and from time to time an elegant chariot rode past, with a uniformed coachman in front and liveried servants standing behind. Ragged children darted among the traffic and turned cartwheels under the horses' hoofs for the amusement of the crowd, some of whom threw a few coppers in their direction.

Teddy Burke was oblivious to the excitement, and to the rich array of goods on display in the shopwindows. His attention was wholly fixed upon the quarry, a fine lady wearing a heavy flounced crinoline skirt of deep purple. In a few moments he would dip her as she walked along the street.

His gang was in formation. One stall had taken up a position three paces ahead; another was five paces back. True to their title, the stalls would create disorder and confusion should anything go wrong with the intended dip.

The quarry was moving, but that did not worry Teddy Burke. He planned to work her on the fly, the most difficult kind of dip, as she moved from one shop to the next.

"Right, here we go," he said, and the stickman moved alongside him. It was the stickman's job to take the pogue once Teddy had snaffled it, thus leaving Teddy clean, should there be any hue and cry and a constable to stop him.

Together with the stickman, he moved so close to the woman he could smell her perfume. He was moving along her right side, for a woman's dress had only one pocket, and that was on the right.

Teddy carried an overcoat draped across his left arm. A sensible person might have asked why a gentleman would carry an overcoat on such a warm day; but the coat looked new, and he could have conceivably just picked it up from a fitting at one of the nearby shops. In any case, the overcoat concealed the movement of his right arm across his body to the woman's skirt. He fanned the dress delicately, to determine if a purse was there. His fingers touched it; he took a deep breath, praying that the coins would not clink, and lifted it out of the pocket.

Immediately he eased away from the woman, shifted his overcoat to his other arm, and in the course of that movement passed the purse to the stickman. The stickman drifted off. Ahead and behind, the stalls moved out in different directions. Only Teddy Burke, now clean, continued to walk along the Strand, pausing before a shop that displayed cut-glass and crystal decanters imported from France.

A tall gent with a red beard was admiring the wares in the

window. He did not look at Teddy Burke. "Nice pull," he said.

Teddy Burke blinked.

The speaker was too well-dressed, too square-rigged, to be a plainclothes crusher, and he certainly wasn't a nose, or informer. Teddy Burke said carefully, "Are you addressing me, sir?"

"Yes," the man said. "I said that was a very nice pull. You tool her off?"

Teddy Burke was profoundly insulted. A tool was a wire hook that inferior dippers employed to snare a purse if their fingers were too shaky for the job. "Beg your pardon, sir. I don't know your meaning, sir."

"I think you do, well enough," the man said. "Shall we walk awhile?"

Teddy Burke shrugged and fell into step alongside the stranger. After all, he was clean; he had nothing to fear. "Lovely day," he said.

The stranger did not answer. They walked for some minutes in silence. "Do you think you can be less effective?" the man asked after a time.

"How do you mean, sir?"

"I mean," the man said, "can you buzz a customer and come out dry?"

"On purpose?" Teddy Burke laughed. "It happens often enough without trying, I can tell you that."

"There's five quid for you, if you can prove yourself a prize bungler."

Teddy Burke's eyes narrowed. There were plenty of magsmen about, sharp con men who often employed an unwitting accomplice, setting him up to take a fall in some elaborate scheme. Teddy Burke was nobody's fool. "Five quid's no great matter."

"Ten," the man said, in a weary voice.

"I have to think of me boys."

"No," the man said, "this is you, alone."

"What's the lay, then?" Teddy Burke said.

"Lots of bustle, a ruck touch, just enough to set the quarry to worry, make him pat his pockets."

"And you want me to come up dry?"

"Dry as dust," the man said.

"Who's the quarry, then?" Teddy Burke said.

"A gent named Trent. You'll touch him with a bungler's dip in front of his offices, just a roughing-up, like."

"Where's the office, then?"

"Huddleston & Bradford Bank."

Teddy Burke whistled. "Westminster. Sticky, that is. There's enough crushers about to make a bloody army."

"But you'll be dry. All you've to do is worry him."

Teddy Burke walked a few moments, looking this way and that, taking the air and thinking things over. "When will it be, then?"

"Tomorrow morning. Eight o'clock sharp."

"All right."

The red-bearded gentleman gave him a five-pound bill, and informed him he would get the rest when the job was done.

"What's it all about, then?" Teddy Burke asked.

"Personal matter," the man replied, and slipped away into the crowd.

CHAPTER 8

The Holy Land

Between 1801 and 1851, London tripled in size. With a population of two and a half million, it was by far the largest city in the world, and every foreign observer was astonished at its dimensions. Nathaniel Hawthorne was speechless; Henry James was fascinated and appalled at its "horrible numerosity"; Dostoevsky found it "as vast as an ocean . . . a Biblical sight, some prophecy out of the Apocalypse being fulfilled before your very eyes."

And yet London continued to grow. At the mid-century, four thousand new dwellings were under construction at any one time, and the city was literally exploding outward. Already, the now familiar pattern of expansion was termed "the flight to the suburbs." Outlying areas that at the turn of the century had been villages and hamlets—Marylebone, Islington, Camden, St. John's Wood, and Bethnal Green—were thoroughly built up, and the newly affluent middle classes were deserting the central city for these areas, where the air was better, the noise less bothersome, and the atmosphere in general more pleasant and "countrified."

Of course, some older sections of London retained a character of great elegance and wealth, but these were often cheek to jowl with the most dismal and shocking slums. The proximity of great riches and profound squalor also impressed foreign observers, particularly since the slums, or rookeries, were refuges and breeding places for "the criminal class." There were sections of London where a thief might rob a mansion and literally cross a street to disappear into a tangled maze of alleyways and dilapidated buildings crammed with humanity and so dangerous that even an armed policeman did not dare pursue the culprit.

The genesis of slums was poorly understood at the time; indeed, the very term "slums" did not become widely accepted until 1890. But in a vague way the now familiar pattern was recognized: a region of the city would be cut off from circulation by newly constructed thoroughfares that bypassed it; businesses would depart; disagreeable industries would move in, creating local noise and air pollution and further reducing the attractiveness of the area; ultimately, no one with the means to live elsewhere would choose to reside in such a place, and the region would become decrepit, badly maintained, and overpopulated by the lowest classes.

Then, as now, these slums existed in part because they were profitable for landlords. A lodging house of eight rooms might take on a hundred boarders, each paying a shilling or two a week to live in "hugger-mugger promiscuity," sleeping with as many as twenty members of the same or opposite sex in the same room. (Perhaps the most bizarre example of lodgings of the period was the famous waterfront sailors' "penny hangs." Here a drunken seaman slept the night for a penny, draping himself across chest-high ropes, and hanging like clothes on a line.)

While some proprietors of lodging houses, or netherskens, lived in the area—and often accepted stolen goods in lieu of rent—many owners were substantial citizens, landlords *in absentia* who employed a tough deputy to collect the rents and keep some semblance of order.

During this period there were several notorious rookeries, at Seven Dials, Rosemary Lane, Jacob's Island, and Ratcliffe Highway, but none was more famous than the six acres in central London that comprised the rookery of St. Giles, called "the Holy Land." Located near the theatre district of Leicester Square, the prostitute center of the Haymarket, and the fashionable shops of Regent Street, the St. Giles rookery was strategically located for any criminal who wanted to "go to ground."

Contemporary accounts describe the Holy Land as "a dense mass of houses so old they only seem not to fall, through which narrow and tortuous lanes curve and wind. There is no privacy here, and whoever ventures in this region finds the streets—by courtesy so called—thronged with loiterers, and sees, through half-glazed windows, rooms crowded to suffocation." There are references to "the stagnant gutters . . . the filth choking up dark passages . . . the walls of bleached soot, and doors falling from their hinges . . . and children swarming everywhere, relieving themselves as they please."

Such a squalid, malodorous and dangerous tenement was no place for a gentleman, particularly after nightfall on a foggy summer evening. Yet in late July, 1854, a red-bearded man in fashionable attire walked fearlessly through the smoke-filled, cramped and narrow lanes. The loiterers and vagrants watching him no doubt observed that his silver-headed cane looked ominously heavy, and might conceal a blade. There was also a bulge about the trousers that implied a barker tucked in the waistband. And the very boldness of such a foolhardy incursion probably intimidated many of those who might be tempted to waylay him.

Pierce himself later said, "It is the demeanor which is respected among these people. They know the look of fear, and likewise its absence, and any man who is not afraid makes them afraid in turn."

Pierce went from street to stinking street, inquiring after a certain woman. Finally he found a lounging soak who knew her.

"It's Maggie you want? Little Maggie?" the man asked, leaning against a yellow gas lamppost, his face deep shadows in the fog.

"She's a judy, Clean Willy's doll."

"I know of her. Pinches laundry, doesn't she? Aye, she does a bit of snow, I'm sure of it." Here the man paused significantly, squinting.

Pierce gave him a coin. "Where shall I find her?"

"First passing up, first door to yer right," the man said. Pierce continued on.

"But it's no use your bothering," the man called after him. "Willy's in the stir now—in Newgate, no less—and he has only the cockchafer on his mind."

Pierce did not look back. He walked down the street, passing vague shadows in the fog, and here and there a woman whose clothing glowed in the night—matchstick dippers with patches of phosphorous on their garments. Dogs barked; children cried; whispers and groans and laughter were conveyed to him through the fog. Finally he arrived at the nethersken, with its bright rectangle of yellow light at the entrance, shining on a crudely hand-painted sign which read:

LOGINS FOR

THRAVELERS

Pierce glanced at the sign, then entered the building, pushing his way past the throng of dirty, ragged children clustered about the stairs; he cuffed one briskly, to show them there was to be no plucking at his pockets. He climbed the creaking stairs to the second floor, and asked after the woman named Maggie. He was told she was in the kitchen, and so he descended again, to the basement.

The kitchen was the center of every lodging house, and at this hour it was a warm and friendly place, a focus of heat and rich smells, while the fog curled gray and cold outside the windows. A half-dozen men stood by the fire, talking and drinking; at a side table, several men and women played cards while others sipped bowls of steaming soup; tucked away in the corners were musical instruments, beggars' crutches, hawkers' baskets, and peddlers' boxes. He found

Maggie, a dirty child of twelve, and drew her to one side. He gave her a gold guinea, which she bit. She flashed a half-smile.

"What is it, then, guv?" She looked appraisingly at his fine clothes, a calculating glance far beyond her years. "A bit of a tickle for you?"

Pierce ignored the suggestion. "You dab it up with Clean Willy?"

She shrugged. "I did. Willy's in."

"Newgate?"

"Aye."

"You see him?"

"I do, once and again. I goes as his sister, see."

Pierce pointed to the coin she clutched in her hand. "There's another one of those if you can downy him a message."

For a moment, the girl's eyes glowed with interest. Then they went blank again. "What's the lay?"

"Tell Willy, he should break at the next topping. It's to be Emma Barnes, the murderess. They'll hang her in public for sure. Tell him: break at the topping."

She laughed. It was an odd laugh, harsh and rough. "Willy's in Newgate," she said, "and there's no breaks from Newgate —topping or no."

"Tell him *he* can," Pierce said. "Tell him to go to the house where he first met John Simms, and all will be well enough."

"Are you John Simms?"

"I am a friend," Pierce said. "Tell him the next topping and he's over the side, or he's not Clean Willy."

She shook her head. "How can he break from Newgate?"

"Just tell him," Pierce said, and turned to leave.

At the door to the kitchen, he looked back at her, a skinny child, stoop-shouldered in a ragged secondhand dress spattered with mud, her hair matted and filthy.

"I'll tell," she said, and slipped the gold coin into her shoe.

He turned away from her and retraced his steps, leaving the
Holy Land. He came out of a narrow alley, turned into
Leicester Square, and joined the crowd in front of the May-
berry Theatre, blending in, disappearing.

C H A P T E R   9

The Routine of Mr. Edgar Trent

Respectable London was quiet at night. In the era before the
internal combustion engine, the business and financial districts at the center of the town were deserted and silent
except for the quiet footsteps of the Metropolitan Police constables making their twenty-minute rounds.

As dawn came, the silence was broken by the crowing of
roosters and the mooing of cows, barnyard sounds incongruous in an urban setting. But in those days there was plenty
of livestock in the central city, and animal husbandry was
still a major London industry—and indeed, during the day, a
major source of traffic congestion. It was not uncommon for
a fine gentleman to be delayed in his coach by a shepherd
with his flock moving through the streets of the city. London
was the largest urban concentration in the world at that time,
but by modern standards the division between city and country life was blurred.

Blurred, that is, until the Horse Guards clock chimed
seven o'clock, and the first of that peculiarly urban phenomenon—commuters—appeared on their way to work, conveyed by "the Marrowbone stage"; that is, on foot. These
were the armies of women and girls employed as seamstresses

in the sweatshops of West End dress factories, where they worked twelve hours a day for a few shillings a week.

At eight o'clock, the shops along the great thoroughfares took down their shutters; apprentices and assistants dressed the windows in preparation for the day's commerce, setting out what one sarcastic observer called "the innumerable whim-whams and fribble-frabble of fashion."

Between eight and nine o'clock was rush hour, and the streets became crowded with men. Everyone from government clerks to bank cashiers, from stockbrokers to sugar-bakers and soap-boilers, made their way to work on foot, in omnibuses, tandems, dogcarts—altogether a rattling, noisy, thickly jammed traffic of vehicles and drivers who cursed and swore and lashed at their horses.

In the midst of this, the street sweepers began their day's labors. In the ammonia-rich air, they collected the first droppings of horse dung, dashing among the carts and omnibuses. And they were busy: an ordinary London horse, according to Henry Mayhew, deposited six tons of dung on the streets each year, and there were at least a million horses in the city.

Gliding through the midst of this confusion, a few elegant broughams, with gleaming dark polished wood carriages and delicately sprung, lacy-spoked wheels, conveyed their substantial citizens in utter comfort to the day's employment.

Pierce and Agar, crouched on a rooftop overlooking the imposing façade of the Huddleston & Bradford Bank across the way, watched as one such brougham came down the street toward them.

"There he is now," Agar said.

Pierce nodded. "Well, we shall know soon enough." He checked his watch. "Eight-twenty nine. Punctual, as usual."

Pierce and Agar had been on the rooftop since dawn. They had watched the early arrival of the tellers and clerks; they had seen the traffic in the street and on the sidewalks grow more brisk and hurried with each passing minute.

Now the brougham pulled up to the door of the bank, and the driver jumped down to open the door. The president of Huddleston & Bradford stepped down to the pavement. Mr. Edgar Trent was near sixty, his beard was gray, and he had a considerable paunch; whether he was balding or not, Pierce could not discern, for a high top hat covered his head.

"He's a fat one, isn't he," Agar said.

"Watch, now," Pierce said.

At the very moment that Mr. Trent stepped to the ground, a well-dressed young man jostled him roughly, muttered a brief apology over his shoulder, and moved on in the rush-hour crowd. Mr. Trent ignored the incident. He walked the few steps forward to the impressive oak doors of the bank.

Then he stopped, halting in mid-stride.

"He's realized," Pierce said.

On the street below, Trent looked after the well-dressed young man, and immediately patted his side coat pocket, feeling for some article. Apparently, what he sought was still in its place; his shoulders dropped in relief, and he continued on into the bank.

The brougham clattered off; the bank doors swung shut.

Pierce grinned and turned to Agar. "Well," he said, "that's that."

"That's what?" Agar said.

"That's what we need to know."

"What do we need to know, then?" Agar said.

"We need to know," Pierce said slowly, "that Mr. Trent brought his key with him today, for this is the day of—" He broke off abruptly. He had not yet informed Agar of the plan, and he saw no reason to do so until the last minute. A man with a tendency to be a soak, like Agar, could loosen his tongue at an unlikely time. But no drunk could split what he did not know.

"The day of what?" Agar persisted.

"The day of reckoning," Pierce said.

"You're a tight one," Agar said. And then he added, "Wasn't that Teddy Burke, trying a pull?"

"Who's Teddy Burke?" Pierce said.

"A swell, works the Strand."

"I wouldn't know," Pierce said, and the two men left the building rooftop.

"Cor, you're a tight one," Agar said again. "That *was* Teddy Burke."

Pierce just smiled.

In the coming weeks, Pierce learned a great deal about Mr. Edgar Trent and his daily routine. Mr. Trent was a rather severe and devout gentleman; he rarely drank, never smoked or played at cards. He was the father of five children; his first wife had died in childbirth some years before and his second wife, Emily, was thirty years his junior and an acknowledged beauty, but she was as severe in disposition as her husband.

The Trent family resided at No. 17 Highwater Road, Mayfair, in a large Georgian mansion with twenty-three rooms, not including servants' quarters. Altogether, twelve servants were employed: a coach driver, two liverymen, a gardener, a doorman, a butler, a cook and two kitchen assistants, and three maids. There was also a governess for the three youngest children.

The children ranged in age from a four-year-old son to a twenty-nine-year-old daughter. All lived in the house. The youngest child had a tendency to somnambulation, so that there were often commotions at night that roused the entire household.

Mr. Trent kept two bulldogs, which were walked twice a day, at seven in the morning and at eight-fifteen at night, by the cook's assistants. The dogs were penned in a run at the back of the house, not far from the tradesmen's entrance.

Mr. Trent himself followed a rigid routine. Each day, he arose at 7 a.m., breakfasted at 7:30, and departed for work at

8:10, arriving at 8:29. He invariably lunched at Simpson's at one o'clock, for one hour. He left the bank promptly at 7 p.m., returning home no later than 7:20. Although he was a member of several clubs in town, he rarely frequented them. Mr. Trent and his wife went out of an evening twice in the course of a week; they generally gave a dinner once a week and occasionally a large party. On such evenings, an extra maid and manservant would be laid on, but these people were obtained from adjacent households; they were very reliable and could not be bribed.

The tradesmen who came each day to the side entrance of the house worked the entire street, and they were careful never to associate with a potential thief. For a fruit or vegetable hawker, a "polite street" was not easily come by, and they were all a close-mouthed lot.

A chimney sweep named Marks worked the same area. He was known to inform the police of any approach by a lurker seeking information. The sweep's boy was a simpleton; nothing could be got from him.

The constable patrolling the street, Lewis, made his rounds once every seventeen minutes. The shift changed at midnight; the night man, Howell, made his rounds once every sixteen minutes. Both men were highly reliable, never sick or drunk, and not susceptible to bribes.

The servants were content. None had been recently hired, nor had any been recently discharged; they were all well-treated and loyal to the household, particularly to Mrs. Trent. The coach driver was married to the cook; one of the liverymen was sleeping with one of the upstairs maids; the other two maids were comely and did not, apparently, lack for male companionship—they had found lovers among the serving staff of nearby households.

The Trent family took an annual seaside holiday during the month of August, but they would not do so this year, for Mr. Trent's business obligations were such that he was required to remain in town the whole of the summer. The family occasionally weekended in the country at the home of Mrs. Trent's parents, but during these outings most of the servants remained in the mansion. At no time, it seemed, were there fewer than eight people residing in the house.

All this information Pierce accumulated slowly and carefully, and often at some risk. Apparently he adopted various disguises when he talked with servants in pubs and on the street; he must also have loitered in the neighborhood, observing the patterns of the house, but this was a dangerous practice. He could, of course, hire a number of "crows" to scout the area for him, but the more people he hired, the more likely it was that rumors of an impending burglary of the Trent mansion would get out. In that case, the already formidable problems of cracking the house would be increased. So he did most of the reconnaissance himself, with some help from Agar.

According to his own testimony, by the end of August Pierce was no further ahead than he had been a month before. "The man afforded no purchase," Pierce said, speaking of Trent. "No vices, no weaknesses, no eccentricities, and a wife straight from the pages of a handbook on dutiful attention to the running of a happy household."

Clearly, there was no point in breaking into a twenty-three-room mansion on the off chance of coming upon the hidden key. Pierce had to have more information, and as he continued his surveillance it became evident that this information could be obtained only from Mr. Trent himself, who alone would know the location of the key.

Pierce had failed in every attempt to strike up a personal acquaintance with Mr. Trent. Henry Fowler, who shared with Pierce an occasional gentleman's evening on the town, had been approached on the subject of Trent, but Fowler had said the man was religious, proper, and rather a bore in conversation; and he added that his wife, though pretty, was equally tedious. (These comments, when brought forward in trial testimony, caused Mr. Fowler considerable embarrassment, but then Mr. Fowler was confronted with much greater embarrassments later.)

Pierce could hardly press for an introduction to such an unappetizing couple. Nor could he approach Trent directly, pretending business with the bank; Henry Fowler would rightly expect that Pierce would bring any business to him. Nor did Pierce know anyone except Fowler who was acquainted with Trent.

In short, Pierce had no gammon to play, and by the first of August he was considering several desperate ploys—such as staging an accident in which he would be run down by a cab in front of the Trent household, or a similar episode in front of the bank. But these were cheap tricks and, to be effective, they would require some degree of genuine injury to Pierce. Understandably, he was not happy at the prospect, and kept postponing the matter.

Then, on the evening of August 3rd, Mr. Trent suddenly changed his established routine. He returned home at his usual time, 7:20, but he did not go indoors. Instead, he went directly to the dog run at the back of the house, and put one of his bulldogs on a leash. Petting the animal elaborately, he climbed back into his waiting carriage and drove off.

When Pierce saw that, he knew he had his man.

A Made Dog

Not far from Southwark Mint was the livery stable of Jeremy Johnson & Son. It was a smallish establishment, quartering perhaps two dozen horses in three wooden barns, with hay, saddles, bridles, and other apparatus hanging from rafters. A casual visitor to this stable might be surprised to hear, instead of the whinny of horses, the predominant sound of barking, growling, snarling dogs. But the meaning of those sounds was clear enough to frequenters of the place, and no cause for particular comment. Throughout London, there were many reputable establishments that operated a side business of training fighting dogs.

Mr. Jeremy Johnson, Sr., led his red-bearded customer back through the stables. He was a jovial old man with most of his teeth missing. "Bit of an old gummer myself," he said, chuckling. "Doesn't hurt the drinking, though, I'll tell you that." He slapped the hindquarters of a horse to push it out of the way. "Move on, move on," he said, then looked back at Pierce. "Now what is it you'll be wanting?"

"Your best," Pierce said.

"That's what all the gentlemen are wanting," Mr. Johnson said, with a sigh. "None wants else than the best."

"I am very particular."

"Oh, I can see that," Johnson said. "I can see that, indeed. You're seeking a learner, so as to polish him yourself?"

"No," Pierce said, "I want a fully made dog."

"That's dear, you know."

"I know."

"Very dear, very dear," Johnson mumbled, moving back through the stable. He pushed open a creaking door, and they came into a small courtyard at the rear. Here were three wood-boarded circular pits, each perhaps six feet in diameter, and caged dogs on all sides. The dogs yelped and barked as they saw the men.

"Very dear, a made dog," Johnson said. "Takes a proper long training to have a good made dog. Here's how we do. First we gives the dog to a coster, and he jogs the dog day and day again—to toughen him, you know."

"I understand," Pierce said impatiently, "but I—"

"Then," Johnson continued, "then we puts the learner in with an old gummer—or a young gummer, as the case is now. Lost our gummer a fortnight past, so we took this one"—he pointed to a caged dog—"and yanked all the teeth, so he's the gummer now. Very good gummer he is, too. Knows how to worry a learner—very agile, this gummer is."

Pierce looked at the gummer. It was a young and healthy dog, barking vigorously. All its teeth were gone, yet it continued to snarl and pull back its lips menacingly. The sight made Pierce laugh.

"Yes, yes, 'tis a bit of a joke," Johnson said, moving around the enclosure, "but not when you get to this one here. Not here, there's no joking. Here's the finest taste dog in all London, I warrant."

This was a mongrel, larger than a bulldog, and parts of its body had been shaved. Pierce knew the routine: a young dog was first trained in sparring bouts with an old and toothless veteran; then it was put into the pit with a "taste dog," which was expendable but had good spirit. It was in the course of sparring with the taste dog that the learner acquired the final skills to go for the kill. The usual practice was to shave the vulnerable parts of the taste dog, encouraging the learner to attack those areas.

"This taster," Johnson said, "this taster has put the touches on more champions than you can name. You know Mr. Benderby's dog, the one that bested the Manchester killer last month? Well, this taster here trained Mr. Benderby's dog. And also Mr. Starrett's dog, and—oh, a dozen others, all top fighting dogs. Now Mr. Starrett himself, he comes back to me and wants to buy this very taster. Says he wants to have him to worry a badger or two. You know what he offers me? Fifty quid, he offers me. And you know what I say? Not on your life, I say, not fifty quid for this taster."

Johnson shook his head a little sadly.

"Not for badgers, anyhow," he said. "Badgers are no proper worry for any fighting dog. No, no. A proper fighting dog is for your dogs, or, if need be, for your rats." He squinted at Pierce. "You want your dog for ratting? We have special trained ratters," Mr. Johnson said. "A touch less dear, is why I mention it."

"I want your very best made dog."

"And you shall have it, I warrant. Here is the devil's own, right here." Johnson paused before a cage. Inside, Pierce saw a bulldog that weighed about forty pounds. The dog growled but did not move. "See that? He's a confident one. He's had a good mouthful or two, and he's well made. Vicious as ever I saw. Some dogs have the instinct, you know—can't be taught 'em, they just have the instinct to get a good mouthful straightaway. This here one, he's got the instinct."

"How much?" Pierce said.

"Twenty quid."

Pierce hesitated.

"With the studded leash, and the collar and muzzle, all in," Johnson added.

Pierce still waited.

"He'll do you proud, I warrant, very proud."

After a lengthy silence, Pierce said, "I want your *best* dog." He pointed to the cage. "This dog has never fought. He has no scars. I want a trained veteran."

"And you shall have him," Johnson said, not blinking. He moved two cages down. "This one here has the killer instinct, the taste of blood, and quick? Why, quicker than your eye, he is, this one. Took the neck off old Whitington's charger a week past, at the pub tourney—perhaps you was there and saw him."

Pierce said, "How much?"

"Twenty-five quid, all in."

Pierce stared at the animal for a moment, then said, "I want the best dog you have."

"This is the very same, I swear it—the very dog that's best of the lot."

Pierce crossed his arms over his chest and tapped his foot on the ground.

"I swear it, sir, twenty-five quid, a gentleman's fancy and most excellent in all respects."

Pierce just stared at him.

"Well, then," Johnson said, looking away as if embarrassed, "there *is* one more animal, but he's very special. He has the killer instinct, the taste of blood, the quick move, and a tough hide. This way."

He led Pierce out of the enclosed courtyard to another area, where there were three dogs in somewhat larger pens. They were all heavier than the others; Pierce guessed they must weigh fifty pounds, perhaps more. Johnson tapped the middle cage.

"This'un," he said. "This'un turned felon on me," he said. "Thought I'd have to top him off—he was a felon, pure and simple." Johnson rolled up his sleeve to reveal a set of jagged white scars. "This'un did this to me," he said, "when he turned felon. But I brought him back, nursed him, and trained him special, because he has the spirit, see, and the spirit's everything."

"How much?" Pierce said.

Johnson glanced at the scars on his arm. "This'un I was saving—"

"How much?"

"Couldn't let him go for less'n fifty quid, beg pardon."

"I will give you forty."

"Sold," Johnson said quickly. "You'll take 'im now?"

"No," Pierce said. "I'll call for him soon. For the moment, hold him."

"Then you'll be putting a little something down?"

"I will," Pierce said, and gave the man ten pounds. Then he had him pry open the dog's jaws, and he checked the teeth; and then he departed.

"Damn me," Johnson said after he had gone. "Man buys a made dog, then leaves him. What're we up to today?"

CHAPTER 11

The Destruction of Vermin

Captain Jimmy Shaw, a retired pugilist, ran the most famous of the sporting pubs, the Queen's Head, off Windmill Street. A visitor to that pub on the evening of August 10, 1854, would be greeted by a most peculiar spectacle, for although the pub was notably low-ceilinged, dingy, and cheap, it was filled with all manner of well-dressed gentlemen who rubbed shoulders with hawkers, costers, navvies, and others of the lowest social station. Yet nobody seemed to mind, for everyone shared a state of excited, noisy anticipation. Furthermore, nearly everyone had brought a dog. There were dogs of all sorts: bulldogs, Skye terriers, brown English terriers, and various mongrels. Some nestled in the arms of their owners; others were tied to the legs of tables or to the footrail of the bar. All were the subject of intense discussion and scrutiny: they were hefted into the air to gauge their weight, their limbs were felt for the strength of bones, their jaws opened for a look at the teeth.

A visitor might then observe that the few decorative features of the Queen's Head reflected this same interest in dogs. Studded leather collars hung from the rafters; there were stuffed dogs in dirty glass boxes mounted over the bar; there were prints of dogs by the hearth, including a famous drawing of Tiny, "the wonder dog," a white bulldog whose legendary exploits were known to every man present.

Jimmy Shaw, a burly figure with a broken nose, moved about the room calling, "Give your orders, gentlemen," in a loud voice. At the Queen's Head, even the best gentlemen drank hot gin without complaint. Indeed, no one seemed to notice the tawdry surroundings at all. Nor, for that matter, did anyone seem to mind that most of the dogs were heavily scarred on the face, body, and limbs.

Above the bar, a soot-covered sign read:

EVERY MAN HAS HIS FANCY
RATTING SPORTS IN REALITY

And if people should be uncertain as to the meaning of that sign, their doubts ended at nine o'clock, when Captain Jimmy gave the order to "light up the pit" and the entire assembled company began to file toward the upstairs room, each man carrying his dog, and each man dropping a shilling into the hand of a waiting assistant before ascending the stairs.

The second floor of the Queen's Head was a large room, as low-ceilinged as the ground floor. This room was wholly devoid of furnishings, and dominated by the pit—a circular arena six feet in diameter, enclosed by slat boards four feet high. The floor of the pit was whitewashed, freshly applied each evening.

As the spectators arrived on the second floor, their dogs immediately came alive, jumping in their owners' arms, barking vigorously, and straining on the leashes. Captain Jimmy said sternly, "Now you gentlemen that have fancies—shut 'em up," and there was some attempt to do this, but it was hardly successful, especially when the first cage of rats was brought forth.

At the sight of the rats, the dogs barked and snarled fiercely. Captain Jimmy held the rusty wire cage over his head, waving it in the air; it contained perhaps fifty scampering rats. "Nothing but the finest, gentlemen," he announced. "Every one country born, and not a water-ditch among 'em. Who wants to try a rat?"

By now, fifty or sixty people had crammed into the narrow room. Many leaned over the wooden boards of the pit. There was money in every hand, and lively bargaining. Over the general din, a voice from the back spoke up. "I'll have a try at twenty. Twenty of your best for my fancy."

"Weigh the fancy of Mr. T.," Captain Jimmy said, for he knew the speaker. The assistants rushed up and took the bulldog from the arms of a gray-bearded, balding gentleman. The dog was weighed.

"Twenty-seven pounds!" came the cry, and the dog was returned to its owner.

"That's it, then, gents," Captain Jimmy said. "Twenty-seven pounds is Mr. T.'s fancy dog, and he has called for a try at twenty rats. Shall it be four minutes?"

Mr. T. nodded in agreement.

"Four minutes it is, gentlemen, and you may wager as you see fit. Make room for Mr. T."

The gray-bearded gentleman moved up to the edge of the pit, still cradling his dog in his arms. The animal was spotted black and white, and it snarled at the rats opposite. Mr. T. urged his dog on by making snarling and growling noises himself.

"Let's see them," Mr. T. said.

The assistant opened the cage and reached in to grab the rats with his bare hand. This was important, for it proved

that the rats were indeed country animals, and not infected
with any disease. The assistant picked out "twenty of the
finest" and tossed them down into the pit. The animals
scampered around the perimeter, then finally huddled together in one corner, in a furry mass.

"Are we ready?" called Captain Jimmy, brandishing a
stopwatch in his hand.

"Ready," said Mr. T., making growling and snarling
sounds to his dog.

"Blow on 'em! Blow on 'em!" came the cry from the
spectators, and various otherwise quite dignified gentlemen
puffed and blew toward the rats, raising the fur and sending
them into a frenzy.

"Aaannnddd . . . go!" shouted Captain Jimmy, and Mr. T.
flung his dog into the pit. Immediately, Mr. T. crouched
down until his head was just above the wooden rim, and
from this position he urged his dog on with shouted instructions and canine growls.

The dog leapt forward into the mass of rats, striking out
at them, snapping at the necks like the true and well-blooded
sport that he was. In an instant he had killed three or four.

The betting spectators screamed and yelled no less than
the owner, who never took his eyes from the combat. "That's
it!" shouted Mr. T. "That's a dead one, drop 'im, now go!
Grrrrrr! Good, that's another, drop 'im. Go! Grrr-rugh!"

The dog moved quickly from one furry body to the next.
Then one rat caught hold of his nose and clung tightly; the
dog could not shake the rat free.

"Twister! Twister!" shrieked the crowd.

The dog writhed, got free, and raced after the others.
Now there were six rats killed, their bodies lying on the
blood-streaked pit floor.

"Two minutes past," called Captain Jimmy.

"Hi, Lover, good Lover," screamed Mr. T. "Go, boy.
Grrrrh! That's one, now drop 'im. Go, Lover!"

The dog raced around the arena, pursuing its quarry; the

crowd screamed and pounded the wooden slats to keep the animals in a frenzy. At one point Lover had four rats clinging to his face and body, and still he kept going, crunching a fifth in his strong jaws. In the midst of all this furious excitement, no one noticed a red-bearded gentleman of dignified bearing who pushed his way through the crowd until he was standing alongside Mr. T., whose attention remained wholly focused on the dog.

"Three minutes," Captain Jimmy called. There was a groan from several in the crowd. Three minutes gone and only twelve rats dead; those who had bet on Mr. T.'s fancy were going to lose their money.

Mr. T. himself did not seem to hear the time. His eyes never left the dog; he barked and yelped; he twisted his body, writhing with the dog he owned; he snapped his jaws and screamed orders until he was hoarse.

"Time!" shouted Captain Jimmy, waving the stopwatch. The crowd sighed and relaxed. Lover was pulled from the arena; the three remaining rats were deftly scooped up by the assistants.

The ratting match was over; Mr. T. had lost.

"Bloody good try," said the red-bearded man, in consolation.

The paradoxes inherent in Mr. Edgar Trent's behavior at the Queen's Head pub—indeed, in his very presence in such surroundings—require some explanation.

In the first place, a man who was the president of a bank, a devout Christian, and a pillar of the respectable community would never think to associate himself with members of the lower orders. Quite the contrary: Mr. Trent devoted considerable time and energy to keeping these people in their proper place, and he did so with the firm and certain knowledge that he was helping to maintain good social order.

Yet there were a few places in Victorian society where members of all classes mingled freely, and chief among these were sporting events—the prize ring, the turf, and, of course, the baiting sports. All these activities were either disreputable or flatly illegal, and their supporters, derived from every stratum of society, shared a common interest that permitted them to overlook the breakdown of social convention upon such occasions. And if Mr. Trent saw no incongruity in his presence among the lowest street hawkers and costers, it is also true that the hawkers and costers, usually tongue-tied and uneasy in the presence of gentlemen, were equally relaxed at these sporting events, laughing and nudging freely men whom they would not dare to touch under ordinary circumstances.

Their common interest—animal baiting—had been a cherished form of amusement throughout Western Europe since medieval times. But in Victorian England animal sports were dying out rapidly, the victim of legislation and changing public tastes. The baiting of bulls or bears, common at the turn of the century, was now quite rare; cockfighting was found only in rural centers. In London in 1854, only three animal sports remained popular, and all concerned dogs.

Nearly every foreign observer since Elizabethan times has commented on the affection Englishmen lavish upon their dogs, and it is odd that the very creature most dear to English hearts should be the focus of these flagrantly sadistic "sporting events."

Of the three dog sports, dogs set against other dogs was considered the highest "art" of animal sports. This sport was sufficiently widespread that many London criminals made a good living working exclusively as dog thieves, or "fur-pullers." But dogfights were relatively uncommon, since they were ordinarily battles to the death, and a good fighting dog was an expensive article.

Even less common was badger-baiting. Here a badger would be chained in an arena, and a dog or two set loose to worry the animal. The badger's tough hide and sharp bite made the spectacle particularly tense and highly popular, but a scarcity of badgers limited the sport.

Ratting was the most common dog sport, particularly at the mid-century. Although technically illegal, it was conducted for decades with flagrant disregard for the law. Throughout London there were signs reading, "Rats Wanted" and "Rats Bought and Sold"; there was, in fact, a minor industry in ratcatching, with its own specialized rules of the trade. Country rats were most prized, for their fighting vigor and their absence of infection. The more common sewer rats, readily identified by their smell, were timid and their bites more likely to infect a valuable fighting dog. When one recognizes that the owner of a sporting pub with a well-attended rat pit might buy two thousand rats a week—and a good country rat could fetch as much as a shilling—it is not surprising that many individuals made a living as ratcatchers. The most famous was "Black Jack" Hanson, who went about in a hearse-like wagon, offering to rid fashionable mansions of pests for absurdly low rates, so long as he could "take the critters live."

There is no good explanation for why Victorians at all levels of society looked away from the sport of ratting, but they were conveniently blind. Most humane writing of the period deplores and condemns cockfighting—which was already very rare—without mentioning dog sports at all. Nor is there any indication that reputable gentlemen felt any unease at participating in ratting sports; for these gentlemen considered themselves "staunch supporters of the destruction of vermin," and nothing more.

One such staunch supporter, Mr. T., retired to the downstairs rooms of the Queen's Head pub, which was now virtually deserted. Signaling the solitary barman, he called for a glass of gin for himself and some peppermint for his fancy.

Mr. T. was in the process of washing his dog's mouth out

with peppermint—to prevent canker—when the red-bearded gentleman came down the stairs and said, "May I join you for a glass?"

"By all means," Mr. T. said, continuing to minister to his dog.

Upstairs, the sound of stomping feet and shouting indicated the beginning of another episode of the destruction of vermin. The red-bearded stranger had to shout over the din. "I perceive you are a gentleman of sporting instinct," he said.

"And unlucky," Mr. T. said, equally loudly. He stroked his dog. "Lover was not at her best this evening. When she is in a state, there is none to match her, but at times she lacks bustle." Mr. T. sighed regretfully. "Tonight was such a one." He ran his hands over the dog's body, probing for deep bites, and wiped the blood of several cuts from his fingers with his handkerchief. "But she came off well enough. My Lover will fight again."

"Indeed," the red-bearded man said, "and I shall wager upon her again when she does."

Mr. T. showed a trace of concern. "Did you lose?"

"A trifle. Ten guineas, it was nothing."

Mr. T. was a conservative man, and well enough off, but not disposed to think of ten guineas as "a trifle." He looked again at his drinking companion, noticing the fine cut of his coat and the excellent white silk of his neckcloth.

"I am pleased you take it so lightly," he said. "Permit me to buy you a glass, as a token of your ill fortune."

"Never," returned the red-bearded man, "for I count it no ill fortune at all. Indeed, I admire a man who may keep a fancy and sport her. I should do so myself, were I not so often abroad on business."

"Oh, yes?" said Mr. T., signaling to the barman for another round.

"Quite," said the stranger. "Why, only the other day, I was offered a most excellently made dog, close upon a felon, with the tastes of a true fighter. I could not make the purchase, for I have no time myself to look after the animal."

"Most unfortunate," said Mr. T. "What was the price asked?"

"Fifty guineas."

"Excellent price."

"Indeed."

The waiter brought more drinks. "I am myself in search of a made dog," Mr. T. said.

"Indeed?"

"Yes," Mr. T. said. "I should like a third to complement my stable, with Lover and Shantung—that is the other dog. But I don't suppose . . ."

The red-bearded gentleman paused discreetly before answering. The training, buying, and selling of fighting dogs was, after all, illegal. "If you wish," Pierce said at last, "I could inquire whether the animal is still available."

"Oh, yes? That would be very good of you. Very good indeed." Mr. T. had a sudden thought. "But were I you, I should buy it myself. After all, while you were abroad, your wife could instruct the servants in the care of the beast."

"I fear," replied the red-bearded man, "that I have devoted too much of my energies these past years to the pursuit of business concerns. I have never married." And then he added, "But of course I should like to."

"Of course," Mr. T. said, with a most peculiar look coming over his face.

CHAPTER 12

The Problem of Miss Elizabeth Trent

Victorian England was the first society to constantly gather statistics on itself, and generally these figures were a source of unabashed pride. Beginning in 1840, however, one trend worried the leading thinkers of the day: there were increasingly more single women than men. By 1851, the number of single women of marriageable age was reliably put at 2,765,000 —and a large proportion of these women were the daughters of the middle and upper classes.

Here was a problem of considerable dimension and gravity. Women of lower stations in life could take jobs as seamstresses, flower girls, field workers, or any of a dozen lowly occupations. These women were of no pressing concern; they were slovenly creatures lacking in education and a discriminating view of the world. A. H. White reports, in tones of astonishment, that he interviewed a young girl who worked as a matchbox maker, who "never went to church or chapel. Never heard of 'England' or 'London' or the 'sea' or 'ships.' Never heard of God. Does not know what He does. Does not know whether it is better to be good or bad."

Obviously, in the face of such massive ignorance, one must simply be grateful that the poor child had discovered some way to survive in society at all. But the problem presented by the daughters of middle- and upper-class households was different. These young ladies possessed education and a taste for genteel living. And they had been raised from birth for no other purpose than to be "perfect wives."

It was terribly important that such women should marry. The failure to marry—spinsterhood—implied a kind of dreadful crippling, for it was universally acknowledged that "a woman's true position was that of administratrix, mainspring, guiding star of the home," and if she was unable to perform this function, she became a sort of pitiful social misfit, an oddity.

The problem was made more acute by the fact that well-born women had few alternatives to wifehood. After all, as one contemporary observer noted, what occupations could they find "without losing their position in society? A lady, to be such, must be a mere lady, and nothing else. She must not work for profit, or engage in any occupation that money can command, lest she invade the rights of the working classes, who live by their labor. . . ."

In practice, an unmarried upper-class woman could use the one unique attribute of her position, education, and become a governess. But by 1851, twenty-five thousand women were already employed as governesses and there was, to say the least, no need for more. Her other choices were much less appealing: she might be a shop assistant, a clerk, a telegraphist, or a nurse, but all these occupations were more suitable for an ambitious lower-class woman than a firmly established gentlewoman of quality.

If a young woman refused such demeaning work, her spinsterhood implied a considerable financial burden upon the household. Miss Emily Downing observed that "the daughters of professional men . . . cannot but feel themselves a burden and a drag on the hard-won earnings of their fathers; they must know—if they allow themselves to think at all—that they are a constant cause of anxiety, and that should they not get married, there is every probability of their be-

ing, sooner or later, obliged to enter the battle of life utterly
unprepared and unfitted for the fight."

In short, there was intense pressure for marriage—any
sort of decent marriage—felt by fathers and daughters alike.
The Victorians tended to marry relatively late, in their
twenties or thirties, but Mr. Edgar Trent had a daughter
Elizabeth, now twenty-nine and of "wholly marriageable
condition"—meaning somewhat past her prime. It could not
have escaped Mr. Trent's attention that the red-bearded
gentleman might be in need of a wife. The gentleman himself expressed no reluctance to marry, but rather had indicated that the exigencies of business had kept him from
pursuing personal happiness. Thus there was no reason to believe that this well-dressed, evidently well-to-do young man
with a sporting instinct might not be drawn to Elizabeth.
With this in mind, Mr. Trent contrived to invite Mr. Pierce
to his house on Highwater Road for Sunday tea, on the pre-
text of discussing the purchase of a fighting dog from Mr.
Pierce. Mr. Pierce, somewhat reluctantly, accepted the invitation.

Elizabeth Trent was not called as a witness at the trial
of Pierce, out of deference to her finer sensibilities. But
popular accounts of the time give us an accurate picture
of her. She was of medium height, rather darker in complexion than was the fashion, and her features were, in the
words of one observer, "regular enough without being what
one might call pretty." Then, as now, journalists were inclined to exaggerate the beauty of any woman involved in a
scandalous event, so that the absence of compliments about
Miss Trent's appearance probably implies "an unfortunate
aspect."

She apparently had few suitors, save for those openly
ambitious fellows eager to marry a bank president's daughter,
and these she staunchly rejected, with her father's un-

doubtedly mixed blessing. But she must surely have been impressed with Pierce, that "dashing, intrepid, fine figure of a man with charm to burn."

By all accounts, Pierce was equally impressed by the young lady. A servant's testimony records their initial meeting, which reads as if it came from the pages of a Victorian novel.

Mr. Pierce was taking tea on the rear lawn with Mr. Trent and Mrs. Trent, an "acknowledged beauty of the town." They watched as bricklayers in the back yard patiently erected a ruined building, while nearby a gardener planted picturesque weeds. This was the last gasp of a nearly one-hundred-year English fascination with ruins; they were still so fashionable that everyone who could afford a decent ruin installed one on his grounds.

Pierce watched the workmen for a while. "What is it to be?" he inquired.

"We thought a water mill," Mrs. Trent said. "It will be so delightful, especially if there is the rusted curve of the waterwheel itself. Don't you think so?"

"We are building the rusted wheel at a goodly expense," Mr. Trent grumbled.

"It is being constructed of previously rusted metal, saving us a good deal of bother," Mrs. Trent added. "But of course we must wait for the weeds to grow up around the site before it takes on the proper appearance."

At that moment Elizabeth arrived, wearing white crinoline. "Ah, my darling daughter," Mr. Trent said, rising, and Mr. Pierce rose with him. "May I present Mr. Edward Pierce, my daughter Elizabeth."

"I confess I did not know you had a daughter," Pierce said. He bowed deeply at the waist, took her hand, and seemed about to kiss it but hesitated. He appeared greatly flustered by the young woman's arrival on the scene.

"Miss Trent," he said, releasing her hand awkwardly. "You take me quite by surprise."

"I cannot tell if that is to my advantage or no," Elizabeth Trent replied, quickly taking a seat at the tea table and holding out her hand until a filled cup was put in it.

"I assure you, it is wholly to your advantage," Mr. Pierce replied. And he was reported to have colored deeply at this remark.

Miss Trent fanned herself; Mr. Trent cleared his throat; Mrs. Trent, the perfect wife, picked up a tray of biscuits and said, "Will you try one of these, Mr. Pierce?"

"With gratitude, Madam," Mr. Pierce replied, and no one present doubted the sincerity of his words.

"We are just discussing the ruins," Mr. Trent said, in a somewhat overloud voice. "But prior to that Mr. Pierce was telling us of his travels abroad. He has recently returned from New York, in point of fact."

It was a cue; his daughter picked it up neatly. "Really?" she said, fanning herself briskly. "How utterly fascinating."

"I fear it is more so in the prospect than the telling," Mr. Pierce replied, avoiding the glance of the young woman to such a degree that all observed his abashed reticence. He was clearly taken with her; and the final proof was that he addressed his remarks to Mrs. Trent. "It is a city like any other in the world, if truth be told, and chiefly distinguished by the lack of niceties which we residents of London take for granted."

"I have been informed," Miss Trent ventured, still fanning, "that there are native predators in the region."

"I should be delighted if I could regale you," Mr. Pierce said, "with endless adventures with the Indians—for so they are called, in America as in the East—but I fear I have no adventures to report. The wilderness of America does not begin until the Mississippi is crossed."

"Have you done so?" asked Mrs. Trent.

"I have," Mr. Pierce replied. "It is a vast river, many times more broad than the Thames, and it marks the boundary in America between civilization and savagery. Although lately they are constructing a railway across that vast colony"—he permitted himself the condescending reference to America, and Mr. Trent guffawed—"and I expect with the coming of the railway, the savagery will soon vanish."

"How quaint," Miss Trent said, apparently unable to think of anything else to say.

"What business took you to New York?" Mr. Trent asked.

"If I may be so bold," Mr. Pierce continued, ignoring the question, "and if the delicate ears of the ladies present shall not be offended, I shall give an example of the savagery which persists in the American lands, and the rude way of life which many persons there think nothing remarkable. Do you know of buffaloes?"

"I have read of them," said Mrs. Trent, her eyes flashing. According to some of the testimony of the servants, she was as taken with Mr. Pierce as was her stepdaughter, and her demeanor created a minor scandal within the Trent household. Mrs. Trent said, "These buffaloes are large beasts, like wild cows, and shaggy."

"Precisely so," Mr. Pierce said. "The western portion of the American country is widely populated with these buffalo creatures, and many persons make their livelihood—such as it is—in hunting them."

"Have you been to California, where there is gold?" asked Miss Trent abruptly.

"Yes," Pierce said.

"Let the man finish his tale," Mrs. Trent said, rather too sharply.

"Well," Pierce said, "the buffalo hunters, as they are known, sometimes seek the flesh of the animals, which is reckoned like venison, and sometimes the hide, which also has value."

"They lack tusks," Mr. Trent said. Mr. Trent had lately financed an elephant-killing expedition on behalf of the bank, and at this very moment an enormous warehouse at dockside

was filled with five thousand ivory tusks. Mr. Trent had
gone to inspect these goods for himself, a vast room of white
curving tusks, most impressive.

"No, they have no tusks, although the male of the species
possesses horns."

"Horns, I see. But not of ivory."

"No, not ivory."

"I see."

"Please go on," Mrs. Trent said, her eyes still flashing.

"Well," Pierce said, "the men who ki— who dispatch these
buffaloes are called buffalo hunters, and they utilize rifles
for their purposes. On occasion they organize themselves
into a line to drive the beasts over some cliff in a mass. But
that is not common. Most frequently, the beast is dispatched
singly. In any event—and here I must beg excuses for the
crudity of what I must report of this crude countryside—
once the beast has terminated existence, its innards are removed."

"Very sensible," Mr. Trent said.

"To be sure," Pierce said, "but here is the peculiar part.
These buffalo hunters prize as the greatest of delicacies one
portion of the innards, that being the small intestines of the
beast."

"How are they prepared?" Miss Trent asked. "By roast-
ing over a fire, I expect."

"No, Madam," Pierce said, "for I am telling you a tale
of abject savagery. These intestines which are so prized, so
much considered a delicacy, are consumed upon the spot, in
a state wholly uncooked."

"Do you mean *raw?*" asked Mrs. Trent, wrinkling her
nose.

"Indeed, Madam, as we would consume a raw oyster, so
do the hunters consume the intestine, and that while it is still
warm from the newly expired beast."

"Dear God," said Mrs. Trent.

"Now, then," Pierce continued, "it happens upon occasion

that two men may have joined in the killing, and immediately afterward each falls upon one end of the prized intestines. Each hunter races the other, trying to gobble up this delicacy faster than his opponent."

"Gracious," Miss Trent said, fanning herself more briskly.

"Not only that," Pierce said, "but in their greedy haste, the buffalo hunter often swallows the portions whole. This is a known trick. But his opponent, recognizing the trick, may in the course of eating pull from the other the undigested portion straightaway from his mouth, as I might pull a string through my fingers. And thus one man may gobble up what another has earlier eaten, in a manner of speaking."

"Oh, dear," said Mrs. Trent, turning quite pale.

Mr. Trent cleared his throat. "Remarkable."

"How quaint," said Miss Trent bravely, with a quivering voice.

"You really must excuse me," said Mrs. Trent, rising.

"My dear," Mr. Trent said.

"Madam, I hope I have not distressed you," said Mr. Pierce, also rising.

"Your tales are quite remarkable," Mrs. Trent said, turning to leave.

"My dear," Mr. Trent said again, and hastened after her.

Thus Mr. Edward Pierce and Miss Elizabeth Trent were briefly alone on the back lawn of the mansion, and they were seen to exchange a few words. The content of their conversation is not known. But Miss Trent later admitted to a servant that she found Mr. Pierce "quite fascinating in a rough-and-ready way," and it was generally agreed in the Trent household that young Elizabeth was now in possession of that most valuable of all acquisitions, a "prospect."

CHAPTER 13

A Hanging

The execution of the notorious axe murderess Emma Barnes on August 28, 1854, was a well-publicized affair. On the evening prior to the execution, the first of the crowds began to gather outside the high granite walls of Newgate Prison, where they would spend the night in order to be assured of a good view of the spectacle the following morning. That same evening, the gallows was brought out and assembled by the executioner's assistants. The sound of hammering would continue long into the night.

The owners of nearby rooming houses that overlooked Newgate square were pleased to rent their rooms for the evening to the better class of ladies and gents eager to get a room with a good view over the site for a "hanging party." Mrs. Edna Molloy, a virtuous widow, knew perfectly well the value of her rooms, and when a well-spoken gentleman named Pierce asked to hire the best of them for the night, she struck a hard bargain: twenty-five guineas for a single evening.

That was a considerable sum of money. Mrs. Molloy could live comfortably for a year on that amount, but she did not let the fact influence her, for she knew what it was worth to Mr. Pierce himself—the cost of a butler for six months, or the price of one or two good ladies' dresses, and nothing more substantial than that. The very proof of his indifference lay in the ready way he paid her, on the spot, in gold guineas. Mrs. Molloy did not wish to risk offending him by biting the coins in front of him, but she would bite them as soon as she was alone. One couldn't be too careful with gold guineas, and she had been fooled more than once, even by gentlemen.

The coins were genuine, and she was much relieved. Thus she paid little attention when, later in the day, Mr. Pierce and his party filed upstairs to the hired room. The party consisted of two other men and two women, all smartly turned out in good clothes. She could tell by their accents that the men were not gentlemen, and the women were no better than they looked, despite the wicker baskets and bottles of wine they carried.

When the party entered the room and closed the door behind them, she did not bother to listen at the keyhole. She'd have no trouble from them, she was sure of it.

Pierce stepped to the window and looked down at the crowd, which gathered size with each passing minute. The square was dark, lit only by the glare of torches around the scaffolding; by that hot, baleful light he could see the crossbar and trap taking shape.

"Never make it," Agar said behind him.

Pierce turned. "He has to make it, laddie."

"He's the best snakesman in the business, the best anybody ever heard speak of, but he can't get out of there," Agar said, jerking his thumb toward Newgate Prison.

The second man now spoke. The second man was Barlow, a stocky, rugged man with a white knife scar across his forehead, which he usually concealed beneath the brim of his hat. Barlow was a reformed buzzer turned rampsman—a pickpocket who had degenerated to plain mugging—whom Pierce had hired, some years back, as a buck cabby. All rampsmen were thugs at heart, and that was precisely what a cracksman like Pierce wanted for a buck cabby, a man holding the reins to the cab, ready to make the getaway—or ready for a bit of a shindy, if it came to that. And Barlow was loyal; he had worked for Pierce for nearly five years now.

Barlow frowned and said, "If it can be done, he'll do it. Clean Willy can do it if it can be done." He spoke slowly, and gave the impression of a man who formed his thoughts with slowness. Pierce knew he could be quick in action, however.

Pierce looked at the women. They were the mistresses of Agar and Barlow, which meant they were also their accomplices. He did not know their names and he did not want to know. He regretted the very idea that they must be present at this occasion—in five years, he had never seen Barlow's woman—but there was no way to avoid it. Barlow's woman was an obvious soak; you could smell the gin breath across the room. Agar's woman was little better, but at least she was sober.

"Did you bring the trimmings?" Pierce asked.

Agar's woman opened a picnic basket. In it, he saw a sponge, medicinal powders, and bandages. There was also a carefully folded dress. "All I was told, sir."

"The dress is small?"

"Aye, sir. Barely more'n a child's frock, sir."

"Well enough," Pierce said, and turned back to look at the square once more. He paid no attention to the gallows or the swelling crowd. Instead he stared at the walls of Newgate Prison.

"Here's the supper, sir," said Barlow's woman. Pierce looked back at the supplies of cold fowl, jars of pickled onion, lobster claws, and a packet of dark cigars.

"Very good, very good," he said.

Agar said, "Are you playing the noble, sir?" This was a reference to a well-known magsman's con. It was said sarcastically, and Agar later testified that Pierce didn't care for the comment. He turned back with his long coat open at the waist to reveal a revolver jammed into the waistband of his trousers.

"If any of you steps aside," he said, "you'll have a barker up your nose, and I'll see you in lavender." He smiled thinly. "There are worse things, you know, than transportation to Australia."

"No offense," Agar said, looking at the gun. "No offense at all, no offense—it was only in the manner of a joke."

Barlow said, "Why'd we need a snakesman?"

Pierce was not sidetracked. "Bear my words carefully," he said. "Any of you steps aside and you'll stop a shot before you can say Jack Robin. I mean every word." He sat down at the table. "Now then," he said, "I'll have a leg of that chicken, and we shall disport ourselves as best we can while we wait."

Pierce slept part of the night; he was awakened at daybreak by the crowd that jammed the square below. The crowd had now swollen to more than fifteen thousand noisy, rough people, and Pierce knew that the streets would be filled with ten or fifteen thousand more, making their way to see the hanging on their route to work. Employers hardly bothered to keep up a pretense of strictness on any Monday morning when there was a hanging; it was an accepted fact that everybody would be late to work, and especially today, with a woman to be hanged.

The gallows itself was now finished; the rope dangled in the air above the trap. Pierce glanced at his pocketwatch. It was 7:45, just a short time before the execution itself.

In the square below, the crowd began to chant: "Oh, my, think I'm going to die! Oh, my, think I'm going to die!" There was a good deal of laughter and shouting and stamping of feet. One or two fights broke out, but they could not be sustained in the tightly packed crush of the crowd.

They all went to the window to watch.

Agar said, "When do you think he'll make his move?"

"Right at eight, I should think."

"I'd do it a bit sooner, myself."

Pierce said, "He'll make his move whenever he thinks best."

The minutes passed slowly. No one in the room spoke.

Finally, Barlow said, "I knew Emma Barnes—never thought she'd come to this."

Pierce said nothing.

At eight o'clock, the chimes of St. Sepulchre signaled the hour, and the crowd roared in anticipation. There was the soft jingle of a prison bell, and then a door in Newgate opened and the prisoner was led out, her wrists strapped behind her. In front was a chaplain, reciting from the Bible. Behind was the city executioner, dressed in black.

The crowd saw the prisoner and shouted "Hats off!" Every man's hat was removed as the prisoner slowly stepped up the scaffolding. Then there were cries of "Down in front! Down in front!" They were, for the most part, unheeded.

Pierce kept his gaze on the condemned woman. Emma Barnes was in her thirties, and looked vigorous enough. The firm lines and muscles of her neck were clearly visible through her open-necked dress. But her eyes were distant and glazed; she did not really seem to see anything. She took up her position and the city executioner turned to her, making slight adjustments, as if he were a seamstress positioning a dressmaker's dummy. Emma Barnes stared above the crowd. The rope was fitted to a chain around her neck.

The clergyman read loudly, keeping his eyes fixed on the Bible. The city executioner strapped the woman's legs together with a leather strap; this occasioned a good deal of fumbling beneath her skirts; the crowd made raucous comments.

Then the executioner stood, and slipped a black hood over the woman's head. And then, at a signal, the trap opened with a wooden *crack!* that Pierce heard with startling distinctness; and the body fell, and caught, and hung instantly motionless.

"He's getting better at it," Agar said. The city executioner was known for botching executions, leaving the hanged prisoner to writhe and dangle for several minutes before he died. "Crowd won't like it," Agar added.

The crowd, in fact, did not seem to mind. There was a

moment of utter silence, and then the excited roar of discussion. Pierce knew that most of the crowd would remain in the square, watching for the next hour, until the dead woman was cut down and placed in a coffin.

"Will you take some punch?" asked Agar's tart.

"No," Pierce said. And then he said, "Where is Willy?"

Clean Willy Williams, the most famous snakesman of the century, was inside Newgate Prison beginning his escape. He was a tiny man, and he had been famous in his youth for his agility as a chimney sweep's apprentice; in later years he had been employed by the most eminent cracksmen, and his feats were now legendary. It was said that Clean Willy could climb a surface of glass, and no one was quite certain that he couldn't.

Certainly the guards of Newgate, knowing the celebrity of their prisoner, had kept a close watch on him these many months, just in case. Yet they also knew that escape from Newgate was flatly impossible. A resourceful man might make a go of it from Ponsdale, where routines were notoriously lax, the walls low, and the guards not averse to the feel of gold coin and were known to look the other way. Ponsdale, or Highgate, or any of a dozen others, but never Newgate.

Newgate Prison was the most secure in all England. It had been designed by George Dance, "one of the most meticulous intellects of the Age of Taste," and every detail of the building had been set forth to emphasize the harsh facts of confinement. Thus the proportions of the window arches had been "subtly thickened in order to intensify the painful narrowness of the openings," and contemporary observers applauded the excellence of such cruel effects.

The reputation of Newgate was not merely a matter of aesthetics. In the more than seventy years since 1782, when the building was finished, no convict had ever escaped. And this was hardly surprising: Newgate was surrounded on all sides with granite walls fifty feet high. The stones were so

finely cut that they were said to be impossible to scale. Yet
even if one could manage the impossible, it was to no avail,
for encircling the top of the walls was an iron bar, fitted
with revolving, razor-sharp spiked drums. And the bar was
also fitted with spikes. No man could get past that obstacle.
Escape from Newgate was inconceivable.

With the passing months, as the guards grew familiar with
the presence of little Willy, they ceased to watch him closely.
He was not a difficult prisoner. He never broke the rule of
silence, never spoke to a fellow inmate; he suffered the "cockchafer"—or treadmill—for the prescribed fifteen-minute intervals without complaint or incident; he worked at oakum-
picking with no surcease. Indeed, there was some grudging
respect for the reformed aspect of the little man, for the cheerful way he went about the routine. He was a likely candidate
for a ticket-of-leave, a foreshortened sentence, in a year or so.

Yet at eight in the morning on that Monday, August 28,
1854, Clean Willy Williams had slipped to a corner of the
prison where two walls met, and with his back to the angle
he was skinning straight up the sheer rock surface, bracing
with his hands and feet. He dimly heard the chanting of the
crowd: "Oh, my, think I'm going to die!" as he reached the
top of the wall, and without hesitation grabbed the bar with
its iron spikes. His hands were immediately lacerated.

From childhood, Clean Willy had had no sensation in his
palms, which were thickly covered with calluses and scar
tissue. It was the custom of homeowners of the period to
keep a hearth burning right to the moment when the chimney
sweep and his child assistant arrived to clean the flue, and if
the child scorched his hands in hastening up the still-hot
chimney, that was not any great concern. If the child didn't
like the work, there were plenty of others to take his place.

Clean Willy's hands had been burned again and again,
over a period of years. So he felt nothing now as the blood
trickled down from his slashed palms, ran in rivulets along

his forearms, and dripped and spattered on his face. He paid no attention at all.

He moved slowly along the revolving spike wheels, down the full length of one wall, then to the second wall, and then to the third. It was exhausting work. He lost all sense of time, and never heard the noise of the crowd that followed the execution. He continued to make his way around the perimeter of the prison yard until he reached the south wall. There he paused and waited while a patrolling guard passed beneath him. The guard never looked up, although Willy later remembered that drops of his own blood landed on the man's cap and shoulders.

When the guard was gone, Willy clambered over the spikes—cutting his chest, his knees, and his legs, so that the blood now ran very freely—and jumped fifteen feet down to the roof of the nearest building outside the prison. No one heard the sound of his landing, for the area was deserted; everybody was attending the execution.

From that roof he jumped to another, and then another, leaping six- and eight-foot gaps without hesitation. Once or twice, he lost his grip on the shingles and slates of the roofs, but he always recovered. He had, after all, spent much of his life on rooftops.

Finally, less than half an hour from the time he began to inch his way up the prison wall, he slipped through a gabled window at the back of Mrs. Molloy's lodging house, padded down the hallway, and entered the room rented, at considerable expense, by Mr. Pierce and his party.

Agar recalled that Willy presented "a ghastly aspect, most fearsome," and he added that "he was bleeding like a stuck saint," although this blasphemous reference was expunged from the courtroom records.

Pierce directed the swift treatment of the man, who was barely conscious. He was revived with the vapors of ammo-

nium chloride from a cut-glass inhaler. His clothes were
stripped off by the women, who pretended no modesty but
worked quickly; his many wounds were staunched with styp-
tic powder and sticking plaster, then bound with surgical
bandages. Agar gave him a sip of coca wine for energy, and
Burroughs & Wellcome beef-and-iron wine for sustenance.
He was forced to down two Carter's Little Nerve Pills and
some tincture of opium for his pain. This combined treatment brought the man to his senses, and enabled the women
to clean his face, douse his body with rose water, and bundle
him into the waiting dress.

When he was dressed, he was given a sip of Bromo Caffein
for further energy, and told to act faint. A bonnet was placed
over his head, and boots laced on his feet; his bloody prison
garb was stuffed in the picnic basket.

No one among the crowd of more than twenty thousand
paid the slightest attention when the well-dressed party of
hangers-on departed Mrs. Molloy's boarding house—with
one woman of their party so faint that she had to be carried
by the men, who hustled her into a waiting cab—and rattled
off into the morning light. A faint woman was a common
enough sight and, in any case, nothing to compare to a woman
turning slowly at the end of the rope, back and forth, back
and forth.

CHAPTER 14

A Georgian Disgrace

It is usually estimated that seven-eighths of the structures in Victorian London were actually Georgian. The face of the city and its general architectural character were legacies of that earlier era; the Victorians did not begin to rebuild their capital in any substantial way until the 1880s. This reluctance reflected the economics of urban building. For most of the century, it simply was not profitable to tear down old structures, even those badly suited to their modern functions. Certainly the reluctance was not aesthetic—the Victorians loathed the Georgian style, which Ruskin himself termed "the *ne plus ultra* of ugliness."

Thus it is perhaps not surprising that the *Times*, in reporting that a convict had escaped from Newgate Prison, observed that "the virtues of this edifice have been clearly overstated. Not only is escape from its confines possible, it is mere child's play, for the fleeing villain had not yet attained his majority. It is time for this public disgrace to be torn down."

The article went on to comment that "the Metropolitan Police has dispatched groups of armed officers into the rookeries of the town, in order to flush out the escaped man, and there is every expectation of his apprehension."

There were no follow-up reports. One must remember that during this period, jailbreaks were, in the words of one commentator, "quite as common as illegitimate births," and nothing so ordinary was really newsworthy. At a time when the curtains of the windows of Parliament were being soaked in

lime to protect the members against the cholera epidemic
while they debated the conduct of the Crimean campaign,
the newspapers could not be bothered with a minor felon
from the dangerous classes who had been lucky enough to
make a clean getaway.

A month later, the body of a young man was found float-
ing in the Thames, and police authorities identified him as the
escaped convict from Newgate. It received barely a para-
graph in the *Evening Standard;* the other newspapers did not
mention it at all.

CHAPTER 15

The Pierce Household

After his escape, Clean Willy was taken to Pierce's house in
Mayfair, where he spent several weeks in seclusion while his
wounds healed. It is from his later testimony to police that
we first learn of the mysterious woman who was Pierce's
mistress, and known to Willy as "Miss Miriam."

Willy was placed in an upstairs room, and the servants
were told that he was a relative of Miss Miriam's who had
been run down by a cab on New Bond Street. From time to
time, Willy was tended by Miss Miriam. He said of her that
she was "well carried, a good figure, and well-spoke, and she
walked here and there slow, never hurrying." This last sentiment was echoed by all the witnesses, who were impressed by
the ethereal aspect of the young woman; her eyes were said
to be especially captivating, and her grace in movement was
called "dreamlike" and "phantasmagorical."

Apparently this woman lived in the house with Pierce,

although she was often gone during the day. Clean Willy was never very clear about her movements, and in any case he was often sedated with opium, which may also account for the ghostly qualities he saw in her.

Willy recalled only one conversation with her. He asked, "Are you his canary, then?" Meaning was she Pierce's accomplice in burglary.

"Oh no," she said, smiling. "I have no ear for music."

From this he assumed she was not involved in Pierce's plans, although this was later shown to be wrong. She was an integral part of the plan, and was probably the first of the thieves to know Pierce's intentions.

At the trial, there was considerable speculation about Miss Miriam and her origins. A good deal of evidence points to the conclusion that she was an actress. This would explain her ability to mimic various accents and manners of different social classes; her tendency to wear make-up in a day when no respectable woman would let cosmetics touch her flesh; and her open presence as Pierce's mistress. In those days, the dividing line between an actress and a prostitute was exceedingly fine. And actors were by occupation itinerant wanderers, likely to have connections with criminals, or to be criminals themselves. Whatever the truth of her past, she seems to have been his mistress for several years.

Pierce himself was rarely in the house, and on occasion he was gone overnight. Clean Willy recalled seeing him once or twice in the late afternoon, wearing riding clothes and smelling of horses, as if he had returned from an equestrian excursion.

"I didn't know you were a horse fancier," Willy once said.

"I'm not," Pierce replied shortly. "Hate the bloody beasts."

Pierce kept Willy indoors after his wounds were healed, waiting for his "terrier crop" to grow out. In those days, the surest way to identify an escaped convict was by his short haircut. By late September, his hair was longer, but still Pierce did not allow him to leave. When Willy asked why, Pierce said, "I am waiting for you to be recaptured, or found dead."

This statement puzzled Willy, but he did as he was told. A few days later, Pierce came in with a newspaper under his arm and told him he could leave. That same evening Willy went to the Holy Land, where he expected to find his mistress, Maggie. He found that Maggie had taken up with a footpad, a rough sort who made his way by "swinging the stick"—that is, by mugging. Maggie showed no interest in Willy.

Willy then took up with a girl of twelve named Louise, whose principal occupation was snowing. She was described in court as "no gofferer, mind, and no clean-starcher, just a bit of plain snow now and then for the translator. Simple, really." What was meant by this passage, which required considerable explanation to the presiding magistrates, was that Willy's new mistress was engaged in the lowest form of laundry stealing. The better echelons of laundry stealers, the gofferers and clean-starchers, stole from high-class districts, often taking clothes off the lines. Plain ordinary snowing was relegated to children and young girls, and it could be lucrative enough when fenced to "translators," who sold the clothing as second-hand goods.

Willy lived off this girl's earnings, never venturing outside the sanctuary of the rookery. He had been warned by Pierce to keep his mouth shut, and he never mentioned that he had had help in his break from Newgate. Clean Willy lived with his judy in a lodging house that contained more than a hundred people; the house was a well-known buzzer's lurk. Willy lived and slept with his mistress in a bed he shared with twenty other bodies of various sexes, and Louise reported of this period, "He took his ease, and spent his time cheerful, and waited for the cracksman to give his call."

CHAPTER 16

Rotten Row

Of all the fashionable sections of that fashionable city of London, none compared to the spongy, muddy pathway in Hyde Park called the Ladies' Mile, or Rotten Row. Here, weather permitting, were literally hundreds of men and women on horseback, all dressed in the greatest splendor the age could provide, radiant in the golden sunshine at four in the afternoon.

It was a scene of bustling activity: the horsemen and horsewomen packed tightly together; the women with little uniformed foot pages trotting along behind their mistresses, or sometimes accompanied by stern, mounted duennas, or sometimes escorted by their beaus. And if the spectacle of Rotten Row was splendid and fashionable, it was not entirely respectable, for many of the women were of dubious character. "There is no difficulty," wrote one observer, "in guessing the occupation of the dashing *equestrienne* who salutes half-a-dozen men at once with whip or with a wink, and who sometimes varies the monotony of a safe seat by holding her hands behind her back while gracefully swerving over to listen to the compliments of a walking admirer."

These were members of the highest class of prostitute and, like it or not, respectable ladies often found themselves competing with these smartly turned-out demimondes for masculine attention. Nor was this the only arena of such competition; it occurred at the opera, and the theatre as well. More than one young lady found that her escort's gaze was fixed not on the performance but on some high box where an elegant woman returned his glances with open, frank interest.

Victorians claimed to be scandalized by the intrusion of prostitutes into respectable circles, but despite all the calls for reform and change, the women continued to appear gaily for nearly a half-century more. It is usual to dismiss Victorian prostitution as a particularly gaudy manifestation of that society's profound hypocrisy. But the issue is really more complex; it has to do with the way that women were viewed in Victorian England.

This was an era of marked sexual differentiation in dress, manner, attitude, and bearing. Even pieces of furniture and rooms within the house were viewed as "masculine" or "feminine"; the dining room was masculine, the drawing room feminine, and so on. All this was assumed to have a biological rationale:

"It is evident," wrote Alexander Walker, "that the man, possessing reasoning faculties, muscular power, and courage to employ it, is qualified for being a protector; the woman, being little capable of reasoning, feeble, and timid, requires protecting. Under such circumstances, the man naturally governs: the woman naturally obeys."

With minor variations, this belief was repeated again and again. The power of reasoning was small in women; they did not calculate consequences; they were governed by their emotions, and hence required strict controls on their behavior by the more rational and levelheaded male.

The presumed intellectual inferiority of the female was reinforced by her education, and many well-bred women probably were the simpering, tittering, pathologically delicate fools that populate the pages of Victorian novels. Men could not expect to share much with their wives. Mandell Creighton wrote that he found "ladies in general very unsatisfactory mental food; they seem to have no particular thoughts or ideas, and though for a time it is flattering to one's vanity to think one may teach them some, it palls after a while. Of course at a certain age, when you have a house and so on, you get a wife as part of its furniture, and find her a very comfortable institution; but I doubt greatly whether there were ever many men who had thoughts worth recounting, who told these thoughts to their wives at first, or who expected them to appreciate them."

There is good evidence that both sexes were bored silly by this arrangement. Women, stranded in their vast, servant-filled households, dealt with their frustrations in spectacular displays of hysterical neurosis: they suffered loss of hearing, speech, and sight; they had choking fits, fainting spells, loss of appetite, and even loss of memory. In the midst of a seizure they might make copulating movements or writhe in such arcing spasms that their heads would touch their heels. All these bizarre symptoms, of course, only reinforced the general notion of the frailty of the female sex.

Frustrated men had another option, and that was recourse to prostitutes, who were often lively, gay, witty—indeed, all the things it was inconceivable for a woman to be. On a simpler level, men found prostitutes agreeable because they could, in their company, discard the strained formalities of polite society and relax in an atmosphere of "unbuttoned easiness." This freedom from restraints was at least as important as the availability of sexual outlets *per se*, and it is probably this appeal that gave the institution such a broad base within society and allowed prostitutes to intrude boldly into acceptable arenas of Victorian society, such as Rotten Row.

Beginning in late September, 1854, Edward Pierce began to meet Miss Elizabeth Trent on riding excursions in Rotten Row. The first encounter was apparently accidental but later, by a sort of unstated agreement, they occurred with regularity.

Elizabeth Trent's life began to form itself around these afternoon meetings: she spent all morning preparing for them, and all evening discussing them; her friends complained that she talked incessantly of Edward; her father complained of his daughter's insatiable demand for new dresses. She seemed, he said, "to require *as a necessity* a new garment every day, and she would prefer two."

The unattractive young woman apparently·never thought it strange that Mr. Pierce should single her out from among the throng of stunning beauties on Rotten Row; she was completely captivated by his attentions. At the trial, Pierce summarized their conversations as "light and trivial," and recounted only one in detail.

This occurred sometime in the month of October, 1854. It was a time of political upheaval and military scandal; the nation had suffered a severe blow to its self-esteem. The Crimean War was turning into a disaster. When it began, J. B. Priestley notes, "the upper classes welcomed the war as a glorified large-scale picnic in some remote and romantic place. It was almost as if the Black Sea had been opened to tourism. Wealthy officers like Lord Cardigan decided to take their yachts. Some commanders' wives insisted upon going along, accompanied by their personal maids. Various civilians cancelled their holidays elsewhere to follow the army and see the sport."

The sport quickly became a debacle. The British troops were badly trained, badly supplied, and ineptly led. Lord Raglan, the military commander, was sixty-five and "old for his age." Raglan often seemed to think he was still fighting Waterloo, and referred to the enemy as "the French," although the French were now his allies. On one occasion he was so confused that he took up an observation post behind the Russian enemy lines. The atmosphere of "aged chaos" deepened, and by the middle of the summer even the wives of officers were writing home to say that "nobody appears to have the least idea what they are about."

By October, this ineptitude culminated in Lord Cardigan's charge of the Light Brigade, a spectacular feat of heroism which decimated three-quarters of his forces in a successful effort to capture the wrong battery of enemy guns.

Clearly the picnic was over, and nearly all upper-class

Englishmen were profoundly concerned. The names of Cardigan, Raglan, and Lucan were on everyone's lips. But on that warm October afternoon in Hyde Park, Mr. Pierce gently guided Elizabeth Trent into a conversation about her father.

"He was most fearfully nervous this morning," she said.

"Indeed?" Pierce said, trotting alongside her.

"He is nervous every morning when he must send the gold shipments to the Crimea. He is a different man from the very moment he arises. He is distant and preoccupied in the extreme."

"I am certain he bears a heavy responsibility," Pierce said.

"So heavy, I fear he may take to excessive drink," Elizabeth said, and laughed a little.

"I pray you exaggerate, Madam."

"Well, he acts strangely, and no mistake. You know he is entirely opposed to the consumption of any alcohol before nightfall."

"I do, and most sensible, too."

"Well," Elizabeth Trent continued, "I suspect him of breaking his own regulation, for each morning of the shipments he goes alone to the wine cellar, with no servants to accompany him or to hold the gas lanterns. He is insistent upon going alone. Many times my stepmother has chided him that he may stumble or suffer some misfortune on the steps to the basement. But he will have none of her entreaties. And he spends some time in the cellar, and then emerges, and makes his journey to the bank."

"I think," Pierce said, "that he merely checks the cellar for some ordinary purpose. Is that not logical?"

"No, indeed," Elizabeth said, "for at all times he relies upon my stepmother to deal in the stocking and care of the cellar, and the decanting of wines before dinners, and such matters."

"Then his manner is most peculiar. I trust," Pierce said gravely, "that his responsibilities are not placing an overgreat burden upon his nervous system."

"I trust," the daughter answered, with a sigh. "Is it not a lovely day?"

"Lovely," Pierce agreed. "Unspeakably lovely, but no more lovely than you."

Elizabeth Trent tittered, and replied that he was a bold rogue to flatter her so openly. "One might even suspect an ulterior motive," she said, laughing.

"Heavens, no," Pierce said, and to further reassure her he placed his hand lightly, and briefly, over hers.

"I am so happy," she said.

"And I am happy with you," Pierce said, and this was true, for he now knew the location of all four keys.

PART II

The
KEYS

November, 1854–February, 1855

CHAPTER 17

The Necessity of a Fresh

Mr. Henry Fowler, seated in a dark recess of the taproom at the lunch hour, showed every sign of agitation. He bit his lip, he twisted his glass in his hands, and he could hardly bring himself to look into the eyes of his friend Edward Pierce. "I do not know how to begin," he said. "It is a most embarrassing circumstance."

"You are assured of my fullest confidence," Pierce said, raising his glass.

"I thank you," Fowler said. "You see," he began, then faltered. "You see, it is"—he broke off, and shook his head—"most dreadfully embarrassing."

"Then speak of it forthrightly," Pierce advised, "as one man to another."

Fowler gulped his drink, and set the glass back on the table with a sharp clink. "Very well. Plainly, the long and the short of it is that I have the French malady."

"Oh, dear," Pierce said.

"I fear I have overindulged," said Fowler sadly, "and now I must pay the price. It is altogether most wretched and vexing." In those days, venereal disease was thought to be the consequence of sexual overactivity. There were few cures, and fewer doctors willing to treat a patient with the illness. Most hospitals made no provision for gonorrhea and syphilis at all. A respectable man who contracted these diseases became an easy target for blackmail; thus Mr. Fowler's reticence.

"How may I help you?" Pierce asked, already knowing the answer.

"I maintained the hope—not falsely, I pray—that as a bachelor, you might have knowledge—ah, that you might make an introduction on my behalf to a fresh girl, a country girl."

Pierce frowned. "It is no longer so easy as it once was."

"I know that, I know that," Fowler said, his voice rising heatedly. He checked himself, and spoke more quietly. "I understand the difficulty. But I was hoping . . ."

Pierce nodded. "There is a woman in the Haymarket," he said, "who often has a fresh or two. I can make discreet inquiries."

"Oh, *please*," said Mr. Fowler, his voice tremulous. And he added, "It is most painful."

"All I can do is inquire," Pierce said.

"I should be forever in your debt," Mr. Fowler said. "It is most painful."

"I shall inquire," Pierce said. "You may expect a communication from me in a day or so. In the meanwhile, do not lose cheer."

"Oh, thank you, thank you," Fowler said, and called for another drink.

"It may be expensive," Pierce warned.

"Damn the expense, man. I swear I will pay anything!" Then he seemed to reconsider this comment. "How much do you suppose?"

"A hundred guineas, if one is to be assured of a true fresh."

"A hundred guineas?" He looked unhappy.

"Indeed, and only if I am fortunate enough to strike a favorable bargain. They are much in demand, you know."

"Well, then, it shall be," Mr. Fowler said, gulping another drink. "Whatever it is, it shall be."

Two days later, Mr. Fowler received by the newly instituted penny post a letter addressed to him at his offices at the Huddleston & Bradford Bank. Mr. Fowler was much re-assured by the excellent quality of the stationery, and the fine penmanship displayed by the unmistakably feminine hand.

Nov. 11, 1854

Sir,

Our mutual acquaintance, Mr. P., has requested that I inform you when next I knew of any lady—*fresh*. I am pleased to recommend to you a very pretty fair young girl, just come from the country, and I think you will like her very much. If it is convenient for you, you may meet her in four days' time at Lichfield Street, at the bottom of St. Martin's Lane, at eight o'clock. She shall be there waiting for you, and suitable arrangements for private quarterings have been made nearby.

I remain, Sir, your most obedient
humble servant,
M.B.

South Moulton Street

There was no mention of the price of the girl, but Mr. Fowler hardly cared. His private parts were now swollen and extremely tender, so much so, in fact, that he could think of nothing else as he sat at his desk and tried to conduct the business of the day. He looked again at the letter and again felt reassured by the excellent impression it made. In every aspect, it smacked of the utmost reliability, and that was important. Fowler knew that many virgins were nothing of the sort, but rather young girls initiated a score of times over, with their "demure state" freshly renewed by the application of a small seamstress's stitch in a strategic place.

He also knew that intercourse with a virgin was not uniformly accepted as a cure for venereal disease. Many men swore the experience produced a cure; others rejected the idea. It was often argued that the failures resulted from the

fact that the girl was not genuinely fresh. Thus Mr. Fowler
looked at the stationery and the penmanship, and found there
the reassurance he hoped to find. He sent off a quick note of
vague thanks to his friend Pierce for his assistance in this
matter.

CHAPTER 18

The Carriage Fakement

On the same day that Mr. Fowler was writing a letter of
thanks to Mr. Pierce, Mr. Pierce was preparing to crack the
mansion of Mr. Trent. Involved in this plan were five people:
Pierce, who had some inside knowledge of the layout of the
house; Agar, who would make the wax impression of the
key; Agar's woman, who would act as "crow," or lookout;
and Barlow, who would be a "stall," providing diversion.

There was also the mysterious Miss Miriam. She was essential to the planned housebreak, for she would carry out what
was called "the carriage fakement." This was one of the most
clever methods of breaking into a house. For its effect, the
carriage fakement relied upon a solid social custom of the day
—the tipping of servants.

In Victorian England, roughly 10 percent of the entire
population was "in service," and nearly all were poorly paid.
The poorest paid were those whose tasks brought them in
contact with visitors and house guests: the butler and the
hall porter relied on tips for most of their annual income.
Thus the notorious disdain of the porter for insubstantial
callers—and thus, too, the "carriage fakement."

By nine o'clock on the evening of November 12, 1854,

Pierce had his confederates in their places. The crow, Agar's woman, lounged across the street from the Trent mansion. Barlow, the stall, had slipped down the alley toward the tradesman's entrance and the dog pens at the back of the house. Pierce and Agar were concealed in shrubbery right next to the front door. When all was in readiness, an elegant closed carriage drew up to the curb in front of the house, and the bell was rung.

The Trent household's hall porter heard the ring, and opened the door. He saw the carriage drawn up at the curb. Dignified and conscious of tips, the porter was certainly not going to stand in the doorway and shout into the night to inquire what was wanted. When, after a moment, no one emerged from the carriage, he went down the steps to the curb to see if he could be of service.

Inside the carriage he saw a handsome, refined woman who asked if this was the residence of Mr. Robert Jenkins. The porter said it was not, but he knew of Mr. Jenkins; the house was around the corner, and he gave directions.

While this was happening, Pierce and Agar slipped into the house through the open front door. They proceeded directly to the cellar door. This door was locked, but Agar employed a twirl, or picklock, and had it open in a moment. The two men were inside the cellar, with the door closed behind them, by the time the porter received his shilling from the lady in the carriage. The porter tossed the coin in the air, caught it, walked back to the house, and locked up the door once more, never suspecting he had been tricked.

That was the carriage fakement.

In the light of a narrow-beam lantern, Pierce checked his watch. It was 9:04. That gave them an hour to find the key before Barlow provided his diversion to cover their escape.

Pierce and Agar moved stealthily down the creaking stairs into the depths of the cellar. They saw the wine racks, locked behind iron gratings. These new locks yielded easily to Agar's attentions. At 9:11, they swung the grating door open and entered the wine cellar proper. They immediately began the search for the key.

There was no way to be clever about the search. It was a slow and painstaking business. Pierce could make only one assumption about the hiding place: since Mr. Trent's wife was the person who usually went into the cellar, and since Mr. Trent did not want her coming across the key by accident, the banker probably hid his key at some inconveniently high location. They first searched the tops of the racks, feeling with their fingers. It was dusty, and there was soon a good deal of dust in the air.

Agar, with his bad lungs, had difficulty suppressing his cough. Several times his stifled grunts were sufficiently loud to alarm Pierce, but the Trent household never heard them.

Soon it was 9:30. Now, Pierce knew, time was beginning to work against them. Pierce searched more frantically and became impatient, hissing his complaints to Agar, who wielded the spot of light from the hot shaded lantern.

Ten more minutes passed, and Pierce began to sweat. And then, with startling suddenness, his fingers felt something cold on the top of the wine-rack crossbars. The object fell to the ground with a metallic clink. A few moments of scrambling around on the earthen floor of the cellar, and they had the key. It was 9:45.

Pierce held it into the spot from the lantern. In darkness, Agar groaned.

"What is it?" Pierce whispered.

"That's not it."

"What do you mean?"

"I mean it's not the ruddy key, it's the wrong one."

Pierce turned the key over in his hands. "Are you sure?" he whispered, but even as he spoke he knew Agar was right. The key was dusty and old; there was grime in the crevices of the prongs. Agar spoke his thoughts.

"Nobody's touched her in ten years."

Pierce swore, and continued his search, while Agar held the lantern. Agar looked at the key critically.

"Damn me but she's odd," he whispered. "I never seen the likes of it. Small as she is, delicate-like, could be a lady's twirl to some female trifle, you ask me—"

"—Shut up," Pierce hissed.

Agar fell silent. Pierce searched, feeling his heart thump in his chest, not looking at his clock, not wanting to know the time. Then his fingers again felt cold metal. He brought it into the light.

It was a shiny key.

"That's for a safe," Agar said when he saw it.

"Right," Pierce said, sighing. He took the lantern and held it for Agar. Agar fished two wax blanks from his pockets. He held them in his hands to warm them a moment, and then he pressed the key into them, first one side, then the other.

"Time?" he whispered.

"Nine-fifty-one," Pierce said.

"I'll do another," Agar said, and repeated the process with a second set of blanks. This was common practice among the most adept screwsmen, for one never knew when a blank might be later injured after a break-in. When he had two sets, Pierce returned the key to its hiding place.

"Nine-fifty-seven."

"Crikey, it's close."

They left the wine cellar, locking it behind them, and slipped up the stairs to the basement door. Then they waited.

Barlow, lurking in the shadows near the servants' quarters, checked his own pocket watch and saw it was ten o'clock. He had a moment of hesitation. On the one hand, every minute his accomplices spent inside the Trent household was dangerous; on the other hand, they might not have finished their work, despite the planned schedule. He had no wish to be the villain, greeted by the spectacle of their angry faces when they made their escape.

Finally he muttered to himself, "Ten is ten," and, carrying a bag, he moved back to the dog kennels. Three dogs were there, including the new gift of a made dog from Mr. Pierce. Barlow bent over the run and pushed four squeaking rats out of the bag and into the enclosure. Immediately, the dogs began to yelp and bark, raising a terrible din.

Barlow slipped off into the shadows as he saw the lights come on in one window after another in the servants' quarters.

Pierce and Agar, hearing the commotion, opened the cellar door and moved into the hallway, locking that door behind them. There was the sound of running footsteps at the back of the house. They unfastened the locks and bolts of the front door, let themselves out, and disappeared into the night.

They left behind them only one sign of their visit: the unlocked front door. They knew that in the morning the hall porter, being first to arise, would come upon the front door and find the locks open. But the porter would remember the incident of the carriage the night before, and would assume that he had forgotten to lock up afterward. He might secretly suspect a housebreak, but as the day went on and nothing was discovered missing, he would forget all about it.

In any case, no burglary of the Trent residence was ever reported to authorities. The mysterious commotion of the dogs was explained by the bodies of the dead rats in the kennel. There was some discussion of how the rats had found their way into the dog run, but the Trent household was large and busy, and there was no time for idle speculation on trivial matters.

Thus, by dawn of November 13, 1854, Edward Pierce had the first of the four keys he needed. He immediately directed his attention to obtaining the second key.

CHAPTER 19

The Assignation

Mr. Henry Fowler could scarcely believe his eyes. There, in the faint glow of the street gas lamp, was a delicate creature, rosy-cheeked and wonderfully young. She could not be much past the age of consent of twelve, and her very posture, bearing, and timid manner bespoke her tender and uninitiated state.

He approached her; she replied softly, halting, with downcast eyes, and led him to a brothel lodging house not far distant. Mr. Fowler eyed the establishment with some trepidation, for the exterior was not particularly prepossessing. Thus it was a pleasant surprise when the child's gentle knock at the door received an answer from an exceedingly beautiful woman, whom the child called "Miss Miriam." Standing in the hallway, Fowler saw that this accommodation house was not one of those crude establishments where beds rented for five shillings an hour and the proprietor came round and rapped on the door with a stick when the time was due; on the contrary, here the furnishings were plush velvet, with rich drapings, fine Persian carpets, and appointments of taste and quality. Miss Miriam comported herself with extraordinary dignity as she requested one hundred and fifty pounds; her manner was so wellborn that Fowler paid without a quibble, and he proceeded directly to an upstairs room with the little girl, whose name was Sarah.

Sarah explained that she had lately come from Derbyshire, that her parents were dead, that she had an older brother off in the Crimea, and a younger brother in the poorhouse. She talked of all these events almost gaily as they ascended the stairs. Fowler thought he detected a certain overexcited quality to her speech; no doubt the poor child was nervous at her first experience, and he reminded himself to be gentle.

The room they entered was as superbly furnished as the downstairs sitting room; it was red and elegant, and the air was softly perfumed with the scent of jasmine. He looked about briefly, for a man could never be too careful. Then he bolted the door and turned to face the girl.

"Well, now," he said.

"Sir?" she said.

"Well, now," he said. "Shall, we, ah . . ."

"Oh, yes, of course, sir," she said, and the simple child began to undress him. He found it extraordinary, to stand in the midst of this elegant—very nearly *decadent*—room and have a little child who stood barely to his waist reach up with her little fingers and pluck at his buttons, undressing him. Altogether, it was so remarkable he submitted passively, and soon was naked, although she was still attired.

"What is this?" she asked, touching a key around his neck on a silver chain.

"Just a—ah—key," he replied.

"You'd best take it off," she said, "it may harm me."

He took it off. She dimmed the gaslights, and then disrobed. The next hour or two was magical to Henry Fowler, an experience so incredible, so astounding he quite forgot his painful condition. And he certainly did not notice that a stealthy hand slipped around one of the heavy red velvet drapes and plucked away the key from atop his clothing; nor did he notice when, a short time later, the key was returned.

"Oh, sir," she cried, at the vital moment. "Oh, *sir!*"

And Henry Fowler was, for a brief instant, more filled with life and excitement than he could ever remember in all his forty-seven years.

CHAPTER 20

The Coopered Ken

The ease with which Pierce and his fellow conspirators obtained the first two keys gave them a sense of confidence that was soon to prove false. Almost immediately after obtaining Fowler's key, they ran into difficulties from an unexpected quarter: the South Eastern Railway changed its routine for the dispatcher's offices in London Bridge Station.

The gang employed Miss Miriam to watch the routine of the offices, and in late December, 1854, she returned with bad news. At a meeting in Pierce's house, she told both Pierce and Agar that the railway company had hired a jack who now guarded the premises at night.

Since they had been planning to break in at night, this was sour news indeed. But according to Agar, Pierce covered his disappointment quickly. "What's his rig?" he asked.

"He comes on duty at lock-up each night, at seven sharp," Miss Miriam said.

"And what manner of fellow is he?"

"He's a ream escop," she replied, meaning a real policeman. "He's forty or so; square-rigged, fat. But I'll wager he doesn't sleep on the job, and he's no lushington."

"Is he armed?"

"He is," she said, nodding.

"Where's he lurk, then?" Agar said.

"Right at the door. Sits up at the top of the steps by the door, and does not move at all. He has a small paper bag at

his side, which I think is his supper." Miss Miriam could not
be sure of that, because she dared not remain watching the
station office too late in the day for fear of arousing suspicion.

"Crikey," Agar said in disgust. "Sits right by the door?
He's coopered that ken."

"I wonder why they put on a night guard," Pierce said.

"Maybe they knew we were giving it the yack," Agar
said, for they had kept the office under surveillance, off and
on, for a period of months, and someone might have noticed.

Pierce sighed.

"No gammon now," Agar said.

"There's always a gammon," Pierce said.

"It's coopered for sure," Agar said.

"Not coopered," Pierce said, "just a little more difficult
is all."

"How you going to knock it over, then?" Agar said.

"At the dinner hour," he said.

"In broad daylight?" Agar said, aghast.

"Why not?" Pierce said.

The following day, Pierce and Agar watched the midday
routine of the office. At one o'clock, the London Bridge
Station was crowded with passengers coming and going;
porters hauling luggage behind elegant travelers on their way
to coaches; hawkers shouting refreshments for sale; and three
or four policemen moving around, keeping order and watching for buzzers—pickpockets—since train stations were becoming their new favorite haunt. The dipper would nail his
quarry as he boarded the train, and the victim would not
discover the robbery until he was well out of London.

The association of pickpockets with train stations became
so notorious that when William Frith painted one of the most
famous pictures of his generation, "The Railway Station," in
1862, the chief focus of the composition was two detectives
pinching a thief.

Now the London Bridge Station had several Metropolitan

Police constables. And the railway companies had private guards as well.

"It's fair aswarm with miltonians," Agar said unhappily, looking around the station platforms.

"Never mind that," Pierce said. He watched the railway office.

At one o'clock, the clerks clambered down the iron stairs, chattering among themselves, off to lunch. The traffic manager, a stern gentleman in muttonchop whiskers, remained inside. The clerks were back at two o'clock, and the office routine resumed.

The next day, the manager went to lunch but two of the clerks remained behind, skipping lunch.

By the third day, they knew the pattern: one or more of the men in the office went to lunch for an hour at one o'clock, but the office was never left unattended. The conclusion was clear.

"No daylight gammon," Agar said.

"Perhaps Sunday," Pierce said, thinking aloud.

In those days—and indeed to the present day—the British railway system strongly resisted operations on the Sabbath. It was considered unnecessary and unseemly for any company to do business on Sunday, and the railways in particular had always shown an oddly moralistic bent. For example, smoking on railway carriages was forbidden long after smoking became a widespread custom in society; a gentleman who wished to enjoy a cigar was obliged to tip the railroad porter—another forbidden act—and this state of affairs continued, despite the intense pressure of public opinion, until 1868, when Parliament finally passed a law forcing the railroads to allow passengers to smoke.

Similarly, although everyone agreed that the most God-fearing men sometimes needed to travel on the Sabbath, and although the popular custom of weekend excursions provided ever more pressure for Sunday schedules, the railroads fought stubbornly against this trend. In 1854, the South Eastern Railway ran only four trains on Sunday, and the other line that used London Bridge, the London & Greenwich Railway, ran only six trains, less than half the usual number.

Pierce and Agar checked the station the following Sunday, and found a double guard posted outside the traffic manager's office; one jack stationed himself near the door, and the second was positioned near the foot of the stairs.

"Why?" Pierce asked when he saw the two guards. "Why, in God's name, *why?*"

In later courtroom testimony, it emerged that the South Eastern Railway management changed hands in the fall of 1854. Its new owner, Mr. Willard Perkins, was a gentleman of philanthropic bent whose concern for the lower classes was such that he introduced a policy of employing more people at all positions on the line, "in order to provide honest work for those who might otherwise be tempted into lawlessness and improvident promiscuity." The extra personnel were hired for this reason alone; the railway never suspected a robbery, and indeed Mr. Perkins was greatly shocked when his line was eventually robbed.

It is also true that at this time the South Eastern Railway was trying to build new access lines into downtown London, and this caused the displacement of many families and the destruction of their houses. Thus this philanthropic endeavor had a certain public-relations aspect in the minds of the railway owners.

"No gammon on Sunday," Agar said, looking at the two guards. "Perhaps Christmas?"

Pierce shook his head. It was possible that security might be relaxed on Christmas Day, but they could not depend on that. "We need something routine," he said.

"There's nothing to be done by day."

"Yes," Pierce said. "But we don't know the full night routine. We never had an all-night watch." At night the station was deserted, and loiterers and tramps were briskly ordered off by the policemen making their rounds.

"They'll shoo away a canary," Agar said. "And perhaps collar him as well."

"I was thinking of a canary in a lurk," Pierce said. A concealed man could remain all night in the station.

"Clean Willy?"

"No," Pierce said. "Clean Willy is a mouth and a flat, without a downy bone in his body. He's glocky."

"It's true he's glocky," Agar said.

Clean Willy, dead at the time of the trial, was noted in courtroom testimony to be of "diminished faculties of reasoning"; this was reported by several witnesses. Pierce himself said, "We felt we could not trust him to do the surveillance. If he were apprehended, he would put down on us —reveal our plans—and never know the difference."

"Who shall we have instead?" Agar said, looking around the station.

"I was thinking of a skipper," Pierce said.

"A skipper?" Agar said, in surprise.

"Yes," Pierce said. "I think a skipper would do nicely. Do you happen to know of a bone skipper?"

"I can find one. But what's the lurk, then?"

"We'll pack him in a crate," Pierce said.

Pierce then arranged for a packing crate to be built and delivered to his residence. Agar obtained, by his own accounting, "a very reliable skipper," and arrangements were made to send the crate to the railway station.

The skipper, named Henson, was never found, nor was there much attempt to track him down; he was a very minor figure in the entire scheme, and by his very nature was somebody not worth bothering with. For the term "skipper" did not imply an occupation, but rather a way of life, and more specifically a way of spending the night.

During the mid-century, London's population was growing at the rate of 20 percent per decade. The number of people in the city was increasing by more than a thousand per day, and even with massive building programs and densely crowded slums, a sizable fraction of the population lacked both shelter and the means to pay for it. Such people spent their nights outdoors, wherever the police with the dreaded bull's-eye lanterns would leave them alone. The favorite places were the so-called "Dry-Arch Hotels," meaning the arches of railway bridges, but there were other haunts: ruined buildings, shop doorways, boiler rooms, omnibus depots, empty market stalls, under hedges, any place that provided a kip. "Skippers" were people who routinely sought another kind of shelter: barns and outhouses. At this time even rather elegant households frequently lacked indoor plumbing; the outhouse was a fixture among all classes, and it was increasingly found in public places as well. The skipper would wedge himself into these narrow confines and sleep away the night.

At his trial, Agar spoke proudly of the way he had procured a reliable skipper. Most of the night people were muck-snipes or tramps, wholly down and out; skippers were a little more enterprising than most, but they were still at the bottom of the social order. And they were often soaks; no doubt their intoxication helped them tolerate their fragrant resting places.

The reason Pierce wanted a skipper, of course, was to obtain someone who could tolerate cramped quarters for many hours. The man Henson was reported to have found his shipping crate "ever so wide" as he was nailed into it.

This crate was placed strategically within London Bridge Station. Through the slats, Henson was able to watch the behavior of the night guard. After the first night, the crate was hauled away, painted another color, and returned to the station again. This routine was followed three nights in succession. Then Henson reported his findings. None of the thieves was encouraged.

"The jack's solid," he told Pierce. "Regular as this very clock." He held up the stopwatch Pierce had given him to time the activities. "Comes on at seven prompt, with his little paper bag of supper. Sits on the steps, always alert, never a snooze, greeting the crusher on his rounds."

"What are the rounds?"

"First crusher works to midnight, goes every eleven minutes round the station. Sometimes he goes twelve, and once or twice thirteen minutes, but regular, it's eleven for him. Second crusher works midnight to the dawn. He's a flummut crusher, keeps to no beat but goes this way and that, popping up here and there like a jack-in-a-box, with a wary eye in all directions. And he's got himself two barkers at his belt."

"What about the jack who sits by the office door?" Pierce said.

"Solid, like I say, ream solid. Comes at seven, chats with the first crusher—he don't care for the second crusher, he cools him with a steady eye, he does. But the first crusher he likes, chats now and again with him, but never a stop in the crusher's rounds, just a little chat."

"Does he ever leave his place?" Pierce said.

"No," the skipper said. "He sits right there, and then he hears the bells of Saint Falsworth ringing the hour, and each time they ring he cocks his head and listens. Now at eleven o'clock, he opens his bag, and eats his tightener, always at the ringing of the clock. Now he eats for maybe ten, fifteen minutes, and he has a bottle of reeb"—beer—"and then the crusher comes around again. Now the jack sits back, taking his ease, and he waits until the crusher comes once more. Now it's half past eleven or thereabouts. And then the crusher passes him by, and the jack goes to the loo."

"Then he *does* leave his place," Pierce said.

"Only for the pisser."

"And how long is he gone?"

"I was thinking you might want to know," Henson said, "so I clocked it proper. He's gone sixty-four seconds one

night, and sixty-eight the next night, and sixty-four the third
night. Always at the same time of the night, near about
eleven-thirty. And he's back to his post when the guard
makes the last round, quarter to midnight, and then 'the other
crusher comes on to the beat."

"He did this every night?"

"Every night. It's the reeb does it. Reeb makes a man have
a powerful urge."

"Yes," Pierce said, "beer does have that effect. Now does
he leave his post at any other time?"

"Not to my eye."

"And you never slept?"

"What? When I'm sleeping here all the day through on
your nice bed, here in your lodgings, and you ask if I kip
the night away?"

"You must tell me the truth," Pierce said, but without
any great sense of urgency.

(Agar later testified: "Pierce asks him the questions, see,
but he shows no interest in the matter, he plays like a flimp
or a dub buzzer, or a mutcher, no interest or importance, and
this because he don't want the skipper to granny that a bone
lay is afoot. Now the skipper should have done, we went to
a lot of trouble on his account, and he could have put down
on us to the miltonians, and for a pretty penny, too, but he
hasn't the sense, otherwise why'd he be a skipper, eh?"

(This statement put the court into an uproar. When His
Lordship requested an explanation, Agar said with an expression of surprise that he had just explained it as best he
could. It required several minutes of interrogation to make it
clear that Agar meant that Pierce had pretended to be a "flimp
or dub buzzer"—that is, a snatch-pickpocket or a low-grade
thief, or a "mutcher," a man who rolled drunks—in order to
deceive the skipper, so that the skipper would not comprehend that a good criminal plan was being worked out. Agar
also said that the skipper should have figured it out for himself and "put down" on them—that is, squealed to the police

—but he lacked the sense to do so. This was only one of several instances in which incomprehensible criminal slang halted courtroom proceedings.)

"I swear, Mr. Pierce," the skipper said. "I swear I never slept a bit."

"And the jack never left except that one time each night?"

"Aye, and every night the same. He's regular as this jerry" —he held up his stopwatch—"that jack is."

Pierce thanked the skipper, paid him a half-crown for his troubles, allowed himself to be whined and cajoled into paying an additional half-crown, and sent the man on his way. As the door closed on the skipper, Pierce told Barlow to "worry" the man; Barlow nodded and left the house by another exit.

When Pierce returned to Agar, he said, "Well? Is it a coopered ken?"

"Sixty-four seconds," Agar said, shaking his head. "That's not your kinchin lay"—not exactly robbing children.

"I never said it was," Pierce said. "But you keep telling me you're the best screwsman in the country, and here's a fitting challenge for your talents: is it a coopered ken?"

"Maybe," Agar said. "I got to practice the lay. And I need to cool it close up. Can we pay a visit?"

"Certainly," Pierce said.

CHAPTER 21

An Audacious Act

"Of recent weeks," wrote the *Illustrated London News* on December 21, 1854, "the incidence of bold and brutal street banditry has reached alarming proportions, particularly of an evening. It would appear that the faith Mr. Wilson placed in street gas lighting as a deterrent to blackguard acts has been unjustified, for the villains are ever bolder, preying upon an unsuspecting populace with the utmost audacity. Only yesterday a constable, Peter Farrell, was lured into an alley, whereupon a band of common thugs fell upon him, beating him and taking all of his possessions and even his very uniform. Nor must we forget that just a fortnight past, Mr. Parkington, M.P., was viciously assaulted in an open, well-lighted place while walking from Parliament to his club. This epidemic of garrotting must receive the prompt attention of authorities in the near future."

The article went on to describe the condition of Constable Farrell, who was "faring no better than could be expected." The policeman gave the story that he had been called by a well-dressed woman who was arguing with her cabdriver, "a surly thug of a fellow with a white scar across the forehead." When the policeman interceded in the dispute, the cabby fell on him, swearing and cursing and beating him with a neddy, or blackjack; and when the unfortunate policeman came to his senses, he discovered he had been stripped of his clothing.

In 1854, many urban-dwelling Victorians were concerned

over what was viewed as an upsurge in street crime. Later periodic "epidemics" of street violence finally culminated in a pedestrian panic during the years 1862 and 1863, and the passage of the "Garrotting Act" by Parliament. This legislation provided unusually stiff penalties for offenders, including flogging in installments—to allow the prisoners to recover before their next scheduled beating—and hanging. Indeed, more people were hanged in England in 1863 than in any year since 1838.

Brutal street crime was the lowest form of underworld activity. Rampsmen and footpads were frequently despised by their fellow criminals, who abhorred crude lays and acts of violence. The usual method of footpadding called for a victim, preferably drunk, to be lured into a corner by an accomplice, preferably a woman, whereupon the footpad would "bear up" on the victim, beat him with a cudgel and rob him, leaving him in the gutter. It was not an elegant way to make a living.

The lurid details of a footpadder bearing up on his hapless quarry were the ordinary fare of news reporting. Apparently, no one ever stopped to think how strange the attack on Constable Farrell really was. In fact, it made very little sense. Then, as now, criminals tried wherever possible to avoid confrontations with the police. To "prop a crusher" was merely asking for an all-out manhunt through the rookeries until the culprits were apprehended, for the police took a special interest in attacks on their own kind.

Nor was there any sensible reason to attack a policeman. He was more capable than most victims of defending himself, and he never carried much money; often he had no money at all.

And, finally, there was absolutely no point in stripping a policeman. In those days, stripping was a common crime, usually the work of old women who lured children into alleys and then took all their clothing to sell at a secondhand shop. But you could not take the down off a crusher's dunnage; that is, you could not disguise a policeman's uniform so that it would have resale value. Secondhand shops were always under surveillance, and always accused of taking stolen goods; no "translator" would ever accept a police uniform. It was perhaps the only kind of clothing in all London that had no resale value at all.

Thus the attack on Constable Farrell was not merely dangerous but pointless, and any thoughtful observer would have been led to ponder why it had occurred at all.

CHAPTER 22

The Prad Prig

Sometime in late December, 1854, Pierce met a man named Andrew Taggert in the King's Arms publican house, off Regent Street. Taggert was by then nearly sixty, and a well-known character in the neighborhood. He had survived a long and varied career, which is worth briefly recounting, for he is one of the few participants in The Great Train Robbery whose background is known.

Taggert was born around 1790 outside Liverpool, and came to London near the turn of the century with his unmarried mother, a prostitute. By the age of ten, he was employed in "the resurrection trade," the business of digging up fresh corpses from graveyards to sell to medical schools. He soon acquired a reputation for uncommon daring; it was said that he once transported a stiff through London streets in daylight, with the man propped up in his cart like a passenger.

The Anatomy Act of 1838 ended the business in corpses,

and Andrew Taggert shifted to the smasher's job of "ringing the changes"—disposing of counterfeit money. In this maneuver, a genuine coin would be offered to a shopkeeper for some purchase, and then the smasher would fumble in his purse, saying that he thought he had correct change, and take the original coin back. After a while, he would say, "No, I don't have it, after all," and hand over a counterfeit coin in place of the original. This was petty work, and Taggert soon tired of it. He moved on to a variety of con games, becoming a full-fledged magsman by the middle 1840s. He was apparently very successful in his work; he took a respectable flat in Camden Town, which was not a wholly respectable area. (Charles Dickens had lived there some fifteen years earlier, while his father was in prison.) Taggert also took a wife, one Mary Maxwell, a widow, and it is one of those minor ironies that the master magsman should himself be conned. Mary Maxwell was a coiner specializing in small silver coins. This bit-faker had served time in prison on several occasions, and knew something of the law, which her new husband apparently did not, for she had not married idly.

A woman's legal position was already the subject of active attempts at reform; but at this time women did not have the right to vote, to own property, or to make wills, and the earnings of any married woman who was separated from her husband were still legally the property of her husband. Although the law treated women as near idiots and appeared overwhelmingly to favor men, there were some odd quirks, as Taggert discovered soon enough.

In 1847, the police raided Mary Maxwell Taggert's coining operation, catching her red-handed in the midst of stamping out sixpence pieces. She greeted the raid with equanimity, announced pleasantly that she was married, and told the police the whereabouts of her husband.

By law, a husband was responsible for any criminal activities of his wife. It was assumed that such activity must be the result of the husband's planning and execution, in which the wife was a mere—and perhaps unwilling—participant.

In July, 1847, Andrew Taggert was arrested and convicted of counterfeiting currency and sentenced to eight years in Bridewell Prison; Mary Maxwell was released without so much as a reprimand. She is said to have displayed "a roistering, bantering demeanour" in the courtroom at the time of her husband's sentencing.

Taggert served three years, and was given a ticket-of-leave and allowed to depart. Afterward it was said the steel had gone out of him, a common consequence of a prison term; he no longer had the energy or the confidence to be a magsman, and turned to hoof-snaffling, or horse stealing. By 1854, he was a familiar face in the flash sporting pubs frequented by turfites; he was said to have been involved in the scandal of 1853 in which a four-year-old was passed off as a three-year-old in the Derby. No one was certain but, as a known prad prig, he was thought to have engineered the theft of the most famous prad of recent years: Silver Whistle, a three-year-old from Derbyshire.

Pierce met him in the King's Arms with a most peculiar suggestion, and Taggert gulped his gin as he said, "You want to snaffle a *what?*"

"A leopard," Pierce said.

"Now, where's an honest man like me to find a leopard?" Taggert said.

"I wouldn't know," Pierce said.

"Never in my life," Taggert said, "would I know of any leopard, excepting the bestiaries here and there, which have all manner of beasts."

"That's so," Pierce said calmly.

"Is it to be christened?"

Now this was a particularly difficult problem. Taggert was an expert christener—a man who could conceal the fact that goods were stolen. He could disguise the markings of a horse so that even its owner would not recognize it. But christening a leopard might be harder.

"No," Pierce said. "I can take it as you have it."

"Won't gull nobody."

"It doesn't have to."

"What's it for, then?"

Pierce gave Taggert a particularly severe look and did not reply.

"No harm in asking," Taggert said. "It's not every day a man gets asked to snaffle a leopard, so I ask why—no harm intended."

"It is a present," Pierce said, "for a lady."

"Ah, a lady."

"On the Continent."

"Ah, on the Continent."

"In Paris."

"Ah."

Taggert looked him up and down. Pierce was well dressed. "You could buy one right enough," he said. "Cost you just as dear as buying from me."

"I made you a business proposition."

"So you did, and a proper one, too, but you didn't mention the joeys for me. You just mention you want a knapped leopard."

"I'll pay you twenty guineas."

"Cor, you'll pay me forty and count yourself lucky."

"I'll pay you twenty-five and *you'll* count yourself lucky," Pierce said.

Taggert looked unhappy. He twisted his gin glass in his hands. "All right, then," he said. "When's it to be?"

"Never you mind," Pierce said. "You find the animal and set the lay, and you'll hear from me soon enough." And he dropped a gold guinea on the counter.

Taggert picked it up, bit it, nodded, and touched his cap. "Good day to you, sir," he said.

"Good day," Pierce said.

CHAPTER 23

The Jolly Gaff

The twentieth-century urban dweller's attitude of fear or indifference to a crime in progress would have astounded the Victorians. In those days, any person being robbed or mugged immediately raised a hue and cry, and the victim both expected and got an immediate response from law-abiding citizens around him, who joined in the fray with alacrity in an attempt to catch the bolting villain. Even ladies of breeding were known, upon occasion, to participate in a fracas with enthusiasm.

There were several reasons for the willingness of the populace to get involved in a crime. In the first place, an organized police force was still relatively new; London's Metropolitan Police was the best in England, but it was only twenty-five years old, and people did not yet believe that crime was "something for the police to take care of." Second, firearms were rare, and remain so to the present day in England; there was little likelihood of a bystander stopping a charge by pursuing a thief. And finally, the majority of criminals were children, often extremely young children, and adults were not hesitant to go after them.

In any case, an adept thief took great care to conduct his business undetected, for if any alarm was raised, the chances were that he would be caught. For this very reason thieves often worked in gangs, with several members acting as "stalls" to create confusion in any alarm. Criminals of the day also utilized the fracas—as a staged event—to cover illegal activities, and this maneuver was known as a "jolly gaff."

A good jolly gaff required careful planning and timing, for it was, as the name implied, a form of theatre. On the morning of January 9, 1855, Pierce looked around the cavernous, echoing interior of the London Bridge Station and saw that all his players were in position.

Pierce himself would perform the most crucial role, that of the "beefer." He was dressed as a traveler, as was Miss Miriam alongside him. She would be the "plant."

A few yards distant was the "culprit," a chavy nine years old, scruffy and noticeably (should anyone care to observe it, *too* noticeably) out of place among the crowd of first-class passengers. Pierce had himself selected the chavy from among a dozen children in the Holy Land; the criterion was speed, pure and simple.

Farther away still was the "crusher," Barlow, wearing a constable's uniform with the hat pulled down to conceal the white scar across his forehead. Barlow would permit the child to elude him as the gaff progressed.

Finally, not far from the steps to the railway dispatcher's office was the whole point of the ploy: Agar, dressed out of twig—disguised—in his finest gentleman's clothing.

As it came time for the London & Greenwich eleven-o'clock train to depart, Pierce scratched his neck with his left hand. Immediately, the child came up and brushed rather abruptly against Miss Miriam's right side, rustling her purple velvet dress. Miss Miriam cried, "I've been robbed, John!"

Pierce raised his beef: "Stop, thief!" he shouted, and raced after the bolting chavy. "Stop, thief!"

Startled bystanders immediately grabbed at the youngster, but he was quick and slippery, and soon tore free of the crowd and ran toward the back of the station.

There Barlow in his policeman's uniform came forward menacingly. Agar, as a civic-spirited gentleman, also joined in the pursuit. The child was trapped; his only escape lay in a desperate scramble up the stairs leading to the railway office, and he ran hard, with Barlow, Agar, and Pierce fast on his heels.

The little boy's instructions had been explicit: he was to get up the stairs, into the office, past the desks of the clerks, and back to a high rear window opening out onto the roof of the station. He was to break this window in an apparent attempt to escape. Then Barlow would apprehend him. But he was to struggle valiantly until Barlow cuffed him; this was his signal that the gaff had ended.

The child burst into the South Eastern Railway office, startling the clerks. Pierce dashed in immediately afterward: "Stop him, he's a thief!" Pierce shouted and, in his own pursuit, knocked over one of the clerks. The child was scrambling for the window. Then Barlow, the constable, came in.

"I'll handle this," Barlow said, in an authoritative and tough voice, but he clumsily knocked one of the desks over and sent papers flying.

"Catch him! Catch him!" Agar called, entering the offices.

By now the child was scrambling up onto the station dispatcher's desk, going toward a narrow high window; he cracked the glass with his small fist, cutting himself. The station dispatcher kept saying "Oh, dear, oh, dear," over and over.

"I am an officer of the law, make way!" Barlow shouted.

"Stop him!" Pierce screamed, allowing himself to become quite hysterical. "Stop him, he's getting away!"

Glass fragments from the window fell on the floor, and Barlow and the child rolled on the ground in an uneven struggle that took rather longer to resolve itself than one might expect. The clerks and the dispatchers watched in considerable confusion.

No one noticed that Agar had turned his back on the commotion and picked the lock on the door to the office, trying several of his jangling ring of bettys until he found one that worked the mechanism. Nor did anyone notice when Agar then moved to the side wall cabinet, also fitted with a lock, which he also picked with one key after another until he found one that worked.

Three or four minutes passed before the young ruffian—who kept slipping from the hands of the red-faced constable—was finally caught by Pierce, who held him firmly. At last the constable gave the little villain a good boxing on the ears, and the lad ceased to struggle and handed up the purse he had stolen. He was carted away by the constable. Pierce dusted himself off, looked around the wreckage of the office, and apologized to the clerks and the dispatcher.

Then the other gentleman who had joined in the pursuit said, "I fear, sir, that you have missed your train."

"By God, I have," Pierce said. "Damn the little rascal."

And the two gentlemen departed—the one thanking the other for helping corner the thief, and the other saying it was nothing—leaving the clerks to clean up the mess.

It was, Pierce later reflected, a nearly perfect jolly gaff.

CHAPTER 24

Hykey Doings

When Clean Willy Williams, the snakesman, arrived at Pierce's house late in the afternoon of January 9, 1855, he found himself confronted by a very strange spectacle in the drawing room.

Pierce, wearing a red velvet smoking jacket, lounged in an easy chair, smoking a cigar, utterly relaxed, a stopwatch in his hands.

In contrast, Agar, in shirtsleeves, stood in the center of the room. Agar was bent into a kind of half-crouch; he was watching Pierce and panting slightly.

"Are you ready?" Pierce said.

Agar nodded.

"Go!" Pierce said, and flicked the stopwatch.

To Clean Willy's amazement, Agar dashed across the room to the fireplace, where he began to jog in place, counting to himself, his lips moving, in a low whisper, ". . . seven . . . eight . . . nine . . ."

"That's it," Pierce said. "Door!"

"Door!" Agar said and, in pantomime, turned the handle on an unseen door. He then took three steps to the right, and reached up to shoulder height, touching something in the air.

"Cabinet," Pierce said.

"Cabinet . . ."

Now Agar fished two wax flats out of his pocket, and pretended to make an impression of a key. "Time?" he asked.

"Thirty-one," Pierce said.

Agar proceeded to make a second impression, on a second set of flats, all the while counting to himself. "Thirty-three, thirty-four, thirty-five . . ."

Again, he reached into the air, with both hands, as if closing something.

"Cabinet shut," he said, and took three paces back across the room. "Door!"

"Fifty-four," Pierce said.

"Steps!" Agar said, and ran in place once more, and then sprinted across the room to halt beside Pierce's chair. "Done!" he cried.

Pierce looked at the watch and shook his head. "Sixty-nine." He puffed on his cigar.

"Well," Agar said, in a wounded tone, "it's better than it was. What was the last time?"

"Your last time was seventy-three."

"Well, it's better—"

"—But not good enough. Maybe if you don't close the

cabinet. And don't hang up the keys, either. Willy can do that."

"Do what?" Willy said, watching.

"Open and close the cabinet," Pierce said.

Agar went back to his starting position.

"Ready?" Pierce said.

"Ready," Agar said.

Once again, this odd charade was repeated, with Agar sprinting across the room, jogging in place, pretending to open a door, taking three steps, making two wax impressions, taking three steps, closing a door, jogging in place, and then running across the room.

"Time?"

Pierce smiled. "Sixty-three," he said.

Agar grinned, gasping for breath.

"Once more," Pierce said, "just to be certain."

Later in the afternoon, Clean Willy was given the lay.

"It'll be tonight," Pierce said. "Once it's dark, you'll go up to London Bridge, and get onto the roof of the station. That a problem?"

Clean Willy shook his head. "What then?"

"When you're on the roof, cross to a window that is broken. You'll see it; it's the window to the dispatcher's office. Little window, barely a foot square."

"What then?"

"Get into the office."

"Through the window?"

"Yes."

"What then?"

"Then you will see a cabinet, painted green, mounted on the wall." Pierce looked at the little snakesman. "You'll have to stand on a chair to reach it. Be very quiet; there's a jack posted outside the office, on the steps."

Clean Willy frowned.

"Unlock the cabinet," Pierce said, "with this key." He

nodded to Agar, who gave Willy the first of the picklocks. "Unlock the cabinet, and open it up, and wait."

"What for?"

"Around ten-thirty, there'll be a bit of a shindy. A soak will be coming into the station to chat up the jack."

"What then?"

"Then you unlock the main door to the office, using this key here"—Agar gave him the second key—"and then you wait."

"What for?"

"For eleven-thirty, or thereabouts, when the jack goes to the W.C. Then Agar comes up the steps, through the door you've unlocked, and he makes his waxes. He leaves, and you lock the first door right away. By now, the jack is back from the loo. You lock the cabinets, put the chair back, and go out the window, quiet-like."

"That's the lay?" Clean Willy said doubtfully.

"That's the lay."

"You popped me out of Newgate for this?" Clean Willy said. "This is no shakes, to knock over a deadlurk."

"It's a deadlurk with a jack posted at the door, and it's quiet, you'll have to be quiet-like, all the time."

Clean Willy grinned. "Those keys mean a sharp vamp. You've planned."

"Just do the lay," Pierce said, "and quiet."

"Piece of cake," Clean Willy said.

"Keep those dubs handy," Agar said, pointing to the keys, "and have the doors ready and open when I come in, or it's nommus for all of us, and we're likely nibbed by the crusher."

"Don't want to be nibbed," Willy said.

"Then look sharp, and be ready."

Clean Willy nodded. "What's for dinner?" he said.

CHAPTER 25

Breaking the Drum

On the evening of January 9th, a characteristic London "pea soup" fog, heavily mixed with soot, blanketed the town. Clean Willy Williams, easing down Tooley Street, one eye to the façade of London Bridge Station, was not sure he liked the fog. It made his movements on the ground less noticeable, but it was so dense that he could not see the second story of the terminus building, and he was worried about access to the roof. It wouldn't do to make the climb halfway, only to discover it was a dead end.

But Clean Willy knew a lot about the way buildings were constructed, and after an hour of maneuvering around the station he found his spot. By climbing onto a porter's luggage cart, he was able to jump to a drainpipe, and from there to the sill of the second-story windows. Here a lip of stone ran the length of the second story; he inched along it until he reached a corner in the façade. Then he climbed up the corner, his back to the wall, in the same way that he had escaped from Newgate Prison. He would leave marks, of course; in those days nearly every downtown London building was soot-covered, and Clean Willy's climb left an odd pattern of whitish scrapes going up the corner.

By eight o'clock at night he was standing on the broad roof of the terminus. The main portion of the station was roofed in slate; over the tracks the roofing was glass, and he avoided that. Clean Willy weighed sixty-eight pounds, but he was heavy enough to break the glass roofing.

Moving cautiously through the fog, he edged around the building until he found the broken window Pierce had mentioned. Looking in, he saw the dispatcher's office. He was surprised to notice that it was in some disarray, as if there had been a struggle in the office during the day and the damage only partially corrected.

He reached through the jagged hole in the glass, turned the transom lock, and raised the window. It was a window of rectangular shape, perhaps nine by sixteen inches. He wriggled through it easily, stepped down onto a desk top, and paused.

He had not been told the walls of the office were glass.

Through the glass, he could see down to the deserted tracks and platforms of the station below. He could also see the jack on the stairs, near the door, a paper bag containing his dinner at his side.

Carefully, Clean Willy climbed down off the desk. His foot crunched on a shard of broken glass; he froze. But if the guard heard it, he gave no sign. After a moment, Willy crossed the office, lifted a chair, and set it next to the high cabinet. He stepped onto the chair, plucked the twirl Agar had given him from his pocket, and picked the cabinet lock. Then he sat down to wait, hearing distant church bells toll the hour of nine o'clock.

Agar, lurking in the deep shadows of the station, also heard the church bells. He sighed. Another two and a half hours, and he had been wedged into a cramped corner for two hours already. He knew how stiff and painful his legs would be when he finally made his sprint for the stairs.

From his hiding place, he could see Clean Willy make an entrance into the office behind the guard; and he could see Willy's head when he stood on the chair and worked the cabinet lock. Then Willy disappeared.

Agar sighed again. He wondered, for the thousandth time, what Pierce intended to do with these keys. All he knew was that it must be a devilish flash pull. A few years earlier,

Agar had been in on a Brighton warehouse pull. There had been nine keys involved: one for an outer gate, two for an inner gate, three for the main door, two for an office door, and one for a storeroom. The pogue had been ten thousand quid in B. of E. notes, and the putter-up had spent four months arranging the lay.

Yet here was Pierce, flush if ever a cracksman was, spending eight months now to get four keys, two from bankers, and two from a railway office. It had all cost a pretty penny, Agar was certain of that, and it meant the pogue was well worth having.

But what *was* it? Why were they breaking this drum now? The question preoccupied him more than the mechanics of timing a sixty-four-second smash and grab. He was a professional; he was cool; he had prepared well and was fully confident. His heart beat evenly as he stared across the station at the jack on the stairs, as the crusher made his rounds.

The crusher said to the jack, "You know there's a P.R. on?" A P.R. was a prize-ring event.

"No," said the jack. "Who's it to be?"

"Stunning Bill Hampton and Edgar Moxley."

"Where's it to be, then?" the jack said.

"I hear Leicester," the crusher said.

"Where's your money?"

"Stunning Bill, for my gambit."

"He's a good one," the jack said. "He's tough, is Bill."

"Aye," the crusher said, "I've got a half-crown or two on him says he's tough."

And the crusher went on, making his rounds.

Agar smirked in the darkness. A copper talking big of a five-shilling bet. Agar bet ten quid on the last P.R., between the Lancaster Dervish, John Boynton, and the gammy Kid Ballew. Agar had come off well on that one: odds were two to one; he'd done a bit of winning there.

He tensed the muscles in his cramped legs, trying to get

the circulation going, and then he relaxed. He had a long
wait ahead of him. He thought of his dolly-mop. Whenever
he was working, he thought of his dolly's quim; it was a
natural thing—tension turned a man randy. Then his thoughts
drifted back to Pierce, and the question that Agar had
puzzled over for nearly a year now: what *was* the damn
pull?

The drunken Irishman with the red beard and slouch hat
stumbled through the deserted station singing "Molly Malone." With his shuffling, flatfooted gait, he was a true soak,
and as he walked along, it appeared he was so lost in his
song that he might not notice the guard on the stairs.

But he did, and he eyed the guard's paper bag suspiciously
before making an elaborate and wobbly bow.

"And a good evenin' to you, sir," the drunk said.

"Evening," the guard said.

"And what, may I inquire," said the drunk, standing stiffer,
"is your business up there, eh? Up to no good, are you?"

"I'm guarding these premises here," the guard said.

The drunk hiccuped. "So you say, my good fellow, but
many a rascal has said as much."

"Here, now—"

"I think," the drunk said, waving an accusatory finger in
the air, trying to point it at the guard but unable to aim ac-
curately, "I think, sir, we shall have the police to look you
over, so that we shall know if you are up to no good."

"Now, look here," the guard said.

"You look here, and lively, too," the drunk said, and
abruptly began to shout, "Police! *Po-lice!*"

"Here, now," the guard said, coming down the stairs. "Get
a grip on yourself, you scurvy soak."

"Scurvy soak?" the drunk said, raising an eyebrow and
shaking his fist. "I am a Dubliner, sir."

"I palled that, right enough," the guard snorted.

At that moment, the constable came running around the corner, drawn by the shouts of the drunk.

"Ah, a criminal, officer," said the drunk. "Arrest that scoundrel," he said, pointing to the guard, who had now moved to the bottom of the stairs. "He is up to no good."

The drunk hiccuped.

The constable and the guard exchanged glances, and then open smiles.

"You find this a laughing matter, sir?" said the drunk, turning to the copper. "I see nothing risible. The man is plainly up to no good."

"Come along, now," the constable said, "or I'll have you in lumber for creatin' a nuisance."

"A nuisance?" the drunk said, twisting free of the constable's arm. "I think you and this blackguard are in cahoots, sir."

"That's enough," the constable said. "Come along smartly."

The drunk allowed himself to be led away by the copper. He was last heard to say, "You wouldn't be havin' a daffy of reeb, would you, now?" and the constable assured him he had no drink on his person.

"Dublin," the guard said, sighing, and he climbed back up the stairs to eat his dinner. The distant chimes rang eleven o'clock.

Agar had seen it all, and while he was amused by Pierce's performance, he worried whether Clean Willy had taken the opportunity to open the office door. There was no way to know until he made his own mad dash, in less than half an hour now.

He looked at his watch, he looked at the door to the office, and he waited.

For Pierce, the most delicate part of his performance was the conclusion, when he was led by the constable out onto Tooley Street. Pierce did not want to disrupt the policeman's regular rhythm on the beat, so he had to disengage himself rather rapidly.

As they came into the foggy night air, he breathed deeply. "Ah," he said, "and it's a lovely evening, brisk and invigorating."

The copper looked round at the gloomy fog. "Chill enough for me," he said.

"Well, my dear fellow," Pierce said, dusting himself off and making a show of straightening up, as if the night air had sobered him, "I am most grateful for your ministrations upon this occasion, and I can assure you that I can carry on well from here."

"You're not going to be creating another nuisance?"

"My dear sir," Pierce said, standing still straighter, "what do you take me for?"

The copper looked back at the London Bridge Station. It was his business to stay on the beat; a drunk wandering in was not his responsibility once he was ejected from the premises. And London was full of drunks, especially Irish ones who talked too much.

"Stay clear of trouble, then," the cop said, and let him go.

"A good evening to you, officer," Pierce said, and bowed to the departing crusher. Then he wandered out into the fog, singing "Molly Malone."

Pierce went no farther than the end of Tooley Street, less than a block from the station entrance. There, hidden in the fog, was a cab. He looked up at the driver.

"How'd it carry off?" Barlow asked.

"Smart and tidy," Pierce said. "I gave Willy two or three minutes; it should have been enough."

"Willy's a bit glocky."

"All he has to do," Pierce said, "is twirl two locks, and he's not too glocky to bring that off." He glanced at his watch. "Well, we'll know soon enough."

And he slipped away, in the fog, back toward the station.

At eleven-thirty, Pierce had taken up a position where he could see the dispatch office stairs and the guard. The copper made his round; he waved to the jack, who waved back. The copper went on; the jack yawned, stood, and stretched.

Pierce took a breath and poised his finger on the stopwatch button.

The guard came down the stairs, yawning again, and moved off toward the W.C. He walked several paces, and then was out of sight, around a corner.

Pierce hit the button, and counted softly, "One . . . two . . . three . . ."

He saw Agar appear, running hard, barefooted to make no sound, and dashing up the stairs to the door.

"Four . . . five . . . six . . ."

Agar reached the door, twisted the knob; the door opened and Agar was inside. The door closed.

"Seven . . . eight . . . nine . . ."

"Ten," Agar said, panting, looking around the office. Clean Willy, grinning in the shadows in the corner, took up the count.

"Eleven . . . twelve . . . thirteen . . ."

Agar crossed to the already opened cabinet. He removed the first of the wax blanks from his pocket, and then looked at the keys in the cabinet.

"Crikey!" he whispered.

"Fourteen . . . fifteen . . . sixteen . . ."

Dozens of keys hung in the cabinet, keys of all sorts, large and small, labeled and unlabeled, all hanging on hooks. He broke into a sweat in an instant.

"Crikey!"

"Seventeen . . . eighteen . . . nineteen . . ."

Agar was going to fall behind. He knew it with sickening suddenness: he was already behind on the count. He stared helplessly at the keys. He could not wax them all; which were the ones to do?

"Twenty . . . twenty-one . . . twenty-two . . ."

Clean Willy's droning voice infuriated him; Agar wanted to run across the room and strangle the little bastard. He stared at the cabinet in a rising panic. He remembered what the other two keys looked like; perhaps these two keys were similar. He peered close at the cabinet, squinting, straining: the light in the office was bad.

"Twenty-three . . . twenty-four . . . twenty-five . . ."

"It's no bloody use," he whispered to himself. And then he realized something odd: each hook had only one key, except for a single hook, which had two. He quickly lifted them off. They looked like the others he had done.

"Twenty-six . . . twenty-seven . . . twenty-eight . . ."

He set out the first blank, and pressed one side of the first key into the blank, holding it neatly, plucking it out with his fingernail; the nail on the little finger was long, one of the hallmarks of a screwsman.

"Twenty-nine . . . thirty . . . thirty-one . . ."

He took the second blank, flipped the key over, and pressed it into the wax to get the other side. He held it firmly, then scooped it out.

"Thirty-two . . . thirty-three . . . thirty-four . . ."

Now Agar's professionalism came into play. He was falling behind—at least five seconds off his count now, maybe more—but he knew that at all costs he must avoid confusing the keys. It was common enough for a screwsman under pressure to make two impressions of the same side of a single key; with two keys, the chance of confusion was doubled. Quickly but carefully, he hung up the first finished key.

"Thirty-five . . . thirty-six . . . thirty-seven, Lordy," Clean Willy said. Clean Willy was looking out the glass windows, down to where the guard would be returning in less than thirty seconds.

"Thirty-eight . . . thirty-nine . . . forty . . ."

Swiftly, Agar pressed the second key into his third blank.

He held it there just an instant, then lifted it out. There was a decent impression.

"Forty-one . . . forty-two . . . forty-three . . ."

Agar pocketed the blank, and plucked up his fourth wax plate. He pressed the other side of the key into the soft material.

"Forty-four . . . forty-five . . . forty-six . . . forty-seven . . ."

Abruptly, while Agar was peeling the key free of the wax, the blank cracked in two.

"Damn!"

"Forty-eight . . . forty-nine . . . fifty . . ."

He fished in his pocket for another blank. His fingers were steady, but there was sweat dripping from his forehead.

"Fifty-one . . . fifty-two . . . fifty-three . . ."

He drew out a fresh blank and did the second side again.

"Fifty-four . . . fifty-five . . ."

He plucked the key out, hung it up, and dashed for the door, still holding the final blank in his fingers. He left the office without another look at Willy.

"Fifty-six," Willy said, immediately moving to the door to lock it up.

Pierce saw Agar exit, behind schedule by five full seconds. His face was flushed with exertion.

"Fifty-seven . . . fifty-eight . . ."

Agar sprinted down the stairs, three at a time.

"Fifty-nine . . . sixty . . . sixty-one . . ."

Agar streaked across the station to his hiding place.

"Sixty-two . . . sixty-three . . ."

Agar was hidden.

The guard, yawning, came around the corner, still buttoning up his trousers. He walked toward the steps.

"Sixty-four," Pierce said, and flicked his watch.

The guard took up his post at the stairs. After a moment, he began humming to himself, very softly, and it was awhile until Pierce realized it was "Molly Malone."

CHAPTER 26

Crossing the Mary Blaine Scrob

"The distinction between base avarice and honest ambition may be exceeding fine," warned the Reverend Noel Blackwell in his 1853 treatise, *On the Moral Improvement of the Human Race*. No one knew the truth of his words better than Pierce, who arranged his next meeting at the Casino de Venise, on Windmill Street. This was a large and lively dance hall, brightly lit by myriad gas lamps. Young men spun and wheeled girls colorfully dressed and gay in their manner. Indeed, the total impression was one of fashionable splendor, which belied a reputation as a wicked and notorious place of assignation for whores and their clientele.

Pierce went directly to the bar, where a burly man in a blue uniform with silver lapel markings sat hunched over a drink. The man appeared distinctly uncomfortable in the casino. "Have you been here before?" Pierce asked.

The man turned. "You Mr. Simms?"

"That's right."

The burly man looked around the room, at the women, the finery, the bright lights. "No," he said, "never been before."

"Lively, don't you think?"

The man shrugged. "Bit above me," he said finally, and turned back to stare at his glass.

"And expensive," Pierce said.

The man raised his drink. "Two shillings a daffy? Aye, it's expensive."

"Let me buy you another," Pierce said, raising a gray-gloved hand to beckon the bartender. "Where do you live, Mr. Burgess?"

"I got a room on Moresby Road," the burly man said.

"I hear the air is bad there."

Burgess shrugged. "It'll do."

"You married?"

"Aye."

The bartender came, and Pierce indicated two more drinks. "What's your wife do?"

"She sews." Burgess showed a flash of impatience. "What's this all about, then?"

"Just a little conversation," Pierce said, "to see if you want to make more money."

"Only a fool doesn't," Burgess said shortly.

"You work the Mary Blaine," Pierce said.

Burgess, with still more impatience, nodded and flicked the silver SER letters on his collar: the insignia of the South Eastern Railway.

Pierce was not asking these questions to obtain information; he already knew a good deal about Richard Burgess, a Mary Blaine scrob, or guard on the railway. He knew where Burgess lived; he knew what his wife did; he knew that they had two children, aged two and four, and he knew that the four-year-old was sickly and needed the frequent attentions of a doctor, which Burgess and his wife could not afford. He knew that their room on Moresby Road was a squalid, peeling, narrow chamber that was ventilated by the sulfurous fumes of an adjacent gasworks.

He knew that Burgess fell into the lowest-paid category of railway employee. An engine driver was paid 35 shillings a week; a conductor 25 shillings; a coachman 20 or 21; but a guard was paid 15 shillings a week and counted himself lucky it was not a good deal less.

Burgess's wife made ten shillings a week, which meant that the family lived on a total of about sixty-five pounds a year.

Out of this came certain expenses—Burgess had to provide his own uniforms—so that the true income was probably closer to fifty-five pounds a year, and for a family of four it was a very rough go.

Many Victorians had incomes at that level, but most contrived supplements of one sort or another: extra work, tips, and a child in industry were the most common. The Burgess household had none of these. They were compelled to live on their income, and it was little wonder that Burgess felt uncomfortable in a place that charged two shillings a drink. It was very far beyond his means.

"What's it to be?" Burgess said, not looking at Pierce.

"I was wondering about your vision."

"My vision?"

"Yes, your eyesight."

"My eyes are good enough."

"I wonder," Pierce said, "what it would take for them to go bad."

Burgess sighed, and did not speak for a moment. Finally he said in a weary voice, "I done a stretch in Newgate a few years back. I'm not wanting to see the cockchafer again."

"Perfectly sensible," Pierce said. "And I don't want anybody to blow my lay. We both have our fears."

Burgess gulped his drink. "What's the sweetener?"

"Two hundred quid," Pierce said.

Burgess coughed, and pounded his chest with a thick fist. "Two hundred quid," he repeated.

"That's right," Pierce said. "Here's ten now, on faith." He removed his wallet and took out two five-pound notes; he held the wallet in such a way that Burgess could not fail to notice it was bulging. He set the money on the bar top.

"Pretty a sight as a hot nancy," Burgess said, but he did not touch it. "What's the lay?"

"You needn't worry over the lay. All you need to do is worry over your eyesight."

"What is it I'm not to see, then?"

"Nothing that will get you into trouble. You'll never see the inside of a lockup again, I promise you that."

Burgess turned stubborn. "Speak plain," he said.

Pierce sighed. He reached for the money. "I'm sorry," he said, "I fear I must take my business elsewhere."

Burgess caught his hand. "Not overquick," he said. "I'm just asking."

"I can't tell you."

"You think I'll blow on you to the crushers?"

"Such things," Pierce said, "have been known to happen."

"I wouldn't blow."

Pierce shrugged.

There was a moment of silence. Finally, Burgess reached over with his other hand and plucked away the two five-pound notes. "Tell me what I do," he said.

"It's very simple," Pierce said. "Soon you will be approached by a man who will ask you whether your wife sews your uniforms. When you meet that man, you simply . . . look away."

"That's all?"

"That's all."

"For two hundred quid?"

"For two hundred quid."

Burgess frowned for a moment, and then began to laugh. "What's funny?" Pierce said.

"You'll never pull it," Burgess said. "It's not to be done, that one. There's no cracking those safes, wherever I look. Few months past, there's a kid, works into the baggage car, wants to do those safes. Have a go, I says to him, and he has a go for half an hour, and he gets no further than the tip of my nose. Then I threw him off smartly, bounced him on his noggin."

"I know that," Pierce said. "I was watching."

Burgess stopped laughing.

Pierce withdrew two gold guineas from his pocket and dropped them on the counter. "There's a dolly-mop in the corner—pretty thing, wearing pink. I believe she's waiting for you," Pierce said, and then he got up and walked off.

CHAPTER 27

The Eel-Skinner's Perplexity

Economists of the mid-Victorian period note that increasing numbers of people made their living by what was then called "dealing," an inclusive term that referred to supplying goods and services to the burgeoning middle class. England was then the richest nation on earth, and the richest in history. The demand for all kinds of consumer goods was insatiable, and the response was specialization in manufacture, distribution, and sale of goods. It is in Victorian England that one first hears of cabinetmakers who made only the joints of cabinets, and of shops that sold only certain kinds of cabinets.

The increasing specialization was apparent in the underworld as well, and nowhere more peculiar than in the figure of the "eel-skinner." An eel-skinner was usually a metalworker gone bad, or one too old to keep up with the furious pace of legitimate production. In either case, he disappeared from honest circles, re-emerging as a specialized supplier of metal goods to criminals. Sometimes the eel-skinner was a coiner who could not get the stamps to turn out coins.

Whatever his background, his principal business was making eel-skins, or coshes. The earliest eel-skins were sausage-like canvas bags filled with sand, which rampsmen and gonophs—muggers and thieves—could carry up their sleeves until the time came to wield them on their victims. Later, eel-skins were filled with lead shot, and they served the same purpose.

An eel-skinner also made other articles. A "neddy" was a cudgel, sometimes a simple iron bar, sometimes a bar with a knob at one end. The "sack" was a two-pound iron shot placed in a strong stocking. A "whippler" was a shot with an attached cord, and was used to disable a victim head on; the attacker held the shot in his hand and flung it at the victim's face, "like a horrible yo-yo." A few blows from these weapons were certain to take the starch out of any quarry, and the robbery proceeded without further resistance.

As firearms became more common, eel-skinners turned to making bullets. A few skilled eel-skinners also manufactured sets of bettys, or picklocks, but this was demanding work, and most stuck to simpler tasks.

In early January, 1855, a Manchester eel-skinner named Harkins was visited by a gentleman with a red beard who said he wanted to purchase a quantity of LC shot.

"Easy enough done," the skinner said. "I make all manner of shot, and I can make LC right enough. How much will you have?"

"Five thousand," the gentleman said.

"I beg pardon?"

"I said, I will have five thousand LC shot."

The eel-skinner blinked. "Five thousand—that's a quantity. That's—let's see—six LC to the ounce. Now, then . . ." He stared up at the ceiling and plucked at his lower lip. "And sixteen . . . now, that makes it . . . Bless me, that's more'n fifty pounds of shot all in."

"I believe so," the gentleman said.

"You want fifty pounds of LC shot?"

"I want five thousand, yes."

"Well, fifty pounds of lead, that'll take some doing, and the casting—well, that'll take some doing. That'll take some time, five thousand LC shot will, some time indeed."

"I need it in a month," the gentleman said.

"A month, a month . . . Let's see, now . . . casting at a hundred a mold . . . Yes, well . . ." The eel-skinner nodded. "Right enough, you shall have five thousand within a month. You'll be collecting it?"

"I will," the gentleman said, and then he leaned closer, in a conspiratorial fashion. "It's for Scotland, you know."

"Scotland, eh?"

"Yes, Scotland."

"Oh, well, yes, I see that plain enough," the eel-skinner said, though the reverse was clearly true. The red-bearded man put down a deposit and departed, leaving the eel-skinner in a state of marked perplexity. He would have been even more perplexed to know that this gentleman had visited skinners in Newcastle-on-Tyne, Birmingham, Liverpool, and London, and placed identical orders with each of them, so that he was ordering a total of two hundred and fifty pounds of lead shot. What use could anyone have for that?

CHAPTER 28

The Finishing Touch

London at the mid-century had six morning newspapers, three evening newspapers, and twenty influential weeklies. This period marked the beginning of an organized press with enough power to mold public opinion and, ultimately, political events. The unpredictability of that power was highlighted in January, 1855.

On the one hand, the first war correspondent in history, William Howard Russell, was in Russia with the Crimean troops, and his dispatches to the *Times* had aroused furious indignation at home. The charge of the Light Brigade, the bungling of the Balaclava campaign, the devastating winter when British troops, lacking food and medical supplies, suffered a 50 percent mortality—these were all reported in the press to an increasingly angry public.

By January, however, the commander of British forces, Lord Raglan, was severely ill, and Lord Cardigan—"haughty, rich, selfish and stupid," the man who had bravely led his Light Brigade to utter disaster, and then returned to his yacht to drink champagne and sleep—Lord Cardigan had returned home, and the press everywhere hailed him as a great national hero. It was a role he was only too happy to play. Dressed in the uniform he had worn at Balaclava, he was mobbed by crowds in every city; hairs from his horse's tail were plucked for souvenirs. London shops copied the woolen jacket he had worn in the Crimea—called a "Cardigan"— and thousands were sold.

The man known to his own troops as "the dangerous ass" went about the country delivering speeches recounting his prowess in leading the charge; and as the months passed, he spoke with more and more emotion, and was often forced to pause and revive himself. The press never ceased to cheer him on; there was no sense of the chastisement that later historians have richly accorded him.

But if the press was fickle, public tastes were even more so. Despite all the provocative news from Russia, the dispatches which most intrigued Londoners in January concerned a man-eating leopard that menaced Naini Tal in northern India, not far from the Burmese border. The "Panar man-eater" was said to have killed more than four hundred natives, and accounts were remarkable for their vivid, even lurid, detail. "The vicious Panar beast," wrote one correspondent, "kills for the sake of killing and not for any food. It rarely eats any portion of the body of its victims, although two weeks past it ate the upper torso of an infant after stealing it from its crib. Indeed, the majority of its victims have been children under the age of ten who are unfortunate enough to stray from the center of the village after nightfall. Adult victims are generally mauled and later die of suppurating wounds; Mr. Redby, a hunter of the region, says these infections are caused by rotten flesh lodged in the beast's claws. The Panar killer is exceedingly strong, and has been seen to carry off a fully grown female adult in its jaws, while the victim struggles and cries out most piteously."

These and other stories became the delicious talk of dining rooms among company given to raciness; women colored and tittered and exclaimed, while men—especially Company men who had spent time in India—spoke knowledgeably about the habits of such a beast, and its nature. An interesting working model of a tiger devouring an Englishman, owned by the East India Company, was visited by fascinated crowds. (The model can still be seen in the Victoria and Albert Museum.)

And when, on February 17, 1855, a caged, fully grown leopard arrived at London Bridge Terminus, it created a considerable stir—much more than the arrival, a short time previously, of armed guards carrying strongboxes of gold, which were loaded into the SER luggage van.

Here was a full-sized, snarling beast, which roared and charged the bars of its cage as it was loaded onto the same luggage van of the London-Folkestone train. The animal's keeper accompanied the beast, in order to look after the leopard's welfare, and to protect the luggage-van guard in the event of any unforeseen mishap.

Meanwhile, before the train departed the station, the keeper explained to the crowd of curious onlookers and children that the beast ate raw meat, that it was a female four years old, and that it was destined for the Continent, where it would be a present to a wellborn lady.

The train pulled out of the station shortly after eight o'clock, and the guard on the luggage van closed the sliding side door. There was a short silence while the leopard stalked its cage, and growled intermittently; finally the railway guard said, "What do you feed her?"

The animal's attendant turned to the guard. "Does your wife sew your uniforms?" he asked.

Burgess laughed. "You mean it's to be you?"

The attendant did not answer. Instead, he opened a small leather satchel and removed a jar of grease, several keys, and a collection of files of varied shapes and sizes.

He went immediately to the two Chubb safes, coated the four locks with grease, and began fitting his keys. Burgess watched with only vague interest in the process: he knew that rough-copied wax keys would not work on a finely made safe without polishing and refining. But he was also impressed; he never thought it would be carried off with such boldness.

"Where'd you make the impressions?" he said.

"Here and there," Agar replied, fitting and filing.

"They keep those keys separate."

"Do they," Agar said.

"Aye, they do. How'd you pull them?"

"That's no matter to you," Agar said, still working.

Burgess watched him for a time, and then he watched the leopard. "How much does he weigh?"

"Ask him," Agar said irritably.

"Are you taking the gold today, then?" Burgess asked as Agar managed to get one of the safe doors open. Agar did not answer; he stared transfixed for a moment at the strongboxes inside. "I say, are you taking the gold today?"

Agar shut the door. "No," he said. "Now stop your voker."

Burgess fell silent.

For the next hour, while the morning passenger train chugged from London to Folkestone, Agar worked on his keys. Ultimately, he had opened and closed both safes. When he was finished, he wiped the grease from the locks. Then he cleaned the locks with alcohol and dried them with a cloth.

Finally he took his four keys, placed them carefully in his pocket, and sat down to await the arrival of the train at the Folkestone station.

Pierce met him at the station and helped to unload the leopard.

"How was it?" he asked.

"The finishing touches are done," Agar said, and then he grinned. "It's the gold, isn't it? The Crimean gold—that's the flash pull."

"Yes," Pierce said.

"When?"

"Next month," Pierce said.

The leopard snarled.

PART III

DELAYS
and
DIFFICULTIES

March–May, 1855

CHAPTER 29

Minor Setbacks

The robbers originally intended to take the gold during the next Crimean shipment. The plan was extremely simple. Pierce and Agar were to board the train in London, each checking several heavy satchels onto the baggage van. The satchels would be filled with sewn packets of lead shot.

Agar would again ride in the van, and while Burgess looked away Agar would open the safes, remove the gold, and replace it with lead shot. These satchels would be thrown from the train at a predetermined point, and collected by Barlow. Barlow would then drive on to Folkestone, where he would meet Pierce and Agar.

Meanwhile, the gold strongboxes—still convincingly heavy—would be transferred to the steamer going to Ostend, where the theft would be discovered by the French authorities hours later. By then, enough people would have been involved in the transportation process that there would be no particular reason to fix suspicion on Burgess; and in any case, British-French relations were at a low level because of the Crimean War, and it would be natural that the French would assume the English had carried out the theft, and vice versa. The robbers could count on plenty of confusion to muddy the waters for the police.

The plan seemed utterly foolproof, and the robbers prepared to carry it out on the next gold shipment, scheduled for March 14, 1855.

On March 2nd, "that fiend in human shape," Czar Nicholas I of Russia, died suddenly. News of his death caused considerable confusion in business and financial circles. For several days the reports were doubted, and when his death was finally confirmed, the stock markets of Paris and London responded with large gains. But as a result of the general uncertainty the gold shipment was delayed until March 27th. By then, Agar, who had sunk into a kind of depression after the fourteenth, was desperately ill with an exacerbation of his chest condition, and so the opportunity was missed.

The firm of Huddleston & Bradford was making gold shipments once a month; there were now only 11,000 English troops in the Crimea, as opposed to 78,000 French, and most of the money was paid out directly from Paris. Thus Pierce and his compatriots were obliged to wait until April.

The next shipment was set for April 19th. The robbers at this time were getting their information on shipment schedules from a tart named Susan Lang, a favorite of Henry Fowler's. Mr. Fowler liked to impress the simple girl with episodes reflecting his importance to the world of banking and commerce, and for her part, the poor girl—who could hardly have understood a word he said—seemed endlessly fascinated by everything he told her.

Susan Lang was hardly simple, but somehow she got her facts wrong: the gold went out on April 18th, and when Pierce and Agar arrived at London Bridge Station in time to board the April 19th train, Burgess informed them of their error. To maintain appearances, Pierce and Agar made the trip anyway, but Agar testified in court that Pierce was in "very ugly humor indeed" during the journey.

The next shipment was scheduled for May 22nd. In order to prevent any further snags, Pierce took the rather risky step of opening a line of communication between Agar and Burgess. Burgess could reach Agar at any time through an intermediary, a betting-shop proprietor named Smashing Billy Banks; and Burgess was to get in touch with Banks if there was any change in the planned routine. Agar would check with Banks daily.

On May 10th, Agar returned to Pierce with a piece of ghastly news—the two safes had been removed from the South Eastern Railway's luggage van and returned to the manufacturer, Chubb, for "overhaul."

"Overhaul?" Pierce said. "What do you mean, overhaul?"

Agar shrugged. "That was the cant."

"Those are the finest safes in the world," Pierce said. "They don't go back for an overhaul." He frowned. "What's wrong with them?"

Agar shrugged.

"You bastard," Pierce said, "did you scratch the locks when you put on your finishing touches? I swear, if someone's cooled your scratches—"

"I greased her lovely," Agar said. "I know they look as a routine for scratches. I tell you, she had nary a tickle on her."

Agar's calm demeanor convinced Pierce that the screws-man was telling the truth. Pierce sighed. "Then *why?*"

"I don't know," Agar said. "You know a man who will blow on the doings at Chubb?"

"No," Pierce said. "And I wouldn't want to try a cross. They're not gulled at Chubb's." The safemaker's firm was unusually careful about its employees. Men were hired and fired only with reluctance, and they were continually warned to look for underworld figures who might try to bribe them.

"A little magging, then?" Agar suggested, meaning some conning.

Pierce shook his head. "Not me," he said. "They're just too careful; I'd never be able to slip it to them. . . ."

He stared into the distance thoughtfully.

"What is it?" Agar asked.

"I was thinking," Pierce said, "that they would never sus-pect a lady."

CHAPTER 30

A Visit to Mr. Chubb

What Rolls-Royce would become to automobiles, and Otis to elevators, Chubb's had long since been to safes. The head of that venerable firm, Mr. Laurence Chubb, Jr., did not later remember—or pretended not to remember—a visit by a handsome young woman in May, 1855. But an employee of the company was sufficiently impressed by the lady's beauty to recall her in great detail.

She arrived in a handsome coach, with liveried footmen, and swept imperiously into the firm unattended by any escort. She was extremely well dressed and spoke with a commanding manner; she demanded to see Mr. Chubb himself, and immediately.

When Mr. Chubb appeared a few moments later, the woman announced that she was Lady Charlotte Simms; that she and her invalid husband maintained a country estate in the Midlands, and that recent episodes of thievery in the neighborhood had convinced her that she and her husband needed a safe.

"Then you have come to the best shop in Christendom," said Mr. Chubb.

"So I have been previously informed," Lady Charlotte said, as if not at all convinced.

"Indeed, Madam, we manufacture the finest safes in the world, and in all sizes and varieties, and these excel even the best of the Hamburg German safes."

"I see."

"What is it, specifically, that Madam requires?"

Here Lady Charlotte, for all her imperiousness, seemed to falter. She gestured with her hands. "Why, just some manner of, ah, large safe, you know."

"Madam," said Mr. Chubb severely, "we manufacture single-thickness and double-thickness safes; steel safes and iron safes; lock safes and throwbolt safes; portable safes and fixed safes; safes with a capacity of six cubic inches and safes with a capacity of twelve cubic yards; safes mounted with single locks and double locks—and triple locks, should the customer require it."

This recitation seemed to put Lady Charlotte even further off her form. She appeared nearly helpless—quite the ordinary way of a female when asked to deal with technical matters. "Well," she said, "I, ah, I don't know . . ."

"Perhaps if Madam looks through our catalogue, which is illustrated, and denotes the various aspects and features of our different models."

"Yes, excellent, that would be fine."

"This way, please." Mr. Chubb led her into his office and seated her by his desk. He drew out the catalogue and opened it to the first page. The woman hardly looked at it.

"They seem rather small."

"These are only pictures, Madam. You will notice that the true dimensions are stated beside each. For example, here—"

"Mr. Chubb," she interrupted, in an earnest tone, "I must beg your assistance. The fact is that my husband is recently ill, or he should be conducting this business for himself. In truth, I know nothing of these matters, and should press my own brother into my assistance were he not at this very minute abroad on business. I am quite at a loss and I can tell nothing from pictures. Can you perhaps show me some of your safes?"

"Madam, forgive me," Mr. Chubb said, rushing around the

desk to help her to her feet. "Absolutely, of course. We maintain no showroom, as you might imagine, but if you will
follow me into the workrooms—and I heartily apologize for
any dust, noise, or commotion you may suffer—I can show
you the various safes we make."

He led Lady Charlotte back into the long workroom behind the offices. Here a dozen men were busy hammering,
fitting, welding, and soldering. The noise was so loud that
Mr. Chubb had to shout for Lady Charlotte to hear, and the
good woman herself fairly winced from the din.

"Now, this version here," he said, "has a one-cubic-foot
capacity, and is double-layered, sixteenth-inch tempered steel,
with an insulating layer of dried brick dust of Cornish origin.
It is an excellent intermediate safe for many purposes."

"It is too small."

"Very good, Madam, too small. Now, this one here"—he
moved down the line—"is one of our most recent creations.
It is a single layer of eighth-inch steel with an inner hinge
and a capacity of—" He turned to the workman: "What is
the capacity?"

"This'un here's two and a half," the workman said.

"Two and a half cubic feet," Mr. Chubb said.

"Still too small."

"Very good, Madam. If you will come this way," and he
led her deeper into the workroom. Lady Charlotte coughed
delicately in a cloud of brick dust.

"Now, this model here—" Mr. Chubb began.

"There!" said Lady Charlotte, pointing across the room.
"That's the size I want."

"You mean those two safes over there?"

"Yes, those."

They crossed the room. "These safes," said Mr. Chubb,
"represent the finest examples of our workmanship. They
are owned by the Huddleston & Bradford Bank, and are
employed in the Crimean gold shipments, where naturally

security is of the utmost. However, these are generally sold to institutions, and not to private individuals. I naturally thought—"

"This is the safe I want," she said, and then looked at them suspiciously. "They don't appear very new."

"Oh, no, Madam, they are nearly two years old now."

This seemed to alarm Lady Charlotte. "Two years old. Why are they back? Have they some defect?"

"No, indeed. A Chubb safe has no defects. They have merely been returned for replacement of the undercarriage mounting pins. Two of them have sheared. You see, they travel on the railway, and the vibration from the roadbed works on the bolts which anchor the safes to the luggage-van floor." He shrugged. "These details need not concern you. There is nothing wrong with the safes, and we are making no alterations. We are merely replacing the anchor bolts."

"Now I see these have double locks."

"Yes, Madam, the banking firm requested double-lock mechanisms. As I believe I mentioned, we also install triple locks if the customer requires it."

Lady Charlotte peered at the locks. "Three seems excessive. It must be rather a bore to turn three locks just to open a safe. These locks are burglarproof?"

"Oh, absolutely. So much so that in two years no villain has ever even attempted to break these locks. It would be quite hopeless, in any case. These safes are double-layered eighth-inch tempered steel. There is no breaking these."

Lady Charlotte peered thoughtfully at the safes for some moments, and finally nodded. "Very well," she said, "I shall take one. Please have it loaded into my carriage outside."

"I beg pardon?"

"I said I shall take one safe such as these I see here. It is precisely what I need."

"Madam," Mr. Chubb said patiently, "we must construct the safe to your order."

"You mean you have none for sale?"

"None already built, no, Madam, I am very sorry. Each safe is specially built to the customer's specifications."

Lady Charlotte appeared quite irritated. "Well, can I have one tomorrow morning?"

Mr. Chubb gulped. "Tomorrow morning—um, well, as a rule, Madam, we require six weeks to construct a safe. On occasion we can manufacture one as quickly as four weeks, but—"

"Four weeks? That is a *month*."

"Yes, Madam."

"I wish to purchase a safe *today*."

"Yes, Madam, quite. But as I have attempted to explain, each safe must be built, and the shortest time—"

"Mr. Chubb, you must think me an utter fool. Well, I shall disabuse you of the notion. I have come here for the purpose of buying a safe, and now I discover you have none to sell—"

"Madam, please—"

"—but on the contrary will construct one for me in only a month's time. Within a month the brigands of the neighborhood will very probably have come and gone, and your safe will not in the least interest me, or my husband. I shall take my business elsewhere. Good day to you, sir, and thank you for your time."

With that, Lady Charlotte swept out of the firm of Chubb's. And Mr. Laurence Chubb, Jr., was heard to mutter in a low voice, "Women."

It was in this fashion that Pierce and Agar learned that the overhaul did not include changing the locks on the safes. That was, of course, all they cared about, and so they made their final preparations for the robbery, which they would carry out on May 22, 1855.

CHAPTER 31

The Snakesman Turns Nose

One week later, their plans were thrown into still further disarray. On May 17, 1855, a letter was delivered to Pierce. Written in a graceful and educated hand, it read:

My dear Sir:

I should be most greatly obliged if you could contrive to meet with me at the Palace, Sydenham, this afternoon at four o'clock, for the purpose of discussing some matters of mutual interest.

Most respectfully, I am,

William Williams, Esq.

Pierce looked at the letter in consternation. He showed it to Agar; but Agar could not read, so Pierce read the contents aloud. Agar stared at the penmanship.

"Clean Willy's got himself a screever for this one," he said.

"Obviously," Pierce said. "But why?"

"Perhaps he's touching you up."

"If that's all it is, I'd be happy," Pierce said.

"You going to meet him?"

"Absolutely. Will you crow for me?"

Agar nodded. "You want Barlow? A good cosh could save a mighty trouble."

"No," Pierce said. "That'll set them hounding for sure, a cosh would."

"Right, then," Agar said, "a simple crow. 'Twon't be easy in the Palace."

"I'm sure Willy knows that," Pierce said gloomily.

A word should be said about the Crystal Palace, that magical structure which came to symbolize the Victorian mid-century. An enormous three-story glass building covering nineteen acres, it was erected in 1851 in Hyde Park, to house the Great Exhibition of that year, and it impressed every visitor who saw it. Indeed, even in drawings the Crystal Palace is stunning to the modern eye, and to see more than a million square feet of glass shimmering in the afternoon light must have been a remarkable sight for anyone. It is not surprising that the Palace soon represented the forward-looking, technological aesthetic of the new industrial Victorian society.

But this fabulous structure had a comfortingly haphazard origin. Led by Prince Albert himself, plans for the Great Exhibition began in 1850, and soon ran into arguments about the proposed Exhibition Hall itself, and its location.

Obviously the building would have to be very large. But what kind of building, and where? A competition in 1850 attracted more than two hundred designs, but no winner. Thus the Building Committee drew up a plan of its own for a dreadful brick monstrosity; the structure would be four times as long as Westminster Abbey and boast a dome even larger than that of St. Peter's. It would be located in Hyde Park.

The public balked at the destruction of trees, the inconvenience to riders, the general ruin of the pleasant neighborhood, and so on. Parliament seemed reluctant to permit Hyde Park to be used as the building site.

In the meantime, the Building Committee discovered that their plans required nineteen million bricks. By the summer of 1850, there was insufficient time to make all these bricks and build the Great Hall in time for the exhibition's opening.

There was even some dark talk that the exhibition would have to be canceled, or at least postponed.

It was at this point that the Duke of Devonshire's gardener, Joseph Paxton, came forward with the idea of erecting a large greenhouse to serve as the Exhibition Hall. His original plan for the committee, drawn up on a piece of blotting paper, was eventually accepted for its several virtues.

First, it saved the trees of Hyde Park; second, its chief material, glass, could be manufactured quickly; and third, it could be taken down after the exhibition and reinstalled elsewhere. The committee accepted a bid of £79,800 from a contractor to erect the giant structure, which was completed in only seven months, and was later the focal point of almost universal acclaim.

Thus the reputation of a nation and an empire was saved by a gardener; and thus a gardener was eventually knighted.*

After the exhibition, the Great Hall was taken down and moved to Sydenham, in South-East London. In those days, Sydenham was a pleasant suburban area of fine homes and open fields, and the Crystal Palace made an excellent addition to the neighborhood. Shortly before four o'clock, Edward Pierce entered the vast structure to meet Clean Willy Williams.

The giant hall held several permanent exhibits, the most impressive being full-scale reproductions of the huge Egyptian statues of Ramses II at Abu Simbel. But Pierce paid no attention to these attractions, or to the lily ponds and pools of water everywhere about.

A brass band concert was in progress; Pierce saw Clean Willy sitting in one of the rows to the left. He also saw Agar,

---

* There was only one unforeseen problem with the Crystal Palace. The building contained trees, and the trees contained sparrows, and the sparrows were not housebroken. It was really no laughing matter, especially as the birds couldn't be shot, and they ignored traps set for them. Finally the Queen herself was consulted, and she said, "Send for the Duke of Wellington." The Duke was informed of the problem. "Try sparrow hawks, Ma'am," he suggested, and he was once more victorious.

disguised as a retired army officer, apparently snoozing in another corner. The band played loudly. Pierce slipped into the seat alongside Willy.

"What is it?" Pierce said, in a low voice. He looked at the band, and thought idly that he despised band music.

"I'm needing a turn," Willy said.

"You've been paid."

"I'm needing more," Willy said.

Pierce shot him a glance. Willy was sweating, and he was edgy, but he did not look nervously around as an ordinary nervous man would do.

"You been working, Willy?"

"No."

"You been touched, Willy?"

"No, I swear it, no."

"Willy," Pierce said, "if you've turned nose on me, I'll put you in lavender."

"I swear it," Willy said. "It's no flam—a finny or two is what I need, and that's the end of it."

The band, in a moment of patriotic support for England's allies, struck up the "Marseillaise." A few listeners had the ill grace to boo the selection.

Pierce said, "You're sweating, Willy."

"Please, sir, a finny or two and that'll be the end of it."

Pierce reached into his wallet and withdrew two five-pound notes. "Don't blow on me," Pierce said, "or I'll do what must be done."

"Thank you, sir, thank you," Willy said, and quickly pocketed the money. "Thank you, sir."

Pierce left him there. As he exited the Palace and came out into the park, he walked quickly to Harleigh Road. There he paused to adjust his top hat. The gesture was seen by Barlow, whose cab was drawn up at the end of the street.

Then Pierce walked slowly down Harleigh Road, moving with all appearances of casualness, as a relaxed gent taking the air. His thoughts, whatever they might have been, were interrupted by the wail of a railroad whistle, and a nearby chugging sound. Looking over the trees and roofs of mansions, he saw black smoke puffing into the air. Automatically, he checked his watch: it was the mid-afternoon train of the South Eastern Railway, coming back from Folkestone, going toward London Bridge Station.

CHAPTER 32

Minor Incidents

The train continued on toward London, and so did Mr. Pierce. At the end of Harleigh Road, near St. Martin's Church, he hailed a cab and rode it into town to Regent Street, where he got out.

Pierce walked along Regent Street casually, never once glancing over his shoulder, but pausing frequently to look in the shopwindows along the street, and to watch the reflections in the glass.

He did not like what he saw, but he was wholly unprepared for what he next heard as a familiar voice cried out, "Edward, dear Edward!"

Groaning inwardly, Pierce turned to see Elizabeth Trent. She was shopping, accompanied by a livery boy, who carried brightly wrapped packages. Elizabeth Trent colored deeply. "I—why, I must say, this is an extraordinary surprise."

"I am so pleased to see you," Pierce said, bowing and kissing her hand.

"I—yes, I—" She snatched her hand away and rubbed it with her other. "Edward," she said, taking a deep breath. "Edward, I did not know what had become of you."

"I must apologize," Pierce said smoothly. "I was very suddenly called abroad on business, and I am sure my letter from Paris was inadequate to your injured sensibilities."

"Paris?" she said, frowning.

"Yes. Did you not receive my letter from Paris?"

"Why, no."

"Damn!" Pierce said, and then immediately apologized for his strong language. "It is the French," he said; "they are so ghastly inefficient. If only I had known, but I never suspected—and when you did not reply to me in Paris, I assumed that you were angry. . . ."

"I? Angry? Edward, I assure you," she began, and broke off. "But when did you return?"

"Just three days past," Pierce said.

"How strange," Elizabeth Trent said, with a sudden look of unfeminine shrewdness, "for Mr. Fowler was to dinner a fortnight past, and spoke of seeing you."

"I do not wish to contradict a business associate of your father's, but Henry has the deplorable habit of mixing his dates. I've not seen him for nearly three months." Pierce quickly added: "And how is your father?"

"My father? Oh, my father is well, thank you." Her shrewdness was replaced by a look of hurt confusion. "Edward, I— My father, in truth, spoke some rather unflattering words concerning your character."

"Did he?"

"Yes. He called you a cad." She sighed. "And worse."

"I wholly understand, given the circumstances, but—"

"But now," Elizabeth Trent said, with a sudden determination, "since you are returned to England, I trust we shall be seeing you at the house once more."

Here it was Pierce's turn to be greatly discomfited. "My

dear Elizabeth," he said, stammering. "I do not know how to say this," and he broke off, shaking his head. It seemed that tears were welling up in his eyes. "When I did not hear from you in Paris, I naturally assumed that you were displeased with me, and . . . well, as time passed . . ." Pierce suddenly straightened. "I regret to inform you that I am betrothed."

Elizabeth Trent stared. Her mouth fell open.

"Yes," Pierce said, "it is true. I have given my word."

"But to whom?"

"To a French lady."

"A *French* lady?"

"Yes, I fear it is true, all true. I was most desperately unhappy, you see."

"I do see, sir," she snapped, and turned abruptly on her heel and walked away. Pierce remained standing on the sidewalk, trying to appear as abject as possible, until she had climbed into her carriage and driven off. Then he continued down Regent Street.

Anyone who observed him might have noticed that at the bottom of Regent Street there was nothing about his manner or carriage that indicated the least remorse. He boarded a cab to Windmill Street, where he entered an accommodation house that was a known dolly-mop's lurk, but one of the better class of such establishments.

In the plush velvet hallway, Miss Miriam said, "He's upstairs. Third door on the right."

Pierce went upstairs and entered a room to find Agar seated, chewing a mint. "Bit late," Agar said. "Trouble?"

"I ran into an old acquaintance."

Agar nodded vaguely.

"What did you see?" Pierce said.

"I cooled two," Agar said. "Both riding your tail nice-like. One's a crusher in disguise; the other's dressed as a square-rigged sport. Followed you all the way down Harleigh, and took a cab when you climbed aboard."

Pierce nodded. "I saw the same two in Regent Street."

"Probably lurking outside now," Agar said. "How's Willy?"

"Willy looks to be turning nose," Pierce said.

"Must have done a job."

Pierce shrugged.

"What's to be done with Willy, then?"

"He'll be getting what any gammy trasseno gets."

"I'd bump him," Agar said.

"I don't know about bumping," Pierce said, "but he won't have another chance to blow on us."

"What'll you do with the officers?"

"Nothing for the moment," Pierce said. "I've got to think a bit." And he sat back, lit a cigar, and puffed in silence.

The planned robbery was only five days away, and the police were on to him. If Willy had sung, and loudly, then the police would know that Pierce's gang had broken into the London Bridge Terminus offices.

"I need a new lay," he said, and stared at the ceiling. "A proper flash lay for the miltonians to discover." He watched the cigar smoke curl upward, and frowned.

CHAPTER 33

Miltonians on the Stalk

The institutions of any society are interrelated, even those which appear to have completely opposite goals. Gladstone himself observed: "There is often, in the course of this wayward and bewildered life, exterior opposition, and sincere and even violent condemnation, between persons and bodies

who are nevertheless profoundly associated by ties and relations that they know not of."

Perhaps the most famous example of this, and one well-
recognized by Victorians, was the bitter rivalry between the
temperance societies and the pubs. These two institutions in
fact served similar ends, and ultimately were seen to adopt
the same attractions: the pubs acquired organs, hymn singing,
and soft drinks, and the temperance meetings had professional
entertainers and a new, raucous liveliness. By the time the
temperance groups began buying pubs in order to turn them
dry, the intermixture of these two hostile forces became pronounced indeed.

Victorians also witnessed another rivalry, centering around
a new social institution—the organized police force. Almost
immediately, the new force began to form relationships with
its avowed enemy, the criminal class. These relationships
were much debated in the nineteenth century, and they continue to be debated to the present day. The similarity in
methods of police and criminals, as well as the fact that many
policemen were former criminals—and the reverse—were
features not overlooked by thinkers of the day. And it was
also noted by Sir James Wheatstone that there was a logical
problem inherent in a law-enforcement institution, "for,
should the police actually succeed in eliminating all crime,
they will simultaneously succeed in eliminating themselves as
a necessary adjunct to society, and no organized force or
power will ever eliminate itself willingly."

In London, the Metropolitan Police, founded by Sir Robert
Peel in 1829, was headquartered in a district known as Scotland Yard. Scotland Yard was originally a geographical term,
denoting an area of Whitehall that contained many government buildings. These buildings included the official residence of the surveyor of works to the crown, which was
occupied by Inigo Jones, and later by Sir Christopher Wren.
John Milton lived in Scotland Yard when he was working
for Oliver Cromwell from 1649 to 1651, and it is apparently

from this association that a slang reference for police, two hundred years later, was "miltonian."

When Sir Robert Peel located the new Metropolitan Police in Whitehall, the correct address for the headquarters was No. 4 Whitehall Place, but the police station there had an entrance from Scotland Yard proper, and the press always referred to the police as Scotland Yard, until the term became synonymous with the force itself.

Scotland Yard grew rapidly in its early years; in 1829 the total force was 1,000, but a decade later it was 3,350, and by 1850 it was more than 6,000, and would increase to 10,000 by 1870. The task of the Yard was extraordinary: it was called upon to police crime in an area of nearly seven hundred square miles, containing a population of two and a half million people.

From the beginning, the Yard adopted a posture of deference and modesty in its manner of solving crimes; the official explanations always mentioned lucky breaks of one sort or another—an anonymous informant, a jealous mistress, a surprise encounter—to a degree that was hard to believe. In fact, the Yard employed informers and plainclothesmen, and these agents were the subject of heated debate for the now familiar reason that many in the public feared that an agent might easily provoke a crime and then arrest the participants. Entrapment was a hot political issue of the day, and the Yard was at pains to defend itself.

In 1855, the principal figure in the Yard was Richard Mayne, "a sensible lawyer," who had done much to improve the public attitude toward the Metropolitan Police. Directly under him was Mr. Edward Harranby, and it was Harranby who oversaw the ticklish business of working with undercover agents and informers. Usually Mr. Harranby kept irregular hours; he avoided contact with the press, and from his office could be seen strange figures coming and going, often at night.

In the late afternoon of May 17th, Harranby had a conversation with his assistant, Mr. Jonathan Sharp. Mr. Harranby reconstructed the conversation in his memoirs, *Days on the Force*, published in 1879. The conversation must be taken with some reservations, for in that volume Harranby was attempting to explain why he did not succeed in thwarting Pierce's robbery plans before they were carried out.

Sharp said to him, "The snakesman blew, and we have had a look at our man."

"What sort is he?" Harranby said.

"He appears a gentleman. Probably a cracksman or a swell mobsman. The snakesman says he's from Manchester, but he lives in a fine house in London."

"Does he know where?"

"He says he's been there, but he doesn't know the exact location. Somewhere in Mayfair."

"We can't go knocking on doors in Mayfair," Harranby said. "Can we assist his powers of memory?"

Sharp sighed. "Possibly."

"Bring him in. I'll have a talk with him. Do we know the intended crime?"

Sharp shook his head. "The snakesman says he doesn't know. He's afraid of being mizzled, you know, he's reluctant to blow all he knows. He says this fellow's planning a flash pull."

Harranby turned irritable. "That is of remarkably little value to me," he said. "What, exactly, is the crime? There's our question, and it begs a proper answer. Who is on this gentleman now?"

"Cramer and Benton, sir."

"They're good men. Keep them on his trail, and let's have the nose in my office, and quickly."

"I'll see to it myself, sir," the assistant said.

Harranby later wrote in his memoirs: "There are times in any professional's life when the elements requisite for the deductive process seem almost within one's grasp, and yet they elude the touch. These are the times of greatest frustration, and such was the case of the Robbery of 1855."

CHAPTER 34

The Nose Is Crapped

Clean Willy, very nervous, was drinking at the Hound's Tooth pub. He left there about six and headed straight for the Holy Land. He moved swiftly through the evening crowds, then ducked into an alley; he jumped a fence, slipped into a basement, crossed it, crawled through a passage into an adjoining building, climbed up the stairs, came out onto a narrow street, walked half a block, and disappeared into another house, a reeking nethersken.

Here he ascended the stairs to the second floor, climbed out onto the roof, jumped to an adjacent roof, scrambled up a drainpipe to the third floor of a lodging house, crawled in through a window, and went down the stairs to the basement.

Once in the basement, he crawled through a tunnel that brought him out on the opposite side of the street, where he came up into a narrow mews. By a side door, he entered a pub house, the Golden Arms, looked around, and exited from the front door.

He walked to the end of the street, and then turned in to the entrance of another lodging house. Immediately he knew that something was wrong; normally there were children yelling and scrambling all over the stairs, but now the entrance and stairs were deserted and silent. He paused at the doorway, and was just about to turn and flee when a rope snaked out and twisted around his neck, yanking him into a dark corner.

Clean Willy had a look at Barlow, with the white scar across his forehead, as Barlow strained on the garrotting rope. Willy coughed, and struggled, but Barlow's strength was such that the little snakesman was literally lifted off the floor, his feet kicking in the air, his hands pulling at the rope.

This struggle continued for the better part of a minute, and then Clean Willy's face was blue, and his tongue protruded gray, and his eyes bulged. He urinated down his pants leg, and then his body sagged.

Barlow let him drop to the floor. He unwound the rope from his neck, removed the two five-pound notes from the snakesman's pocket, and slipped away into the street. Clean Willy's body lay huddled in a corner and did not move. Many minutes passed before the first of the children reemerged, and approached the corpse cautiously. Then the children stole the snakesman's shoes, and all his clothing, and scampered away.

CHAPTER 35

Plucking the Pigeon

Sitting in the third-floor room of the accommodation house with Agar, Pierce finished his cigar and sat up in his chair. "We are very lucky," he said finally.

"Lucky? Lucky to have jacks on our nancy five days before the pull?"

"Yes, lucky," Pierce said. "What if Willy blew? He'd tell them we knocked over the London Bridge Terminus."

"I doubt he'd blow so much, right off. He'd likely tickle them for a bigger push." An informant was in the habit of letting out information bit by bit, with a bribe from the police at each step.

"Yes," Pierce said, "but we must take the chance that he did. Now, that's why we are lucky."

"Where's the luck, then?" Agar said.

"In the fact that London Bridge is the only station in the city with two lines operating from it. The South Eastern, and the London & Greenwich."

"Aye, that's so," Agar said, with a puzzled look.

"We need a bone nose to blow on us," Pierce said.

"You giving the crushers a slum?"

"They must have something to keep them busy," Pierce said. "In five days' time, we'll pull the peters on that train, and I don't want the crushers around to watch."

"Where do you want them?"

"I was thinking of Greenwich," Pierce said. "It would be pleasant if they were in Greenwich."

"So you're needing a bone nose to pass them the slang."

"Yes," Pierce said.

Agar thought for a moment. "There's a dolly-mop, Lucinda, in Seven Dials. They say she knows one or two miltonians—dabs it up with them whenever they pinch her, which is often, seeing as how they like the dabbing."

"No," Pierce said. "They wouldn't believe a woman; it'll look like a feed to them."

"Well, there's Black Dick, the turfite. Know him? He's a Jew, to be found about the Queen's Crown of an evening."

"I know him," Pierce nodded. "Black Dick's a lushington, too fond of his gin. I need a true bone nose, a man of the family."

"A man of the family? Then Chokee Bill will do you proper."

"Chokee Bill? That old mick?"

Agar nodded. "Aye, he's a lag, did a stretch in Newgate. But not for long."

"Oh, yes?" Pierce was suddenly interested. A shortened prison sentence often implied that the man had made a deal to turn nose, to become an informer. "Got his ticket-of-leave early, did he?"

"Uncommon early," Agar said. "And the crushers gave him his broker's license quick-like, too. Very odd, seeing as he's a mick." Pawnbrokers were licensed by the police, who shared the usual prejudice against Irishmen.

"So he's in the uncle trade now?" Pierce said.

"Aye," Agar said. "But they say he deals barkers now and again. And they say he's a blower."

Pierce considered this at length, and finally nodded. "Where is Bill now?"

"His uncling shop is in Battersea, on Ridgeby Way."

"I'll see him now," Pierce said, getting to his feet. "I'll have a go at plucking the pigeon."

"Don't make it too easy," Agar warned.

Pierce smiled. "It will take all their best efforts." He went to the door.

"Here, now," Agar called to him, with a sudden thought. "It just came to me mind: what's there for a flash pull in Greenwich, of all places?"

"That," Pierce said, "is the very question the crushers will be asking themselves."

"But *is* there a pull?"

"Of course."

"A flash pull?"

"Of course."

"But what is it, then?"

Pierce shook his head. He grinned at Agar's perplexed look and left the room.

When Pierce came out of the accommodation house, it was twilight. He immediately saw the two crushers lurking at opposite corners of the street. He made a show of looking nervously about, then walked to the end of the block, where he hailed a cab.

He rode the cab several blocks, then jumped out quickly at a busy part of Regent Street, crossed the thoroughfare, and took a hansom going in the opposite direction. To all appearances, he was operating with the utmost cunning. In fact, Pierce would never bother with the crossover fakement to dodge a tail; it was a glocky ploy that rarely worked, and when he glanced out of the small back window of the hansom cab, he saw that he had not thrown off his pursuers.

He rode to the Regency Arms pub house, a notorious place. He entered it, exited from a side door (which was in plain view of the street), and crossed over to New Oxford Street, where he caught another cab. In the process, he lost one of the crushers, but the other was still with him. Now he proceeded directly across the Thames, to Battersea, to see Chokee Bill.

The image of Edward Pierce, a respectable and well-dressed gentleman, entering the dingy premises of a Battersea pawnbroker may seem incongruous from a modern perspective. At the time, it was not at all uncommon, for the pawnbroker served more than the lower classes, and whomever he served, his function was essentially the same: to act as a sort of impromptu bank, operating more cheaply than established banking concerns. A person could buy an expensive article, such as a coat, and hock it one week to pay the rent; reclaim it a few days later, for wearing on Sunday; hock it again on Monday, for a smaller loan; and so on until there was no further need for the broker's services.

The pawnbroker thus filled an important niche in the society, and the number of licensed pawnshops doubled during the mid-Victorian period. Middle-class people were drawn to the broker more for the anonymity of the loan than the cheapness of it; many a respectable household did not wish it known that some of their silver was uncled for cash. This was, after all, an era when many people equated economic prosperity and good fiscal management with moral behavior; and conversely, to be in need of a loan implied some kind of misdeed.

The pawnshops themselves were not really very shady, although they had that reputation. Criminals seeking fences usually turned to unlicensed, secondhand goods "translators," who were not regulated by the police and were less likely to be under surveillance. Thus, Pierce entered the door beneath the three balls with impunity.

He found Chokee Bill, a red-faced Irishman whose complexion gave the appearance of perpetual near strangulation, sitting in a back corner. Chokee Bill jumped to his feet quickly, recognizing the dress and manner of a gentleman.

"Evening, sir," Bill said.

"Good evening," Pierce said.

"How may I be serving you, sir?"

Pierce looked around the shop. "Are we alone?"

"We are, sir, as my name is Bill, sir." But Chokee Bill got a guarded look in his eyes.

"I am looking to make a certain purchase," Pierce said. As he spoke, he adopted a broad Liverpool dockyard accent, though ordinarily he had no trace of it.

"A certain purchase . . ."

"Some items you may have at hand," Pierce said.

"You see my shop, sir," Chokee Bill said, with a wave of his arm. "All is before you."

"This is all?"

"Aye, sir, whatever you may see."

Pierce shrugged. "I must have been told wrongly. Good evening to you." And he headed for the door.

He was almost there when Chokee Bill coughed. "What is it you were told, sir?"

Pierce looked back at him. "I need certain rare items."

"Rare items," Chokee Bill repeated. "What manner of rare items, sir?"

"Objects of metal," Pierce said, looking directly at the pawnbroker. He found all this circumspection tedious, but it was necessary to convince Bill of the genuineness of his transaction.

"Metal, you say?"

Pierce made a deprecating gesture with his hands. "It is a question of defense, you see."

"Defense."

"I have valuables, property, articles of worth. . . . And therefore I need defense. Do you take my meaning?"

"I take your meaning," Bill said. "And I may have such a thing as you require."

"Actually," Pierce said, looking around the shop again, as if to reassure himself that he was truly alone with the proprietor, "actually, I need five."

"*Five barkers?*" Chokee Bill's eyes widened in astonishment.

Now that his secret was out, Pierce became very nervous. "That's right," he said, glancing this way and that, "five is what I need."

"Five's a goodly number," Bill said, frowning.

Pierce immediately edged toward the door. "Well, if you can't snaffle them—"

"Wait, now," Bill said, "I'm not saying can't. You never heard me say can't. All's I said is five is a goodly number, which it is, right enough."

"I was told you had them at hand," Pierce said, still nervous.

"I may."

"Well, then, I should like to purchase them at once."

Chokee Bill sighed. "They're not here, sir—you can count on that—a man doesn't keep barkers about in an uncle shop, no, sir."

"How quickly can you get them?"

As Pierce became more agitated, Chokee Bill became more calm, more appraising. Pierce could almost see his mind working, thinking over the meaning of a request for five pistols. It implied a major crime, and no mistake. As a blower, he might make a penny or two if he knew the details.

"It would be some days, sir, and that's the truth," Bill said.

"I cannot have them now?"

"No, sir, you'd have to give me a space of time, and then I'll have them for you, right enough."

"How much time?"

There followed a long silence. Bill went so far as to mumble to himself, and tick off the days on his fingers. "A fortnight would be safe."

"A fortnight!"

"Eight days, then."

"Impossible," Pierce said, talking aloud to himself. "In eight days, I must be in Greenw—" He broke off. "No," he said. "Eight days is too long."

"Seven?" Bill asked.

"Seven," Pierce said, staring at the ceiling. "Seven, seven . . . seven days . . . Seven days is Thursday next?"

"Aye, sir."

"At what hour on Thursday next?"

"A question of timing, is it?" Bill asked, with a casualness that was wholly unconvincing.

Pierce just stared at him.

"I don't mean to pry, sir," Bill said quickly.

"Then see you do not. What hour on Thursday?"

"Noon."

Pierce shook his head. "We will never come to terms. It is impossible and I—"

"Here, now—here, now. What hour Thursday must it be?"

"No later than ten o'clock in the morning."

Chokee Bill reflected. "Ten o'clock here?"

"Yes."

"And no later?"

"Not a minute later."

"Will you be coming yourself, then, to collect them?"

Once again, Pierce gave him a stern look. "That hardly need concern you. Can you supply the pieces or not?"

"I can," Bill said. "But there's an added expense for the quick service."

"That will not matter," Pierce said, and gave him ten gold guineas. "You may have this on account."

Chokee Bill looked at the coins, turned them over in his palm. "I reckon this is the half of it."

"So be it."

"And the rest will be paid in kind?"

"In gold, yes."

Bill nodded. "Will you be needing shot as well?"

"What pieces are they?"

"Webley 48-bore, rim-fire, holster models, if my guess is right."

"Then I will need shot."

"Another three guineas for shot," Chokee Bill said blandly.

"Done," Pierce said. He went to the door, and paused. "A final consideration," he said. "If, when I arrive Thursday next, the pieces are not waiting, it shall go hard with you."

"I'm reliable, sir."

"It will go very hard," Pierce said again, "if you are not. Think on it." And he left.

It was not quite dark; the street was dimly lit by gas lamps. He did not see the lurking crusher but knew he was there somewhere. He took a cab and drove to Leicester Square, where the crowds were gathering for the evening's theatrical productions. He entered one throng, bought a ticket for a showing of *She Stoops to Conquer*, and then lost himself in the lobby. He was home an hour later, after three cab changes and four duckings in and out of pubs. He was quite certain he had not been followed.

CHAPTER 36

Scotland Yard Deduces

The morning of May 18th was uncommonly warm and sunny, but Mr. Harranby took no pleasure in the weather. Things were going very badly, and he had treated his assistant, Mr. Sharp, with notable ill temper when he was informed of the death of the snakesman Clean Willy in a nethersken in Seven Dials. When he was later informed that his tails had lost the gentleman in the theatre crowd—a man they knew only as Mr. Simms, with a house in Mayfair—Mr. Harranby had flown into a rage, and complained vigorously about the ineptitude of his subordinates, including Mr. Sharp.

But Mr. Harranby's rage was now controlled, for the Yard's only remaining clue was sitting before him, perspiring profusely, wringing his hands, and looking very red-faced. Harranby frowned at Chokee Bill.

"Now, Bill," Harranby said, "this is a most serious matter."

"I know it, sir, indeed I do," Bill said.

"Five barkers tells me there is something afoot, and I mean to know the truth behind it."

"He was tight with his words, he was."

"I've no doubt," Harranby said heavily. He fished a gold guinea out of his pocket and dropped it on his desk before him. "Try to recall," he said.

"It was late in the day, sir, with all respects, and I was not at my best," Bill said, staring pointedly at the gold piece.

Harranby would be damned if he'd give the fellow another. "Many a memory improves on the cockchafer, in my experience," he said.

"I've done no wrong," Bill protested. "I'm honest as the day is long, sir, and I'd keep nothing from you. There's no call to put me in the stir."

"Then try to remember," Harranby said, "and be quick about it."

Bill twisted his hands in his lap. "He comes into the shop near six, he does. Dressed proper, with good manner, but he speaks a wave lag from Liverpool, and he can voker romeny."

Harranby glanced at Sharp, in the corner. From time to time, even Harranby needed some help in translation.

"He had a Liverpool sailor's accent and he spoke criminal jargon," Sharp said.

"Aye, sir, that's so," Bill said, nodding. "He's in the family, and that's for sure. Wants me to snaffle five barkers, and I say five's a goodly number, and he says he wants them quick-like, and he's nervous, and in a hurry, and he's showing plenty of ream thickers to pay up on the spot."

"What did you tell him?" Harranby said, keeping his eyes fixed on Bill. A skilled informant like Chokee Bill was not above playing each side against the other, and Bill could lie like an adept.

"I says to him, five's a goodly number but I can do it in time. And he says how much time, and I says a fortnight. This makes him cool the cockum for a bit, and then he says he needs it quicker than a fortnight. I says eight days. He says eight days is too long, and he starts to say he's off to Greenwich in eight days, but then he catches himself, like."

"Greenwich," Harranby said, frowning.

"Aye, sir, Greenwich was on the tip of his tongue, but he stops down and says it's too long. So I says how long? And he says seven days. So I says I can translate in seven days. And he says what time of the day? I say noontime. And he says noontime's too late. He says no later than ten o'clock."

"Seven days," Harranby said, "meaning Friday next?"

"No, sir. Thursday next. Seven days from yesterday it was."

"Go on."

"So I says, after a hem and a haw, I says I can have his pieces on Thursday at ten o'clock. And he says that's fly enough, but he's no flat, this one, and he says any gammy cockum and it will go hard on me."

Harranby looked at Sharp again. Sharp said, "The gentleman is no fool and warned that if the guns were not ready at the arranged time, it would be hard on Bill."

"And what did you say, Bill?" Harranby inquired.

"I says I can do it, and I promise him. And he gives me ten gold pushes, and I granny they're ream, and he takes his leave and says he'll be back Thursday next."

"What else?" Harranby said.

"That's the lot," Bill said.

There was a long silence. Finally Harranby said, "What do you make of this, Bill?"

"It's a flash pull and no mistake. He's no muck-snipe, this gent, but a hykey bloke who knows his business."

Harranby tugged at an earlobe, a nervous habit. "What in Greenwich has the makings of a proper flash pull?"

"Damn me if I know," Chokee Bill said.

"What have you heard?" Harranby said.

"I keep my lills to the ground, but I heard nothing of a pull in Greenwich, I swear."

Harranby paused. "There's another guinea in it for you if you can say."

A fleeting look of agony passed across Chokee Bill's face. "I wish I could be helping you, sir, but I heard nothing. It's God's own truth, sir."

"I'm sure it is," Harranby said. He waited awhile longer, and finally dismissed the pawnbroker, who snatched up the guinea and departed.

When Harranby was alone with Sharp, he said again, "What's in Greenwich?"

"Damn me if I know," Sharp said.

"You want a gold guinea, too?"

Sharp said nothing. He was accustomed to Harranby's sour moods; there was nothing to do except ride them out. He sat in the corner and watched his superior light a cigarette and puff on it reflectively. Sharp regarded cigarettes as silly, insubstantial little things. They had been introduced the year before by a London shopkeeper, and were mostly favored by troops returning from the Crimea. Sharp himself liked a good cigar, and nothing less.

"Now, then," Harranby said. "Let us begin from the beginning. We know this fellow Simms has been working for months on something, and we can assume he's clever."

Sharp nodded.

"The snakesman was killed yesterday. Does that mean they know we're on the stalk?"

"Perhaps."

"Perhaps, perhaps," Harranby said irritably. "Perhaps is not enough. We must *decide*, and we must do so according to principles of deductive logic. Guesswork has no place in our thinking. Let us stick to the facts of the matter, and follow them wherever they lead. Now, then, what else do we know?"

The question was rhetorical, and Sharp said nothing.

"We know," Harranby said, "that this fellow Simms, after months of preparation, suddenly finds himself, on the eve of his big pull, in desperate need of five barkers. He has had months to obtain them quietly, one at a time, creating no stir. But he postpones it to the last minute. Why?"

"You think he's playing us for a pigeon?"

"We must entertain the thought, however distasteful," Harranby said. "Is it well known that Bill's a nose?"

"Perhaps."

"Damn your perhapses. Is it known or not?"

"Surely there are suspicions about."

"Indeed," Harranby said. "And yet our clever Mr. Simms chooses this very person to arrange for his five barkers. I say it smells of a fakement." He stared moodily at the glowing tip of his cigarette. "This Mr. Simms is deliberately leading us astray, and we must not follow."

"I am sure you are right," Sharp said, hoping his boss's disposition would improve.

"Without question," Harranby said. "We are being led a merry chase."

There was a long pause. Harranby drummed his fingers on the desk. "I don't like it. We are being too clever. We're giving this Simms fellow too much credit. We must assume he is really planning on Greenwich. But what in the name of God is there in Greenwich to steal?"

Sharp shook his head. Greenwich was a seaport town, but it had not grown as rapidly as the larger ports of England. It was chiefly known for its naval observatory, which maintained the standard of time—Greenwich Mean Time—for the nautical world.

Harranby began opening drawers in his desk, rummaging. "Where is the damned thing?"

"What, sir?"

"The schedule, the schedule," Harranby said. "Ah, here it is." He brought out a small printed folder. "London & Greenwich Railway . . . Thursdays . . . Ah. Thursdays there is a train leaving London Bridge Terminus for Greenwich at eleven-fifteen in the morning. Now, what does that suggest?"

Sharp looked suddenly bright-eyed. "Our man wants his guns by ten, so that he will have time to get to the station and make the train."

"Precisely," Harranby said. "All logic points to the fact that he is, indeed, going to Greenwich on Thursday. And we also know he cannot go later than Thursday."

Sharp said, "What about the guns? Buying five at once."

"Well, now," Harranby said, warming to his subject, "you see, by a process of deduction we can conclude that his need for the guns is genuine, and his postponing the purchase to the last minute—on the surface, a most suspicious business—springs from some logical situation. One can surmise several. His plans for obtaining the guns by other means may have been thwarted. Or perhaps he regards the purchase of guns as dangerous—which is certainly the case; everyone knows we pay well for information about who is buying barkers—so he postpones it to the last moment. There may be other reasons we cannot guess at. The exact reason does not matter. What matters is that he needs those guns for some criminal activity in Greenwich."

"Bravo," Sharp said, with a show of enthusiasm.

Harranby shot him a nasty look. "Don't be a fool," he said, "we are little better off than when we began. The principal question still stands before us. *What is there to steal in Greenwich?*"

Sharp said nothing. He stared at his feet. He heard the scratch of a match as Harranby lit another cigarette.

"All is not lost," Harranby said. "The principles of deductive logic can still aid us. For example, the crime is probably a robbery. If it has been planned for many months, it must figure around some stable situation which is predictable months in advance. This is no casual, off-the-cuff snatch."

Sharp continued to stare at his feet.

"No, indeed," Harranby said. "There is nothing casual about it. Furthermore, we may deduce that this lengthy planning is directed toward a goal of some magnitude, a major crime with high stakes. In addition, we know our man is a seafaring person, so we may suspect his crime has something to do with the ocean, or dockyard activities in some way. Thus we may limit our inquiry to whatever exists in the town of Greenwich that fits our—"

Sharp coughed.

Harranby frowned at him. "Do you have something to say?"

"I was only thinking, sir," Sharp said, "that if it is Greenwich, it's out of our jurisdiction. Perhaps we ought to telegraph the local police and warn them."

"Perhaps, perhaps. When will you learn to do without that word? If we were to cable Greenwich, what would we tell them? Eh? What would we say in our cable?"

"I was only thinking—"

"Good God," Harranby said, standing up behind his desk. "Of course! The cable!"

"The cable?"

"Yes, of course, the cable. The cable is in Greenwich, even as we speak."

"Do you mean the Atlantic cable?" Sharp asked.

"Certainly," Harranby said, rubbing his hands together. "Oh, it fits perfectly. Perfectly!"

Sharp remained puzzled. He knew, of course, that the proposed transatlantic telegraph cable was being manufactured in Greenwich; the project had been under way for more than a year, and represented one of the most considerable technological efforts of the time. There were already undersea cables in the Channel, linking England to the Continent. But these were nothing compared to the twenty-five hundred miles of cable being constructed to join England to New York.

"But surely," Sharp said, "there is no purpose in stealing a cable—"

"Not the *cable*," Harranby said. "The *payroll* for the firm. What is it? Glass, Elliot & Company, or some such. An enormous project, and the payroll must be equal to the undertaking. That's our man's objective. And if he is in a hurry to leave on Thursday, he wishes to be there on Friday—"

"*Payday!*" Sharp cried.

"Exactly," Harranby said. "It is entirely logical. You see

the process of deduction carried to its most accurate conclusion."

"Congratulations," Sharp said cautiously.

"A trifle," Harranby said. He was still very excited, and clapped his hands together. "Oh, he is a bold one, our friend Simms. To steal the cable payroll—what an audacious crime! And we shall have him red-handed. Come along, Mr. Sharp. We must journey to Greenwich, and apprise ourselves of the situation at first hand."

CHAPTER 37

Further Congratulations

"And then?" Pierce said.

Miriam shrugged. "They boarded the train."

"How many of them were there?"

"Four altogether."

"And they took the Greenwich train?"

Miriam nodded. "In great haste. The leader was a squarish man with whiskers, and his lackey was clean-shaven. There were two others, jacks in blue."

Pierce smiled. "Harranby," he said. "He must be very proud of himself. He's such a clever man." He turned to Agar. "And you?"

"Fat Eye Lewis, the magsman, is in the Regency Arms asking about a cracker's lay in Greenwich—wants to join in, he says."

"So the word is out?" Pierce said.

Agar nodded.

"Feed it," he said.

"Who shall I say is in?"

"Spring Heel Jack, for one."

"What if the miltonians find him?" Agar said.

"I doubt that they will," Pierce said.

"Jack's under, is he?"

"So I have heard."

"Then I'll mention him."

"Make Fat Eye pay," Pierce said. "This is valuable information."

Agar grinned. "It'll come to him dear, I promise you."

Agar departed, and Pierce was alone with Miriam.

"Congratulations," she said, smiling at him. "Nothing can go wrong now."

Pierce sat back in a chair. "Something can always go wrong," he said, but he was smiling.

"In four days?" she asked.

"Even in the space of an hour."

Later, in his courtroom testimony, Pierce admitted he was astounded at how prophetic his own words were, for enormous difficulties lay ahead—and they would come from the most unlikely source.

CHAPTER 38

A Sharp Business Practice

Henry Mayhew, the great observer, reformer, and classifier of Victorian society, once listed the various types of criminals in England. The list had five major categories, twenty subheadings, and more than a hundred separate entries. To the modern eye, the list is remarkable for the absence of any consideration of what is now called "white-collar crime."

Of course, such crime existed at that time, and there were some flagrant examples of embezzlement, forgery, false accounting, bond manipulation, and other illegal practices that came to light during the mid-century. In 1850, an insurance clerk named Walter Watts was caught after he embezzled more than £70,000, and there were several crimes much larger: Leopold Redpath's £150,000 in forgeries on the Great Northern Railway Company, and Beaumont Smith's £350,000 in counterfeit exchequer bonds, to name two examples.

Then, as now, white-collar crime involved the largest sums of money, was the least likely to be detected, and was punished most leniently if the participants were ever apprehended. Yet Mayhew's list of criminals ignores this sector of crime entirely. For Mayhew, along with the majority of his contemporaries, was firmly committed to the belief that crime was the product of "the dangerous classes," and that criminal behavior sprang from poverty, injustice, oppression, and lack of education. It was almost a matter of definition: a person who was not from the criminal class could not be committing a crime. Persons of a better station were merely "breaking the law." Several factors unique to the Victorian attitude toward upper-class crime contributed to this belief.

First, in a newly capitalistic society, with thousands of emerging businesses, the principles of honest accounting were not firmly established, and accounting methods were understood to be even more variable than they are today. A man might, with a fairly clear conscience, blur the distinction between fraud and "sharp business practices."

Second, the modern watchdog of all Western capitalist countries, the government, was nowhere near so vigilant then. Personal incomes below £150 annually were not taxed, and the great majority of citizens fell beneath this limit. Those who were taxed got off lightly by modern standards, and although people grumbled about the cost of government, there was no hint yet of the modern citizen's frantic scramble to arrange his finances in such a way as to avoid as much tax as possible. (In 1870, taxes amounted to 9 percent of the gross national product of England; in 1961, they were 38 percent.)

Furthermore, the Victorians of all classes accepted a kind of ruthlessness in their dealings with one another that seems outrageous today. To take an example, when Sir John Hall, the physician in charge of the Crimean troops, decided to get rid of Florence Nightingale, he elected to starve her out by ordering that her food rations be halted. Such vicious maneuvers were considered ordinary by everyone; Miss Nightingale anticipated it, and carried her own supplies of food, and even Lytton Strachey, who was hardly disposed to view the Victorians kindly, dismissed this incident as "a trick."

If this is only a trick, it is easy to see why middle-class observers were reluctant to label many kinds of wrongdoing as "crimes"; and the higher an individual's standing within the community, the greater the reluctance.

A case in point is Sir John Alderston and his crate of wine.

Captain John Alderston was knighted after Waterloo, in 1815, and in subsequent years he became a prosperous London citizen. He was one of the owners of the South Eastern Railway from the inception of the line, and had large financial holdings in several coal mines in Newcastle as well. He was, according to all accounts, a portly, tart-spoken gentleman who maintained a military bearing all his life, barking out terse commands in a manner that was increasingly ludicrous as his waistline spread with the passing years.

Alderston's single vice was a passion for card games, acquired during his army days, and his outstanding eccentricity was that he refused to gamble for money, preferring to wager personal articles and belongings instead of hard cash. Apparently this was his way of viewing card-playing as a gentlemanly pastime, and not a vice. The story of his crate of wine, which figures so prominently in The Great Train Robbery of 1855, never came to light until 1914, some forty years after Alderston's death. At that time, his family commissioned an official biography by an author named William Shawn. The relevant passage reads:

> Sir John at all times had a highly developed sense of conscience, which only once caused him any personal qualms. A family member recalls that he returned home one evening, after an outing for card-playing, in a mood of great distress. When asked the cause, he replied: "I cannot bear it."
>
> Upon further inquiry, it emerged that Sir John had been playing cards with several associates, these being men who also owned a share of the railway. In his play, Sir John had lost a case of Madeira, twelve years old, and he was exceedingly reluctant to part with it. Yet he had promised to put it aboard the Folkestone train, for delivery to the winner, who resided in that coastal town, where he oversaw the operation of the railway at its most distant terminus.
>
> Sir John fretted and fussed for three days, condemning the gentleman who had won, and suspecting aloud that the man had cheated in clandestine fashion. With each passing day, he became more convinced of the man's trickery, although there was no evidence for such a belief.
>
> Finally he instructed his manservant to load the crate of wine on the train, placing it in the luggage van with a deal of ceremony and filling-in of forms; the wine was, in fact, insured against loss or injury during the journey.
>
> When the train arrived in Folkestone, the crate was discovered to be empty, and a robbery of the precious wine was presumed. This provided no small commotion among the railway employees. The guard in the van was dismissed and changes in procedures were adopted. Sir John paid his wager with the funds from the insurance.
>
> Many years later, he admitted to his family that he had

loaded an empty crate onto the train, for he could not, he said, bear parting with his precious Madeira. Yet he was overcome with guilt, especially for the discharged railway employee, to whom he contrived to pay an anonymous annual stipend over a period of many years, such that the sum paid was vastly in excess of the value of his wine.

Yet to the last, he felt no remorse for the creditor, one John Banks. On the contrary, during the last days of his mortal existence, when he lay in his bed delirious with fevers, he was often heard to say, "That blasted Banks is no gentleman, and I'll be damned if he'll get my Madeira, do you hear?"

Mr. Banks at this time had been deceased some years. It has been said that many of Sir John's closest associates suspected that he had had a hand in the mysterious disappearance of the wine, but no one dared accuse him. Instead, certain changes were made in the railway security procedures (partly at the behest of the insuring agency). And when, soon after, a consignment of gold was stolen from the railroad, everyone forgot the matter of Sir John's crate of wine, excepting the man himself, for his conscience tormented him to his final days. Thus was the strength of this great man's character.

CHAPTER 39

Some Late Difficulties

On the evening of May 21st, just a few hours before the robbery, Pierce dined with his mistress, Miriam, in his house in Mayfair.

Shortly before nine-thirty that night, their meal was interrupted by the sudden arrival of Agar, who looked very distraught. He came storming into the dining room, making no apologies for his abrupt entrance.

"What is it?" Pierce said calmly.

"Burgess," Agar said, in a breathless voice. "Burgess: he's downstairs."

Pierce frowned. "You brought him *here?*"

"I had to do," Agar said. "Wait until you hear."

Pierce left the table and went downstairs to the smoking room. Burgess was standing there, twitching his blue guard's cap in his hands. He was obviously as nervous as Agar.

"What's the trouble?" Pierce said.

"It's the line," Burgess said. "They've changed it all, and just today—changed everything."

"What have they changed?" Pierce said.

Burgess spoke in a headlong torrent: "I first came to know this morning, you see, I come to work proper at seven sharp, and there's a cooper working on me van, hammering and pounding. And there's a smith as well, and some gentlemen standing about to watch the work. And that's how I find they've changed all manner of things, and just today, changed it all. I mean the running of the car the way that we do, all changed, and I didn't know—"

"What, exactly, have they changed?" Pierce said.

Burgess took a breath. "The line," he said. "The manner of things, the way we do, all fresh changed."

Pierce frowned impatiently. "Tell me what is changed," he said.

Burgess squeezed his hat in his hands until his knuckles were pale. "For one, they have a new jack the line's put on, started today—a new bloke, young one."

"He rides with you in the baggage van?"

"No, sir," Burgess said. "He only works the platform at the station. Stays at the station, he does."

Pierce shot a glance at Agar. It didn't matter if there were more guards at the platform. There could be a dozen guards, for all Pierce cared. "What of it?" he said.

"Well, it's the new rule, you see."

"What new rule?"

"Nobody rides in the baggage car, save me as guard," Burgess said. "That's the new rule, and there's this new jack to keep it proper."

"I see," Pierce said. That was indeed a change.

"There's more," Agar said gloomily.

"Yes?"

Burgess nodded. "They've gone and fitted a lock to the luggage-van door. Outside lock, it is. Now they lock up in London Bridge, and unlock in Folkestone."

"*Damn,*" Pierce said. He began to pace back and forth in the room. "What about the other stops? That train stops in Redhill, and at—"

"They've changed the rules," Burgess said. "That van is never unlocked till Folkestone."

Pierce continued to pace. "Why have they changed the routine?"

"It's on account of the afternoon fast train," Burgess explained. "There's two fast trains, morning train and afternoon train. Seems the afternoon van was robbed last week. Gentleman was robbed of a valuable parcel somehow—collection of rare wine, I hear it to be. Anyhow, he puts a claim to the line or some such. The other guard's been fired, and there's all bloody hell to pay. Dispatcher his very self called me in this morning and dressed me down proper, warning me of this and that. Near cuffed me, he did. And the new jack at the platform's the station dispatcher's nephew. He's the one locks up in London Bridge, just before the train pulls out."

"Rare wines," Pierce said. "God in heaven, *rare wines*. Can we get Agar aboard in a trunk?"

Burgess shook his head. "Not if they do like today. Today, this nephew, his name's McPherson, he's a Scotsman and eager—badly wanting a job, as I look at it—this McPherson makes the passengers open every trunk or parcel large enough to hold a man. Caused a considerable fray, I'll say. This nephew is a stickler. New to the work, you see, and wanting to do it all proper, and that's the way it is."

"Can we distract him and slip Agar in while he's not looking?"

"Not looking? Never's he not looking. He looks like a starved rat after a flake of cheese, looks here and there and everywhere. And when all the baggage's loaded, he climbs in, pokes about in all the corners seeing there's no lurkers. Then he climbs off and locks up."

Pierce plucked his pocket watch from his waistcoat. It was now ten o'clock at night. They had ten hours before the Folkestone train left the next morning. Pierce could think of a dozen clever ways to get Agar past a watchful Scotsman, but nothing that could be quickly arranged.

Agar, whose face was the very picture of gloom, must have been thinking the same thing. "Shall we put off until next month, then?"

"No," Pierce said. He immediately shifted to his next problem. "Now, this lock they've installed on the luggage-van door. Can it be worked from inside?"

Burgess shook his head. "It's a padlock—hooks through a bolt and iron latch, outside."

Pierce was still pacing. "Could it be unlocked during one of the stops—say, Redhill—and then locked again at Tonbridge, further down the line?"

"Be a risk," Burgess said. "She's a fat lock, big as your fist, and it might be noticed."

Pierce continued to pace. For a long time, his footsteps on the carpet and the ticking of the clock on the mantel were the only sounds in the room. Agar and Burgess watched him. Finally Pierce said, "If the van door is locked, how do you get ventilation?"

Burgess, looking a little confused, said, "Oh, there's air enough. That van's shoddy made, and when the train gets to speed, the breeze whistles through the cracks and chinks loud enough to pain your ears."

"I meant," Pierce said, "is there any apparatus for ventilation of the van?"

"Well, there's the slappers in the roof. . . ."

"What're they?" Pierce said.

"Slappers? Slappers—well, to speak true, they're not your proper slappers, on account of the lack of hinging. Many's the time I was wishing they were true slappers, I mean a slapper fit with hinging, and all the more when it rains—then it's a cold puddle inside, I can tell you—"

"What is a slapper?" Pierce interrupted. "Time is short."

"A slapper? A slapper's what your railway folks call a manner of trap. She's a hinged door up in the roof, mounted center, and inside you've a rod to open or shut the slapper. Some of your slappers—I mean proper slappers—they fit two to a coach, facing opposite ways. That's so's one is always away from the wind. Now, other coaches, they've their slappers mounted both the same, but it's a bother in the yards, you see, for it means the coach must be clamped with the slappers backward, and—"

"And you have two of these slappers in the luggage van?"

"Aye, that's true," Burgess said, "but they're not proper, because they're fixed open, you see, no hinging on the van slappers, and so when it rains there I be, soaked through—"

"The slappers give access directly to the interior of the luggage van?"

"They do, direct down." Burgess paused. "But if you're thinking of slipping a bloke through, it can't be done. They're no more than a hand's breadth square, and—"

"I'm not," Pierce said. "Now, you say you have two slappers? Where are they located?"

"On the roof, like I said, center of the roof, and—"

"Where in relation to the length of the car?" Pierce said. His pacing back and forth, and his brusque, irritable manner left Burgess, who was nervous and trying to be helpful, at a complete loss.

"Where . . . in relation . . ." His voice trailed off.

Agar said, "I don't know what you're thinking, but my knee pains me—my left knee here—and that's always a bad sign. I say, quit the lay for a deadly flummut, and be done."

"Shut up," Pierce said, with a sudden flaring anger that made Agar take a step backward. Pierce turned to Burgess. "Now I am asking," he said, "if you look at the van from the side, you see it as a kind of box, a large box. And on the top of this box are the slappers. Now, where are they?"

"Not proper set, and that's God's truth," Burgess said. "A proper slapper's near the ends of the coach, one at each end, so's to allow air to pass end to end, one slapper to the next. That's the way to arrange it for the best—"

"Where are the slappers on the luggage van?" Pierce said, glancing again at his watch. "I care only about the van."

"That's the hell of it," Burgess said. "They're near center, and no more than three paces separate. And they've no hinge. Now when it rains, down comes the water, direct to the center of the van, and there's one great puddle, straightaway in the center."

"You say the slappers are separated by three paces?"

"Three, four, thereabouts," Burgess said. "I never cared to know for certain, but it's certain I hate the damn things, and that's—"

"All right," Pierce said, "you've told me what I need to know."

"I'm glad of that," Burgess said, with a sort of confused relief, "but I swear, there's no way a man or even a chavy can slip down that hole, and once they lock me in—"

Pierce cut him off with a wave of his hand and turned to Agar. "This padlock on the outside. Is it hard to pick?"

"I don't know it," Agar said, "but a padlock's no trick. They're made strong, but they have fat tumblers, on account of their size. Some a man can use his little finger for the betty, and tickle her broke open in a flash."

"Could I?" Pierce said.

Agar stared at him. "Easy enough, but you might take a minute or two." He frowned. "But you heard what he said, you don't dare break her at the station stops, so why—"

Pierce turned back to Burgess. "How many second-class coaches are there on the morning train?"

"I don't know exact. Six, as often as not. Seven near the weekend. Sometimes, midweek they run five, but lately there's six. Now, first class, that's—"

"I don't care about first class," Pierce said.

Burgess fell silent, hopelessly confused. Pierce looked at Agar: Agar had figured it out. The screwsman shook his head. "Mother of God," Agar said, "you've lost your mind, you've gone flat dabeno, sure as I stand here. What do you think, you're Mr. Coolidge?" Coolidge was a well-known mountaineer.

"I know who I am," Pierce said tersely. He turned back to Burgess, whose confusion had steadily increased during the last few minutes until he was now nearly immobilized, his face blank and expressionless, having lost even the quality of bewilderment.

"Is your name Coolidge, then?" Burgess asked. "You said Simms. . . ."

"It's Simms," Pierce said. "Our friend here is only making a joke. I want you to go home now, and sleep, and get up tomorrow and go to work as usual. Just carry on as usual, no matter what happens. Just do your regular day of work, and don't worry about anything."

Burgess glanced at Agar, then back to Pierce. "Will you pull tomorrow, then?"

"Yes," Pierce said. "Now go home and sleep."

When the two men were alone, Agar exploded in anxious fury. "Damn me if I'll voker flams at this dead hour. This is no simple kynchin lay tomorrow. Is that not plain?" Agar threw up his hands. "Make an end to it, I say. Next month, I say."

Pierce remained quiet for a moment. "I've waited a year," he said finally, "and it will be tomorrow."

"You're puckering," Agar said, "just talk, with no sense."

"It can be done," Pierce insisted.

"Done?" Agar exploded again. "Done *how?* Look here, I know you for a clever one, but I'm no flat, and there's no gammoning me. That lay is coopered. It's too damn sad the wine was snaffled, but so it was, and we must know it." Agar was red-faced and frantic; he swung his arms through the air in agitation.

In contrast, Pierce was almost unnaturally still. His eyes surveyed Agar steadily. "There is a bone lay," Pierce said.

"As God is my witness, how?" Agar watched as Pierce calmly went to a sideboard and poured two glasses of brandy. "You'll not put enough of that in me to cloud my eyes," he said. "Now, look plain."

Agar held up his hand, and ticked the points off on his fingers. "I am to ride in the van, you say. But I cannot get in —an eager jack of a Scotsman stands sharp at the door. You heard as much yourself. But fair enough: I trust you to get me in. Now."

He ticked off another finger. "Now, there I be in the van. The Scotsman locks up from the outside. I've no way to touch that lock, so even if I make the switch, I can't open the door and toss out the pogue. I'm locked in proper, all the way to Folkestone."

"Unless I open the door for you," Pierce said. He gave Agar a snifter of brandy.

Agar swallowed it in a single gulp. "Aye, and there's a likely turn. You come back over all those coaches, tripping light over the rooftops, and swing down like Mr. Coolidge over the side of the van to pick the lock and break the drum. I'll see God in heaven first, no mistake."

Pierce said, "I know Mr. Coolidge."

Agar blinked. "No gull?"

"I met him on the Continent last year. I climbed with him in Switzerland—three peaks in all—and I learned what he knows."

Agar was speechless. He stared at Pierce for any sign of deception, scanning the cracksman's face. Mountaineering was a new sport, only three or four years old, but it had captured the popular attention, and the most notable of the English practitioners, such as A. E. Coolidge, had become famous.

"No gull?" Agar said again.

"I have the ropes and tackle up in the closet," Pierce said. "No gull."

"I'll have another daffy," Agar said, holding out his empty glass. Pierce immediately filled it, and Agar immediately gulped it down.

"Well then," he said. "Let's say you *can* betty the lock, hanging on a rope, and break the drum, and then lock up again, with nobody the wiser. How do I get on in the first place, past the Scots jack, with his sharp cool?"

"There is a way," Pierce said. "It's not pleasant, but there is a way."

Agar appeared unconvinced. "Say you put me on in some trunk. He's bound he'll open it and have a see, and there I am. What then?"

"I intend for him to open it and see you," Pierce said.

"You *intend?*"

"I think so, and it will go smoothly enough, if you can take a bit of odor."

"What manner of odor?"

"The smell of a dead dog, or cat," Pierce said. "Dead some days. Do you think you can manage that?"

Agar said, "I swear, I don't get the lay. Let's settle the down with another daffy or two," and he extended his glass.

"That's enough," Pierce said. "There are things for you to do. Go to your lodgings, and come back with your best dunnage, the finest you have, and quickly."

Agar sighed.

"Go now," Pierce said. "And trust me."

When Agar had departed, he sent for Barlow, his cabby.

"Do we have any rope?" Pierce said.

"Rope, sir? You mean hempen rope?"

"Precisely. Do we have any in the house?"

"No, sir. Could you make do with bridle leather?"

"No," Pierce said. He considered a moment. "Hitch up the horse to the flat carriage and get ready for a night's work. We have a few items to obtain."

Barlow nodded and left. Pierce returned to the dining room, where Miriam was still sitting, patient and calm.

"There's trouble?" she said.

"Nothing beyond repair," Pierce said. "Do you have a black dress? I am thinking of a frock of cheap quality, such as a maid might wear."

"I think so, yes."

"Good," he said. "Set it out, you will wear it tomorrow morning."

"Whatever for?" she asked.

Pierce smiled. "To show your respect for the dead," he said.

CHAPTER 40

A False Alarm

On the morning of May 22nd, when the Scottish guard Mc-
Pherson arrived at the platform of the London Bridge Station
to begin the day's work, he was greeted by a most unexpected
sight. There alongside the luggage van of the Folkestone
train stood a woman in black—a servant, by the look of her,
but handsome enough, and sobbing most piteously.

The object of her grief was not hard to discover, for
near the poor girl, set onto a flat baggage cart, was a plain
wooden casket. Although cheap and unadorned, the casket
had several ventholes drilled in the sides. And mounted on
the lid of the casket was a kind of miniature belfry, containing a small bell, with a cord running from the clapper
down through a hole to the innards of the coffin.

Although the sight was unexpected, it was not in the least
mysterious to McPherson—or, indeed, to any Victorian of
the day. Nor was he surprised, as he approached the coffin,
to detect the reeking odor of advanced corporeal decay
emanating from the ventholes, and suggesting that the present
occupant had been dead for some time. This, too, was wholly
understandable.

During the nineteenth century, both in England and in the
United States, there arose a peculiar preoccupation with the
idea of premature burial. All that remains of this bizarre concern is the macabre literature of Edgar Allan Poe and others,
in which premature burial in some form or another appears
as a frequent motif. To modern thinking, it is all exaggerated

and fanciful; it is difficult now to recognize that for the Victorians, premature burial was a genuine, palpable fear shared by nearly all members of society, from the most superstitious worker to the best-educated professional man.

Nor was this widespread fear a simply neurotic obsession. Quite the contrary: there was plenty of evidence to lead a sensible man to believe that premature burials did occur, and that such ghastly happenings were only prevented by some fortuitous event. A case in 1853 in Wales, involving an apparently drowned ten-year-old boy, received wide publicity: "While the coffin lay in the open grave, and the first earth was shovelled upon it, a most frightful noise and kicking ensued from within. The sextons ceased their labors, and caused the coffin to be opened, whereupon the lad stepped out, and called for his parents. Yet the same lad had been pronounced dead many hours past, and the doctor said that he had no respirations nor any detectable pulse, and the skin was cold and gray. Upon sighting the lad, his mother fell into a swoon, and did not revive for some length of time."

Most cases of premature burial involved victims ostensibly drowned, or electrocuted, but there were other instances where a person might lapse into a state of "apparent death, or suspended animation."

In fact, the whole question of when a person was dead was very much in doubt—as it would be again, a century later, when doctors struggled with the ethics of organ transplantation. But it is worth remembering that physicians did not understand that cardiac arrest was wholly reversible until 1950; and in 1850 there was plenty of reason to be skeptical about the reliability of any indicator of death.

Victorians dealt with their uncertainty in two ways. The first was to delay interment for several days—a week was not uncommon—and await the unmistakable olfactory evidence of the beloved one's departure from this world. Indeed, the Victorian willingness to postpone burial sometimes reached extremes. When the Duke of Wellington died, in 1852, there was public debate about the way his state funeral should be conducted; the Iron Duke simply had to wait until these disagreements were settled, and he was not actually buried until more than two months after his death.

The second method for avoiding premature burial was technological; the Victorians contrived an elaborate series of warning and signaling devices to enable a dead person to make known his resuscitation. A wealthy individual might be buried with a length of iron pipe connecting his casket to the ground above, and a trusted family servant would be required to remain at the cemetery, day and night, for a month or more, on the chance that the deceased would suddenly awake and begin to call for help. Persons buried aboveground, in family vaults, were often placed in patented, spring-loaded caskets, with a complex maze of wires attached to arms and legs, so that the slightest movement of the body would throw open the coffin lid. Many considered this method preferable to any other, for it was believed that individuals often returned from a state of suspended animation in a mute or partially paralyzed condition.

The fact that these spring-loaded coffins popped open months or even years later (undoubtedly the result of some external vibration or deterioration in the spring mechanism) only heightened the widespread uncertainty about how long a person might lie dead before coming back to life, even for a moment.

Most signaling devices were costly, and available only to the wealthy classes. Poor people adopted the simpler tactic of burying relatives with some implement—a crowbar, or a shovel—on the vague assumption that if they revived, they could dig themselves out of their predicament.

There was clearly a market for an inexpensive alarm system, and in 1852 George Bateson applied for, and received, a patent for the Bateson Life Revival Device, described as "a most economical, ingenious, and trustworthy mechanism, superior to any other method, and promoting peace of mind amongst the bereaved at all stations of life. Constructed of the finest materials throughout." And there is an additional comment: "A device of proven efficacy, in countless instances in this country and abroad."

"Bateson's belfry," as it was ordinarily known, was a plain iron bell mounted on the lid of the casket, over the deceased's head, and connected by a cord or wire through the coffin to the dead person's hand, "such that the least tremor shall directly sound the alarum." Bateson's belfries attained instant popularity, and within a few years a substantial proportion of coffins were fitted with these bells. During this period, three thousand people died daily in London alone, and Bateson's business was brisk; he was soon a wealthy man and respected as well: in 1859, Victoria awarded him an O.B.E. for his efforts.

As a kind of odd footnote to the story, Bateson himself lived in mortal terror of being buried alive, and caused his workshop to fabricate increasingly complex alarm systems for installation on his own coffin after he died. By 1867, his preoccupation left him quite insane, and he rewrote his will, directing his family to cremate him at his death. However, suspecting that his instructions would not be followed, in the spring of 1868 he doused himself with linseed oil in his workshop, set himself aflame, and died by self-immolation.

On the morning of May 22nd, McPherson had more important things to worry about than the weeping servant girl and the coffin with its belfry, for he knew that today the gold shipment from Huddleston & Bradford would be loaded upon the railway van at any moment.

Through the open door of the van, he saw the guard, Burgess. McPherson waved, and Burgess responded with a nervous, rather reserved greeting. McPherson knew that his uncle, the dispatcher, had yesterday given Burgess a good deal of sharp talk; Burgess was no doubt worried to keep his job, especially as the other guard had been dismissed. McPherson assumed that this accounted for Burgess's tension.

Or perhaps it was the sobbing woman. It would not be the first time a stout man had been put off his mark by a female's piteous cries. McPherson turned to the young girl and proffered his handkerchief.

"There, now, Missy," he said. "There, now . . ." He sniffed the air. Standing close to the coffin, he noticed that the odor seeping out of the ventholes was certainly rank. But he was not so overcome by the smell that he failed to observe the girl was attractive, even in her grief. "There, now," he said again.

"Oh, please, sir," the girl cried, taking his handkerchief and sniffling into it. "Oh, please, can you help me? The man is a heartless beast, he is."

"What man is that?" McPherson demanded, in a burst of outrage.

"Oh, please, sir, that guard upon the line. He will not let me set my dear brother here upon the train, for he says I must await another guard. Oh, I am most wretched," she finished, and dissolved into tears once more.

"Why, the unfeeling rogue, he would not let your brother be put aboard?"

Through sobs and sniffles, the girl said something about rules.

"Rules?" he said. "A pox on rules, I say." He noticed her heaving bosom, and her pretty, narrow waist.

"Please, sir, he is most firm about the other guard—"

"Missy," he said, "I am the other guard, standing here before you, and I'll see your dear brother on the train with no delay, and never you mind that blackguard."

"Oh, sir, I am in your debt," she said, managing a smile through her tears.

McPherson was overwhelmed: he was a young man, and it was springtime, and the girl was pretty, and soon to be in his debt. At the same instant, he felt the greatest compassion and tenderness for her distress. Altogether, he was set spinning with the emotions of the moment.

"Just you wait," he promised, and turned to chastise Burgess for his heartless and overzealous adherence to the rules. But before he could make known his opinion, he saw the first of the gray-uniformed, armed guards of Huddleston & Bradford, bringing the bullion consignment down the platform toward them.

The loading was carried out with sharp precision. First, two guards came down the platform, entered the van, and made a quick search of the interior. Then eight more guards arrived, in neat formation around two flatcarts, each pushed by a gang of grunting, sweating porters—and each piled high with rectangular, sealed strongboxes.

At the van, a ramp was swung down, and the porters joined together to push first one, and then the other, of the laden flatcarts up into the van, to the waiting safes.

Next an official of the bank, a well-rigged gent with an air of authority, appeared with two keys in his hand. Soon after, McPherson's uncle, the dispatcher, arrived with a second pair of keys. His uncle and the bank's man inserted their keys in the safes and opened them.

The bullion strongboxes were loaded into the safes, and the doors were shut with a massive metal clang that echoed in the interior of the luggage van. The keys were twisted in the locks; the safes were secured.

The man from the bank took his keys and departed. McPherson's uncle pocketed his keys and came over to his nephew.

"Mind your work this morning," he said. "Open every parcel large enough to hold a knave, and no exception." He sniffed the air. "What's that ungodly stink?"

McPherson nodded over his shoulder to the girl and the coffin, a short distance away. It was a pitiful sight but his uncle frowned with no trace of compassion. "Scheduled for the morning train, is it?"

"Yes, Uncle."

"See that you open it," the dispatcher said, and turned away.

"But, Uncle—" McPherson began, thinking he would lose his newly gained favor with the girl by insisting on such a thing.

The dispatcher stopped. "No stomach for it? Dear God, you're a delicate one." He scanned the youth's agonized face, misinterpreting his discomfiture. "All right, then. I'm near enough to death that it holds no terrors for me. I'll see to it myself." And the dispatcher strode off toward the weeping girl and her coffin. McPherson trailed reluctantly behind.

It was at that moment that they heard an electrifying, ghastly sound: the ringing of Mr. Bateson's patented bell.

In later courtroom testimony, Pierce explained the psychology behind the plan. "Any guard watches for certain happenings, which he suspects at any moment, and lies in wait for. I knew the railway guard suspected some fakement to smuggle a living body onto the van. Now, a vigilant guard will know a coffin can easily hold a body; he will suspect it less, because it seems such a poor trick for smuggling. It is too obvious.

"Yet, he will likely wonder if the body is truly dead, and if he is vigilant he will call to have the box opened, and spend some moments making a thorough examination of the body to insure that it is dead. He may feel the pulse, or the warmth of the flesh, or he may stick a pin here or there. Now, no living soul can pass such an examination without detection.

"But how different it is if all believe that the body is not dead, but alive, and wrongly incarcerated. Now all emotions are reversed: instead of suspicion, there is hope the body is vital. Instead of a solemn and respectful opening of the casket, there is a frantic rush to break it free, and in this the relatives join in willingly, sure proof there is nothing to hide.

"And then, when the lid is raised and the decomposed remains come to light, how different is the response of the spectators. Their desperate hopes are dashed in an instant; the cruel and ghastly truth is immediately apparent at a moment's glance, and warrants no prolonged investigation. The relatives are bitterly disappointed and wildly distraught. The lid is quickly closed—and all because of reversed expectations. This is simple human nature, as evidenced in every ordinary man."

At the sound of the bell, which rang only once, and briefly, the sobbing girl let out a shriek. At the same instant, the dispatcher and his nephew broke into a run, quickly covering the short distance to the coffin.

By then the girl was in a state of profound hysteria, clawing at the coffin lid with her fingers, mindless that her efforts were ineffectual. "Oh, my dear brother—oh, Richard, dear Richard—oh, God, he lives . . ." Her fingers scrabbled at the wooden surface, and her tugging rocked the coffin so that the bell rang continuously.

The dispatcher and his nephew instantly caught the girl's frantic anxiety, but they were able to proceed with more sense. The lid was closed with a series of metal latches, and they opened them one after another. Apparently it never occurred to either man, in the heat of the moment, that this coffin had more latches than any three others. And certainly the process of opening was more prolonged as the poor girl, in her agony, somehow impeded their efforts with her own.

In a few moments, the men were at a fever pitch of intensity. And all the while, the girl cried, "Oh, Richard—dear God, make haste, he's alive—please, dear God, he lives, praise God . . ." And all the while, the bell rang from the rocking of the coffin.

The commotion drew a crowd of some size, which stood

a few paces back on the platform, taking in the bizarre spectacle.

"Oh, hurry, hurry, lest we are too late," the girl cried, and the men worked frantically at the latches. Indeed, only when they were at the final two latches did the dispatcher hear the girl cry, "Oh, I knew it was not cholera, he was a quack to say it. Oh, I knew . . ."

The dispatcher froze, his hand on the latch. "Cholera?" he said.

"Oh, hurry, hurry," the girl cried. "It is five days now I have waited to hear the bell. . . ."

"You say cholera?" the dispatcher repeated. "Five days?"

But the nephew, who had not stopped throwing off the latches, now flung the coffin lid wide.

"Thank God!" cried the girl, and threw herself down upon the body inside, as if to hug her brother. But she halted in mid-gesture, which was perfectly understandable. With the raising of the lid, a most hideous, fetid, foul stench rolled forth in a near palpable wave, and its source was not hard to determine; the body lying within, dressed in his best Sunday clothes, hands folded across the chest, was already in a state of obvious decomposition.

The exposed flesh at the face and hands was bloated and puffed, a repellent gray-green color. The lips were black, and so was the partially protruding tongue. The dispatcher and his nephew hardly saw more of that horrific spectacle before the feverish girl, with a final scream of heart-wrenching agony, swooned on the spot. The nephew instantly leapt to attend her, and the dispatcher, with no less alacrity, closed the lid and began shutting the latches with considerably more haste than he had displayed in opening them.

The watching crowd, when it heard that the man had died of cholera, dissipated with the same swiftness. In a moment, the station platform was nearly deserted.

Soon the servant girl recovered from her swoon, but she remained in a state of profound distress. She kept asking softly, "How can it be? I heard the bell. Did you not hear the bell? I heard it plain, did you not? The bell rang."

McPherson did his best to comfort her, saying that it must have been some earth tremor or sudden gust of wind that had caused the bell to ring.

The station dispatcher, seeing that his nephew was occupied with the poor child, took it upon himself to supervise the loading of luggage into the van of the Folkestone train. He did this with as much diligence as he could muster after such a distressing experience. Two well-dressed ladies had large trunks and, despite their haughty protests, he insisted that both be unlocked and opened for his inspection. There was only one further incident, when a portly gentleman placed a parrot—or some such multicolored bird—on the van, and then demanded that his manservant be permitted to ride with the bird and look after its needs. The dispatcher refused, explaining the new rules of the railway. The gentleman became abusive, and then offered the dispatcher "a sensible gratuity," but the dispatcher—who viewed the proffered ten shillings with somewhat more interest than he cared to admit, even to himself—was aware that he was being watched by Burgess, the same guard whom he had admonished the day before. Thus the dispatcher was forced to turn down the bribe, to his own displeasure and also that of the gentleman, who stomped off muttering a litany of stinging profanity.

These incidents did nothing to improve the dispatcher's mood, and when at last the malodorous coffin was loaded into the van, the dispatcher took a certain delight in warning Burgess, in tones of great solicitousness, to look after his health, since his fellow passenger had fallen victim to King Cholera.

To this, Burgess made no response at all, except to look nervous and out of sorts—which had been his appearance prior to the admonition. Feeling vaguely dissatisfied, the dispatcher barked a final order to his nephew to get on with the job and lock up the van. Then he returned to his office.

With embarrassment, the dispatcher later testified that he had no recollection of any red-bearded gentleman in the station that day at all.

CHAPTER 41

A Final Inconvenience

In fact, Pierce had been among the crowd that witnessed the dreadful episode of the opened coffin. He saw that the episode proceeded precisely as he had intended, and that Agar, in his hideous make-up, had escaped detection.

When the crowd dissipated, Pierce moved forward to the van, with Barlow at his side. Barlow was carrying some rather odd luggage on a porter's trolley, and Pierce had a moment of disquiet when he saw the dispatcher himself take up the job of supervising the loading of the van. For if anyone considered it, Pierce's behavior was distinctly odd.

To all appearances, he was a prosperous gentleman. But his luggage was unusual, to say the least: five identical satchels of leather. These satchels were hardly the sort of items considered agreeable by gentlemen. The leather was coarse and the stitching at the seams was crude and obvious. If the satchels were unquestionably sturdy, they were also unmistakably ugly.

Yet none was very large, and Pierce could easily have stowed them in the overhead luggage racks of his carriage compartment, instead of the luggage van. The van was ordinarily considered a nuisance, since it meant delays at both the start and the conclusion of the journey.

Finally, Pierce's manservant—he did not employ a railway

porter—loaded the bags onto the luggage van separately. Although the servant was a burly character of evident strength, he was clearly straining under the weight of each satchel.

In short, a thoughtful man might wonder why a gentleman of quality traveled with five small, ugly, extremely heavy, and identical bags. Pierce watched the dispatcher's face while the bags were loaded, one after another. The dispatcher, somewhat pale, never noticed the bags at all, and indeed did not emerge from his distracted state until another gentleman arrived with a parrot, and an argument ensued.

Pierce drifted away, but did not board the train. Instead, he remained near the far end of the platform, apparently curious about the recovery of the woman who had fainted. In fact, he was lingering in the hope of seeing the padlock that he would soon be attempting to pick. When the dispatcher left, with a final sharp rebuke to his nephew, the young woman made her way toward the coaches. Pierce fell into step beside her.

"Are you fully recovered, Miss?" he asked.

"I trust so," she said.

They merged with the boarding crowd at the coaches. Pierce said, "Perhaps you will join me in my compartment for the duration of the journey?"

"You are kind," the girl said, with a slight nod.

"*Get rid of him*," Pierce whispered to her. "I don't care how, just do it."

Miriam had a puzzled look for only a moment, and then a hearty voice boomed out, "Edward! Edward, my dear fellow!" A man was pushing toward them through the crowd.

Pierce waved a delighted greeting. "Henry," he called. "Henry Fowler, what an extraordinary surprise."

Fowler came over and shook Pierce's hand. "Fancy meeting you here," he said. "Are you on this train? Yes? Why, so am I, the fact of the matter—ah . . ." His voice trailed off as he noticed the girl at Pierce's side. He displayed some discomfiture, for in terms of Henry Fowler's social world all the signals were mixed. Here was Pierce, dressed handsomely and showing his usual polish, standing with a girl who was, God knew, pretty enough, but by her dress and manner a very common sort.

Pierce was a bachelor and a blood, and he might travel openly with a mistress for a holiday by the sea, but such a girl would certainly be dressed with gentility, which this girl was not. And contrariwise, were this creature a servant in his household, he would hardly have her out and about in so public a place as a train station unless there was some particular reason for it, but Fowler could not imagine a reason.

Then, too, he perceived that the girl had been weeping; her eyes were red and there were streaks upon her cheeks, and so it was all most perplexing and unusual, and—

Pierce put Fowler out of his misery. "Forgive me," he said, turning to the girl. "I should introduce you, but I do not know your name. This is Mr. Henry Fowler."

The girl, giving him a demure smile, said, "I am Brigid Lawson. How'd you do, sir."

Fowler nodded a vaguely polite greeting, struggling to assume the correct stance toward an obvious servant girl (and therefore not an equal) and a female in distress (and therefore deserving of gentlemanly conduct, so long as her distress sprang from some morally acceptable exigency). Pierce made the situation clearer.

"Miss, ah, Lawson, has just had a most trying encounter," Pierce said. "She is traveling to accompany her deceased brother, who is now situated in the van. But a few moments past, the bell rang, and there was hope of revival and the casket was opened—"

"I see, I see," Fowler said, "most distressing—"

"—but it was a false alarm," Pierce said.

"And thus doubly painful, I am certain," Fowler said.

"I offered to accompany her on the journey," Pierce said.

"And indeed I should do the same," Fowler said, "were I in your place. In fact . . ." He hesitated. "Would it seem an imposition if I joined you both?"

Pierce did not hesitate. "By all means," he said cheerfully. "That is, unless Miss Lawson . . ."

"You are ever so kind, you two are," the girl said, with a brave but grateful smile.

"Well, it's settled, then," Fowler said, also smiling. Pierce saw that he was looking at the girl with interest. "But would you like to come with me? My compartment is just a short way forward." He pointed up the line of first-class coaches.

Pierce, of course, intended to sit in the last compartment of the final first-class coach. From there, he would have the shortest distance to travel, over the tops of the cars, to reach the luggage van at the rear.

"Actually," Pierce said, "I've my own compartment, down there." He pointed toward the back of the train. "My bags are already there, and I've paid the porter, and so on."

"My dear Edward," Fowler said, "How did you get yourself way back there? The choice compartments are all toward the front, where the noise is minified. Come along: I assure you, you'll find a forward compartment more to your liking, and particularly if Miss Lawson feels poorly. . . ." He shrugged as if to suggest the conclusion was obvious.

"Nothing would delight me more," Pierce said, "but in truth I have selected my compartment on the advice of my physician, after experiencing certain distress on railway journeys. This he has attributed to the effects of vibrations originating in the engine, and therefore he's warned me to sit as far back from the source as possible." Pierce gave a short laugh. "He said, in fact, that I should sit second class, but I cannot bring myself to it."

"And little wonder," Fowler said. "There is a limit to healthy living, though you cannot expect a physician to know it. My own once advised me to quit wine—can you imagine the temerity? Very well, then, we shall all ride in your compartment."

Pierce said, "Perhaps Miss Lawson feels, as you do, that a forward carriage would be preferable."

Before the girl could speak, Fowler said, "What? And steal her away from you, leaving you solitary upon the journey? I would not think of it. Come, come, the train will soon leave. Where is your compartment?"

They walked the length of the train to Pierce's compartment. Fowler was in unshakable good spirits, and chattered at length about physicians and their foibles. They stepped into Pierce's compartment and closed the door. Pierce glanced at his watch: it was six minutes to eight. The train did not always leave precisely on schedule, but even so, time was short.

Pierce had to get rid of Fowler. He could not climb out of his compartment onto the roof of the train if there were any strangers—and certainly anyone from the bank—in his compartment. But at the same time, he had to get rid of Fowler in such a way that no suspicion would be aroused; for in the aftermath of the robbery Mr. Fowler would search his memory—and probably be questioned by the authorities —to uncover the least hint of irregularity that might explain who the robbers were.

Mr. Fowler was still talking, but his focus was directed toward the girl, who gave every appearance of rapt and fascinated attention. "It's the most extraordinary luck, running across Edward today. Do you travel this route often, Edward? I myself do it no more than once a month. And you, Miss Lawson?"

"I been on a train before," the girl said, "but I never gone first class; only my mistress, this time she buys me a first ticket, seeing as how, you know . . ."

"Oh, quite, quite," Fowler said, in a hearty, chin-up manner. "One must do all one can for one in times of stress. I

must confess, I am under no little stress myself this morning.
Now, Edward here, he may have guessed the reason for my
travel, and therefore my stress. Eh, Edward? Have you a
guess?"

Pierce had not been listening. He was staring out the window, considering how to get rid of Fowler in the remaining
few minutes. He looked over at Fowler. "Do you think your
bags are safe?" he said.

"My bags? Bags? What—Oh, in my compartment? I have
no bags, Edward. I carry not so much as a case of briefs, for
once in Folkestone, I shall remain there just two hours, hardly
the space of time to take a meal, or some refreshments, or
smoke a cigar, before I am back on the train, homeward
bound."

Smoke a cigar, Pierce thought. Of course. He reached into
his coat pocket, and withdrew a long cigar, which he lit.

"Now, then, dear girl," Fowler said, "our friend Edward
here shall surely have surmised the purpose of my journey,
but I fancy you are still in the dark."

The girl was, in fact, staring at Mr. Fowler with her mouth
slightly open.

"The truth is that this is no ordinary train, and I am no
ordinary passenger. On the contrary, I am the general manager of the banking firm of Huddleston & Bradford, Westminster, and today, aboard this very train—not two hundred
paces from us as we sit here—my firm has stored a quantity
of gold bullion for shipment overseas to our brave troops.
Can you imagine how much? No? Well, then—it is a quantity in excess of twelve thousand pounds, my dear child."

"Cor!" the girl exclaimed. "And you're in charge of all
that?"

"I am indeed." Henry Fowler was looking plainly self-
satisfied, and with reason. He had obviously overwhelmed
the simple girl with his words, and she now regarded him
with dizzy admiration. And perhaps more? She appeared to
have entirely forgotten Pierce.

That is, until Pierce's cigar smoke billowed in gray clouds within the compartment. Now the girl coughed in a delicate, suggestive fashion, as she had no doubt observed her mistress to do. Pierce, staring out the window, did not seem to notice.

The girl coughed again, more insistently. When Pierce still made no response, Fowler took it upon himself to speak. "Are you feeling well?" he inquired.

"I was, but I'm faint. . . ." The girl made a vague gesture toward the smoke.

"Edward," Fowler said. "I believe your tobacco causes Miss Lawson some distress, Edward."

Pierce looked at him and said, "What?"

"I say, would you mind—" Fowler began.

The girl bent forward and said, "I feel quite faint, I fear, please," and she extended a hand toward the door, as if to open it.

"Just look, now," Fowler said to Pierce. Fowler opened the door and helped the girl—who leaned rather heavily upon his arm—into the fresh air.

"I had no idea," Pierce protested. "Believe me, had I but known—"

"You might have inquired before lighting your diabolical contraption," Fowler said, with the girl leaning against him, weak-kneed, so that much of her bosom pressed against his chest.

"I'm most dreadfully sorry," Pierce said. He started to get out himself, to lend assistance.

The last thing Fowler wanted was assistance. "You shouldn't smoke anyway, if your doctor has warned you that trains are hazardous to your health," he snapped. "Come, my dear," he said to the girl, "my compartment is just this way, and we can continue our conversation with no danger of noxious fumes." The girl went willingly.

"Dreadfully sorry," Pierce said again, but neither of them looked back.

A moment later, the whistle blew and the engine began to

chug. Pierce stepped into his compartment, shut the door, and watched London Bridge Station slide away past his window as the morning train to Folkestone began to gather speed.

PART IV

The GREAT TRAIN ROBBERY

May, 1855

CHAPTER 42

A Remarkable Revival

Burgess, locked in the windowless luggage van, knew by now the location of the train at any moment by the sound of the track. He heard first the smooth clacking of the wheels on the well-laid rails of the yard. Then, later, the hollow, more resonant tones as the train crossed Bermondsey on the elevated overpass for several miles, and, still later, a transition to a deader sound and a rougher ride, signaling the beginning of the southward run outside London and into the countryside.

Burgess had no inkling of Pierce's plan, and he was astonished when the coffin bell began to ring. He attributed it to the vibration and sway of the train, but a few moments later there was a pounding, and then a muffled voice. Unable to make out the words, he approached the coffin.

"Open up, damn you," the voice said.

"Are you alive?" Burgess asked, in tones of wonderment.

"It's Agar, you damnable flat," came the answer.

Burgess hastily began to throw the catches on the coffin lid. Soon after, Agar—covered in a dreadful green paste, smelling horrible, but acting in normal enough fashion—got out of the coffin and said, "I must be quick. Get me those satchels there." He pointed to the five leather valises stacked in a corner of the van.

Burgess hurried to do so. "But the van is locked," he said. "How will it be opened?"

"Our friend," Agar said, "is a mountaineer."

Agar opened the safes and removed the first of the strong-boxes, breaking the seal and taking out the dull gold bars of bullion—each stamped with a royal crown and the initials "H & B." He replaced them with small bags of sewn shot, which he took from the valises.

Burgess watched in silence. The train was now rumbling almost due south, past the Crystal Palace, toward Croyden and Redhill. From there it would go east to Folkestone.

"A mountaineer?" Burgess said finally.

"Yes," Agar said. "He's coming over the tops of the train to unlock us."

"When?" Burgess said, frowning.

"After Redhill, returning to his coach before Ashford. It's all open country there. Almost no chance of being seen." Agar did not glance up from his work.

"Redhill to Ashford? But that's the fastest part of the run."

"Aye, I suppose," Agar said.

"Well, then," Burgess said, "your friend is mad."

CHAPTER 43

The Origin of Audacity

At one point in the trial of Pierce, the prosecutor lapsed into a moment of frank admiration. "Then it is not true," said the prosecutor, "that you had any experience of the recreation of mountaineering?"

"None," Pierce said. "I merely said that to reassure Agar."

"You had not met Mr. Coolidge, nor read extensively on the subject, nor owned any of the particular devices and apparatus considered vital to that activity of mountaineering?"

"No," Pierce said.

"Had you, perhaps, some past experiences of athletic or physical endeavor which persuaded you of your ability to carry out your intended plan?"

"None," Pierce said.

"Well, then," said the prosecutor, "I must inquire, if only for reasons of ordinary human curiosity, what on earth, sir, led you to suppose that without prior training, or knowledge, or special equipment, or athletic prowess—what on earth led you to believe you might succeed in such a palpably dangerous and, may I say, nearly suicidal undertaking as clambering about on a swift-moving railway train? Wherever did you find the audacity for such an act?"

Journalistic accounts mention that at this point the witness smiled. "I knew it would be no difficulty," he said, "despite the appearance of danger, for I had on several occasions read in the press of those incidents which are called railway sway, and I had similarly read of the explanation, offered by engineers, that the forces are caused by the nature of swiftly moving air as shown in the studies of the late Italian, Baroni. Thus, I was assured that these forces would operate to hold my person to the surface of the coach, and I should be utterly safe in my undertaking."

At this point, the prosecutor asked for further elucidation, which Pierce gave in garbled form. The summary of this portion of the trial, as reported in the *Times*, was garbled still further. The general idea was that Pierce—by now almost revered in the press as a master criminal—possessed some knowledge of a scientific principle that had aided him.

The truth is that Pierce, rather proud of his erudition, undertook his climb over the cars with a sense of confidence that was completely unfounded. Briefly, the situation was this:

Beginning around 1848, when railway trains began to at-

tain speeds of fifty or even seventy miles an hour, a bizarre
and inexplicable new phenomenon was noted. Whenever a
fast-moving train passed a train standing at a station, the carriages of both trains had a tendency to be drawn together in
what was called "railway sway." In some cases the carriages
heeled over in such a pronounced fashion that passengers were
alarmed, and indeed there was sometimes minor damage to
coaches.

Railway engineers, after a period of technical chatter, finally
admitted their perplexity outright. No one had the slightest
idea why "railway sway" occurred, or what to do to correct
it. One must remember that trains were then the fastest-
moving objects in human history, and the behavior of such
swift vehicles was suspected to be governed by some set of
physical laws as yet undiscovered. The confusion was precisely that of airplane engineers a century later, when the
"buffeting" phenomenon of an aircraft approaching the speed
of sound was similarly inexplicable, and the means to overcome it could only be guessed at.

However, by 1851 most engineers had decided correctly
that railway sway was an example of Bernoulli's Law, a
formulation of a Swiss mathematician of the previous century
which stated, in effect, that the pressure within a moving
stream of air is less than the pressure of the air surrounding it.

This meant that two moving trains, if they were close
enough, would be sucked together by the partial vacuum of
air between them. The solution to the problem was simple,
and soon adopted: the parallel tracks were set farther apart,
and railway sway disappeared.

In modern times, Bernoulli's Law explains such diverse
phenomena as why a baseball curves, why a sailboat can sail
into the wind, and why an airplane wing lifts the aircraft.
But then, as now, most people did not really understand these
events in terms of physics: most jet-age travelers would probably be surprised to learn that a jet flies because it is literally
sucked upward into the air by a partial vacuum over the wings'

upper surface, and the sole purpose of the engines is to propel the wings forward fast enough to create a stream of passing air that produces this necessary vacuum.

Furthermore, a physicist would dispute even this explanation as not really correct, and would insist that a rigorous explanation of events is even further from the public's "common sense" idea about these phenomena.

In the face of this complexity, one can readily understand Pierce's own confusion, and the erroneous conclusion he drew. Apparently he believed that the airstream around the moving carriage, as described by "Baroni," would act to suck him down to the carriage roof, and thus help him to maintain his footing as he moved from car to car.

The truth is that Bernoulli's Law would not operate in any way on his body. He would simply be a man exposed to a fifty-mile-an-hour blast of rushing air, which could blow him off the train at any moment, and it was absurd for him to attempt what he did at all.

Nor was this the extent of his misinformation. The very fact that high-speed travel was so new left Pierce, along with his contemporaries, with very little sense of the consequences of being thrown from a fast-moving vehicle.

Pierce had seen Spring Heel Jack dead after being thrown from the train. But he had regarded this with no sense of inevitability, as the outcome of some inexorable physical laws. At this time, there was only a vague notion that to be thrown from a speeding train was hazardous, and somewhat more hazardous if the train was moving rapidly. But the nature of the hazard was thought to lie in the precise manner of a person's fall: a lucky man could pick himself up with a few scrapes, while an unlucky man would break his neck on impact. In short, a fall from a train was regarded pretty much like a fall from a horse: some were worse than others, and that was that.

Indeed, during the early history of railroads, there had been a sort of daredevil's sport called "carriage-hopping," favored by the kind of young men who later scaled public buildings and engaged in other madcap escapades. University students were particularly prone to these amusements.

Carriage-hopping consisted of leaping from a moving railway carriage to the ground. Although government officials condemned the practice and railway officials flatly forbade it, carriage-hopping enjoyed a brief vogue from 1830 to 1835. Most hoppers suffered nothing more serious than a few bruises, or at worst a broken bone. The fad eventually lost popularity, but the memory of it bolstered the public belief that a fall from a train was not necessarily lethal.

In fact, during the 1830s, most trains averaged twenty-five miles an hour. But by 1850, when the speed of trains had doubled, the consequences of a fall were quite different, and out of all proportion to a fall at slower speeds. Yet this was not understood, as Pierce's testimony indicates.

The prosecutor asked: "Did you take any manner of precaution against the danger of a fall?"

"I did," Pierce said, "and they caused me no little discomfort. Beneath my ordinary external garb, I wore two pairs of heavy cotton undergarments, which had the effect of making me unpleasantly heated, yet I felt these protective measures necessary."

Thus, wholly unprepared and entirely miscalculating the effects of the physical principles involved, Edward Pierce slung a coil of rope over his shoulder, opened the compartment door, and clambered up onto the roof of the moving carriage. His only true protection—and the source of his audacity—lay in his complete misunderstanding of the danger he faced.

The wind struck him like an enormous fist, screaming about his ears, stinging his eyes, filling his mouth and tugging at his cheeks, burning his skin. He had not removed his long frock coat, and the garment now flapped about him, whipping his legs "so fiercely that it was painful."

For a few moments, he was totally disoriented by the un-expected fury of the shrieking air that passed him; he crouched, clutching the wooden surface of the coach, and paused to get his bearings. He found he could hardly look forward at all, because of the streaking particles of soot blown back from the engine. Indeed, he was rapidly covered with fine black film on his hands and face and clothing. Beneath him, the coach rocked and jolted in an alarming and unpredictable fashion.

He very nearly abandoned his intent in those first moments, but after the initial shock had passed he determined to go forward with his plan. Crawling on his hands and knees, he moved backward to the end of the coach, and paused at the space over the coupling that separated his carriage from the next. This was a gap of some five feet. Some moments passed before he gathered the nerve to jump to the next car, but he did so successfully.

From there he crawled painfully down the length of the car. His frock coat was blown forward, covering his face and shoulders and flapping around his eyes. After some mo-ments of struggle with the garment, he shucked it off and saw it sail away, spun twisting in the air, and eventually fall by the roadside. The whirling coat looked enough like a human form to give him pause; it seemed a kind of warning of the fate that awaited him if he made the slightest error.

Freed of the coat, he was able to make more rapid progress down the second-class coaches; he jumped from one to the next with increasing assurance, and eventually reached the luggage van after a period of time he could not estimate. It seemed an eternity, but he later concluded it had not required more than five or ten minutes.

Once atop the van, he gripped an open slapper, and un-coiled his length of hemp. One end was dropped down the slapper, and after a moment he felt a tug as Agar, inside the van, picked it up.

Pierce turned and moved to the second slapper. He waited

there, his body curled tight against the constant, unyielding blast of the wind, and then a ghastly green hand—Agar's— reached out, holding the end of the rope. Pierce took it; Agar's hand disappeared from view.

Pierce now had his rope slung from one slapper to the next. He tied the loose ends about his belt, and then, hanging on the ropes, eased himself over the side of the van until he was level with the padlock.

In that manner he hung suspended for several minutes while he twirled the padlock with a ring of picks, trying one betty after another and operating, as he later testified with considerable understatement, "with that degree of delicacy which circumstances permitted." Altogether, he tried more than a dozen keys, and he was beginning to despair that any would turn the trick when he heard the scream of the whistle.

Looking forward, he saw the Cuckseys tunnel, and an instant later he was plunged into blackness and churning sound. The tunnel was half a mile long; there was nothing to do but wait. When the train burst into sunlight again, he continued working with the keys, and was gratified when almost immediately one of the picks clicked smoothly in the mechanism. The padlock snapped open.

Now it was a simple matter to remove the lock, swing the crossbar free, and kick the door with his feet until Burgess slid it open. The morning train passed the sleepy town of Godstone, but no one noticed the man dangling on the rope, who now eased down into the interior of the luggage van and collapsed on the floor in absolute exhaustion.

CHAPTER 44

A Problem of Dunnage

Agar testified that in the first moment that Pierce landed inside the luggage van, neither he nor Burgess recognized him: "I cool him first, and I swear I granny he's some muck Indian or nigger, so black he is, and his dunnage torn all about, like he'd gone a proper dewskitch"—as if he'd had a thorough thrashing. "His min's a rag of tatters, and black as all the rest of him, and I says, the cracksman's hired a new bloke to do the lay. And then I see it's him himself, right enough."

Surely the three men must have presented a bizarre picture: Burgess, the guard, neat and tidy in his blue railway uniform; Agar, dressed splendidly in a formal suit, his face and hands a cadaverous bloated green; and Pierce, sagged to his hands and knees, his clothing shredded and sooty black from head to foot.

But they all recovered quickly, and worked with swift efficiency. Agar had completed the switch; the safes were locked up again, with their new treasure of lead shot; the five leather satchels stood by the van door in a neat row, each laden with gold bullion.

Pierce got to his feet and took his watch from his waistcoat, an incongruously clean gold object at the end of a sootblack chain. He snapped it open: it was 8:37.

"Five minutes," he said.

Agar nodded. In five minutes, they would pass the most deserted stretch of track, where Pierce had arranged for Bar-

low to wait and pick up the flung satchels. Pierce sat down
and stared through the open van door at the countryside
rushing past.

"Are you well, then?" Agar asked.

"Well enough," Pierce said. "But I don't cherish going
back."

"Aye, it's frazzled you proper," Agar said. "You're a sight
and no mistake. Will you change when you're snug in the
compartment again?"

Pierce, breathing heavily, was slow to comprehend the
meaning of the words. "Change?"

"Aye, your dunnage." Agar grinned. "You step off at
Folkestone as you stand now and you'll cause no end of stir."

Pierce watched the green, rolling hills flash past, and listened to the rumble of the carriage on the roadbed. Here was
a problem he had never considered and had made no plans
for. But Agar was right: he couldn't step out at Folkestone
looking like a ragged chimney sweep, especially as Fowler
was almost certain to seek him out to say goodbye. "I have
no change," he said softly.

"What say?" Agar said, for the noise of the wind through
the open van door was loud.

"I have no change of clothing," Pierce said. "I never expected . . ." His voice trailed off; he frowned. "I brought no
other clothing."

Agar laughed heartily. "Then you'll play the proper raga-
muffin, as you've made me play the stiff." Agar slapped his
knee. "There's a daffy of justice, I say."

"It's nothing funny," Pierce snapped. "I have acquaintances
on the train who will surely see me and mark the change."

Agar's merriment was quashed instantly. He scratched his
head with a green hand. "And these same of your acquaintances, they'll miss you if you're not there at the station?"

Pierce nodded.

"It's the devil's own trap, then," Agar said. He looked

around the van, at the various trunks and pieces of luggage. "Give me your ring of tickles, and I'll break a pit or two, and we'll find some square-rigged duns to fit you."

He held out his hand to Pierce for the ring of picklocks, but Pierce was looking at his watch. It was now two minutes to the drop-off point. Thirteen minutes after that, the train would stop in Ashford, and by then Pierce had to be out of the luggage van and back in his own compartment. "There's no time," he said.

"It's the only chance—" Agar began, but broke off. Pierce was looking him up and down in a thoughtful way. "No," Agar said. "Damn you, no!"

"We're about the same size," Pierce said. "Now be quick."

He turned away and the screwsman undressed, muttering oaths of all sorts. Pierce watched the countryside. They were close now: he bent to position the satchels at the lip of the open van door.

Now he saw a tree by the roadside, one of the landmarks he'd long since set for himself. Soon there would be the stone fence. . . . There it was . . . and then the old abandoned rusty cart. He saw the cart.

A moment later, he saw the crest of a hill and Barlow in profile beside the coach.

"Now!" he said and, with a grunt, flung one satchel after another out of the moving train. He watched them bounce on the ground, one by one. He saw Barlow hastening down the hill toward them. Then the train went around a curve.

He looked back at Agar, who had stripped to his underclothes, and held his fine duds out for Pierce. "Here you are, and damn your eyes."

Pierce took the clothes, rolled them into as tight a ball as he could manage, wrapped the parcel with Agar's belt, and, without another word, swung out the open door and into the wind. Burgess closed the van door, and a few moments later the guard and Agar heard a clink as the bolt was thrown, and another clink as the padlock was locked once more. They heard the scratching of Pierce's feet as he scrambled up to the roof; and then they saw the rope, which had been taut across the roof from slapper to slapper, suddenly go slack. The rope was pulled out. They heard Pierce's footsteps on the roof a moment longer, and then nothing.

"Damn me, I'm cold," Agar said. "You'd best lock me back up," and he crawled into his coffin.

Pierce had not progressed far on his return journey before he realized he had made still another error in his planning: he had assumed it would take the same amount of time to go from the van to his compartment as it took to go from his compartment to the van. But almost immediately he recognized his mistake.

The return trip, against the blast of the wind, was much slower. And he was further burdened by the parcel of Agar's clothing, which he clutched to his chest, leaving only one hand free to grip the roofing as he crawled forward along the length of the train. His progress was agonizingly slow. Within minutes he realized that he was going to miss his intended schedule, and badly. He would still be crawling along the rooftops when the train reached Ashford Station; and then he would be spotted, and the jig would be up.

Pierce had a moment of profound rage that this final step in the plan should be, in the end, the only thing to go irretrievably wrong. The fact that the error was entirely his own doing merely increased his fury. He gripped the pitching, swaying carriage roof and swore into the wind, but the blast of air was so loud he did not hear his own voice.

He knew, of course, what he must do, but he did not think about it. He continued forward as best he could. He was midway along the fourth of the seven second-class carriages when he felt the train begin to slow beneath him. The whistle screamed.

Squinting ahead, he saw Ashford Station, a tiny red rectangle with a gray roof in the far distance. He could not make out any details, but he knew that in less than a minute the train would be near enough that passengers on the platform could see him on the roof. For a brief moment, he wondered what they would think if they did see him, and then he got up and ran, sprinting forward, leaping from one car to the next without hesitation, half blinded by the smoke that poured from the engine funnel back toward him.

Somehow he made it safely to the first-class coach, swung down, opened the door, dropped into his compartment, and immediately pulled the blinds. The train was now chugging very slowly, and as Pierce collapsed into his seat he heard the hiss of the brakes and the porter's cry: "Ashford Station . . . Ashford . . . Ashford . . ."

Pierce sighed.

They had done it.

CHAPTER 45

The End of the Line

Twenty-seven minutes later, the train arrived at Folkestone, the end of the South Eastern Railway line, and all the passengers disembarked. Pierce emerged from his compartment, appearing, he said, "far better than I deserved, but far from sartorial correctness, to put it lightly."

Although he had hastily employed handkerchief and spittle to clean his face and hands, he had discovered the soot and grime on his flesh to be most recalcitrant. As he had no mir-

ror, he could only guess at the condition of his face, but his
hands were no cleaner than a kind of pale gray. Furthermore,
he suspected that his sandy-colored hair was now a good deal
darker than previously, and he was grateful that most of it
would be covered by his top hat.

But except for the top hat, all his clothing fitted poorly.
Even in an age when most people's clothing fitted poorly,
Pierce felt himself especially noticeable. The trousers were
almost two inches short of an acceptable length, and the cut
of the coat, although elegant enough, was of the extreme and
showy fashion that true gentlemen of breeding avoided as in-
decently *nouveau riche*. And, of course, he reeked of dead
cat.

Thus Pierce stepped out onto the crowded Folkestone platform with an inner dread. He knew that most observers
would put down his appearance as a sham: it was common
enough for men who aspired to be gentlemen to obtain
secondhand goods, which they wore proudly, oblivious to
the ill fit of the garments. But Pierce was all too aware that
Henry Fowler, whose entire conscious being was attuned to
the nuances of social standing, would spot the peculiarity of
Pierce's appearance in an instant, and would wonder what
was amiss. He would almost certainly realize that Pierce had
changed clothing for some reason during the ride, and he
would wonder about that as well.

Pierce's only hope lay in keeping his distance from Fowler.
He planned, if he could, to make off with a distant wave of
goodbye, and an air of pressing business that precluded social
amenities. Fowler would certainly understand a man who
looked after business first. And from a distance, with the in-
tervening throng of people, Pierce's bizarre dress might possibly escape his eye.

As it happened, Fowler came charging through the crowd
before Pierce could spot him. Fowler had the woman beside
him, and he did not look happy.

"Now, Edward," Fowler began crisply, "I should be forever in your debt if you would—" He broke off, and his mouth fell open.

Dear God, Pierce thought. It's finished.

"*Edward*," Fowler said, staring at his friend in astonishment.

Pierce's mind was working fast, trying to anticipate questions, trying to come up with answers; he felt himself break into a sweat.

"Edward, my dear fellow, you look *terrible*."

"I know," Pierce began, "you see—"

"You look ghastly near to death itself. Why, you are positively gray as a corpse. When you told me you suffered from trains, I hardly imagined . . . Are you all right?"

"I believe so," Pierce said, with a heartfelt sigh. "I expect I shall be much improved after I dine."

"Dine? Yes, of course, you must dine at once, and take a draught of brandy, too. Your circulation is sluggish, from the look of you. I should join you myself, but—ah, I see they are now unloading the gold which is my deep responsibility. Edward, can you excuse me? Are you truly well?"

"I appreciate your concern," Pierce began, "and—"

"Perhaps I can help him," the girl said.

"Oh, capital idea," Fowler said. "Most splendid. Splendid. She's a charmer, Edward, and I leave her to you." Fowler gave him a queer look at this last comment, and then he hurried off down the platform toward the luggage van, turning back once to call, "Remember, a good strong draught of brandy's the thing." And then he was gone.

Pierce gave an enormous sigh, and turned to the girl. "How could he miss my clothes?"

"You should see your countenance," she said. "You look horrible." She glanced at his clothes. "And I see you've a dead man's dunnage."

"Mine were torn by the wind."

"Then you have done the pull?"
Pierce only grinned.

Pierce left the station shortly before noon. The girl, Brigid
Lawson, remained behind to supervise the loading of her
brother's coffin onto a cab. Much to the irritation of the
porters, she turned down several waiting cabs at the station,
claiming she had made arrangements in advance for a particular one.

The cab did not arrive until after one o'clock. The driver,
an ugly massive brute with a scar across his forehead, helped
with the loading, then whipped up the horses and galloped
away. No one noticed when, at the end of the street, the cab
halted to pick up another passenger, an ashen-colored gentleman in ill-fitting clothes. Then the cab rattled off, and disappeared from sight.

By noon, the strongboxes of the Huddleston & Bradford
Bank had been transferred, under armed guard, from the
Folkestone railway station to the Channel steamer, which
made the crossing to Ostend in four hours. Allowing for the
Continental time change, it was 5 p.m. when French customs
officials signed the requisite forms and took possession of the
strongboxes. These were then transported, under armed
guard, to the Ostend railway terminus for shipment to Paris
by train the following morning.

On the morning of May 23rd, French representatives of
the bank of Louis Bonnard et Fils arrived at Ostend to open
the strongboxes and verify their contents, prior to placing
them aboard the nine-o'clock train to Paris.

Thus, at about 8:15 a.m. on May 23rd, it was discovered
that the strongboxes contained a large quantity of lead shot,
sewn into individual cloth packets, and no gold at all.

This astounding development was immediately reported to
London by telegraph, and the message reached Huddleston
& Bradford's Westminster offices shortly after 10 a.m. Im-

mediately, it provoked the most profound consternation in that firm's brief but respectable history, and the furor did not abate for months to come.

CHAPTER 46

A Brief History of the Inquiry

Predictably, the initial reaction of Huddleston & Bradford was sheer disbelief that anything was amiss. The French cable had been composed in English and read: GOLD MISSED NOW WHERE IS, and was signed VERNIER, OSTEND.

Confronted by this ambiguous message, Mr. Huddleston announced that there had been, no doubt, some silly delay with the French customs authorities and he predicted the whole business would be unraveled before teatime. Mr. Bradford, who had never made the slightest attempt to conceal his intense and lifelong loathing for all things French, assumed that the filthy Frogs had misplaced the bullion, and were now trying to fix the blame for their own stupidity on the English. Mr. Henry Fowler, who had accompanied the gold shipment to Folkestone and seen it safely onto the Channel steamer, observed that the signature "Vernier" was an unfamiliar name, and speculated that the cable might be some sort of practical joke. This was, after all, a time of increasingly strained relations between the English and their French allies.

Cables requesting—and later demanding—clarification flashed back and forth across the Channel. By noon, it appeared that the steamship crossing from Dover to Ostend had been sunk, and the bullion lost in the mishap. However, by early afternoon it was clear the steamer had had an uneventful passage, but almost everything else was vastly more confused.

Cables were now being fired off to all conceivable parties by the Paris bank, the French railway, the English steamship line, the British railway, and the British bank, in dizzying profusion. As the day wore on, the tone of the messages became more acrimonious and their content more ludicrous. The whole thing reached a sort of pinnacle when the manager of the South Eastern Railway in Folkestone telegraphed the manager of the Britannic Steam Packet Company, also in Folkestone: QUI EST M. VERNIER. To this, the steamship manager shot back YOUR SCURRILOUS ALLEGATIONS SHALL NOT GO UNCHALLENGED.

By teatime in London, the desks of the chief officers of Huddleston & Bradford were heaped with telegrams and cables, and office boys were being dispatched to gentlemen's homes to inform wives that their husbands would not be home for dinner, owing to urgent matters of business. The earlier atmosphere of unruffled calm and disdain for French inefficiency was now fading, replaced by a growing suspicion that something might actually have happened to the gold. And it was increasingly clear that the French were as worried as the English—M. Bonnard himself had taken the afternoon train to the coast, to investigate the situation in Ostend at first hand. M. Bonnard was a notorious recluse, and his decision to travel was viewed as a most significant event.

By seven o'clock in London, when most of the bank's clerks went home for the day, the mood of the officers was openly pessimistic. Mr. Huddleston was snappish; Mr. Bradford had the smell of gin on his breath; Mr. Fowler was pale as a ghost; and Mr. Trent's hands trembled. There was a brief moment of elation around 7:30 p.m., when the customs papers from Ostend, signed by the French the previous day, arrived at the bank. They indicated that at 5 p.m. on May 22nd the designated representative of Bonnard et Fils, one Raymond Vernier, had signed for nineteen sealed strongboxes from Huddleston & Bradford containing, according to the declaration, twelve thousand pounds sterling in bullion. "Here is their bloody death warrant," Mr. Huddleston said, waving the paper in the air, "and if there's been any irregularity, it is wholly upon French heads." But this was an exaggeration of the legal situation, and he himself knew it. Soon after, Mr. Huddleston received a long cable from Ostend:

YOUR CONSIGNMENT NINETEEN (19) STRONG BOXES ARRIVED OSTEND YESTERDAY 22 MAY AT 1700 HOURS ABOARD SHIP "ARLINGTON" SAID CONSIGNMENT ACCEPTED BY OUR REPRE-SENTATIVE WITHOUT BREAKING SEALS WHICH APPEARED INTACT CONSIGNMENT PLACED IN OSTEND STRONG SAFE WITH GUARD NIGHT 22 MAY FOLLOWING OUR CUSTOM NO EVIDENCE TAM-PERING SAFE GUARD CHARACTER RELIABLE MORNING 23 MAY OUR REPRESENTATIVE BROKE SEALS YOUR CONSIGNMENT FOUND CONSISTING QUANTITY LEAD PELLETS FOR GUN BUT NO GOLD PRELIMINARY INQUIRY REGARDING ORIGIN PELLETS SUGGESTS ENGLISH MANUFACTURE REVIEW OF BROKEN SEALS SUGGESTS PREVIOUS BREAK AND SECONDARY SEALING SKILLFUL NATURE NOT AROUSING SUSPICION AT ORDINARY INSPECTION IMMEDIATELY NOTIFYING POLICE OFFICIALS ALSO GOVERNMENT IN PARIS RE-MINDING ALL OF BRITISH ORIGIN BRITISH RAILWAY BRITISH STEAMERSHIP BRITISH SUBJECTS GUARDING THROUGHOUT RE-QUEST YOU INFORM BRITISH AUTHORITIES I AWAIT YOUR SOLU-TION TO THIS TRUE PUZZLE

LOUIS BONNARD, PRESIDENT
BONNARD ET FILS, PARIS
ORIGINEE: OSTEND

Mr. Huddleston's first reaction to the cable was reported to be "a heated and forceful expletive, provoked by the stresses of the moment and the lateness of the hour." He is also said to have commented extensively on the French na-tion, the French culture, and the personal and hygienic habits of the French populace. Mr. Bradford, even more vociferous, expressed his belief in the unnatural French fondness for in-

timacy with barnyard creatures. Mr. Fowler was obviously
intoxicated and Mr. Trent was suffering pains in the chest.
It was nearly ten o'clock at night when the bankers were
finally calm enough for Mr. Huddleston to say to Mr. Bradford: "I shall notify the Minister. You notify Scotland Yard."

Events of subsequent days followed a certain predictable
pattern. The English suspected the French; the French suspected the English; everyone suspected the English railway
officials, who in turn suspected the English steamship officials,
who in turn suspected the French customs officials.

British police officers in France, and French police officers
in England, rubbed shoulders with private detectives hired
by the banks, the railroads, and the shipping line. Everyone
offered some sort of reward for information leading to the
arrest of the villains, and informants on both sides of the
Channel quickly responded with a dazzling profusion of tips
and rumors.

Theories about the lost gold shipment ran the gamut from
the most mundane—a couple of French or English hooligans
stumbling upon a fortuitous opportunity—to the most gran-
diose—an elaborate plot by the highest officials of the French
or English government, engaged in a Machiavellian scheme
intended simultaneously to line their own pockets and to
sour relations with their military allies. Lord Cardigan himself, the great war hero, expressed the opinion that "it must
surely be a clever combination of avarice and statecraft."

Nevertheless, the most widespread belief, on both sides of
the Channel, was that it was some kind of inside job. For one
thing, that was how most crimes were carried out. And, particularly in this case, the complexity and neatness of the theft
surely pointed to inside information and cooperation. Thus
every individual who had the slightest relationship to the
Crimean gold shipment came under scrutiny, and was interrogated by the authorities. The zeal of the police to gather
information led to some unlikely circumstances: the ten-year-

old grandson of the Folkestone harbormaster was tailed by a plainclothesman for several days—for reasons that no one could quite recall later on. Such incidents only increased the general confusion, and the process of interrogation dragged on for months, with each new clue and possibility receiving the full attention of an eager and fascinated press.

No significant progress was made until June 17th, nearly a month after the robbery. Then, at the insistence of the French authorities, the safes in Ostend, aboard the English steamship, and on the South Eastern Railway were all returned to their respective manufacturers in Paris, Hamburg, and London for dismantling and examination of the lock mechanisms. The Chubb safes were discovered to contain telltale scratches inside the locks, as well as traces of metal filings, grease, and wax. The other safes showed no signs of tampering.

This discovery focused new attention on the luggage-van guard Burgess, who had been previously questioned and released. On June 19th, Scotland Yard announced a warrant for his arrest, but the same day the man, his wife, and his two children vanished without a trace. In subsequent weeks of searching, Burgess was not found.

It was then recalled that the South Eastern Railway had suffered another robbery from its luggage van, only a week prior to the bullion theft. The clear implication of generally lax management by railway authorities fed the growing public suspicion that the robbery must have occurred on the London-Folkestone train. And when the South Eastern Railway's hired detectives came forth with evidence that the robbery had been carried out by French villains—an allegation quickly shown to be groundless—the public suspicion hardened into certainty, and the press began to refer to The Great Train Robbery.

All during July and August, 1855, The Great Train Robbery remained a sensational topic in print and conversation. Although no one could figure out quite how it had been done, its evident complexity and audacity soon led to the unquestioned belief that it must have been carried out by Englishmen. The previously suspect French were now deemed too limited and timid even to conceive such a dashing endeavor, to say nothing of bringing it off.

When, in late August, the police in New York City announced they had captured the robbers, and that they were Americans, the English press reacted with frankly scornful disbelief. And, indeed, some weeks later it was learned that the New York police were in error, and that their robbers had never set foot on English soil, but were, in the words of one correspondent, "of that erratic turn of mind, wherein a man will seize upon a publicized event, even if it be notorious, to gain the attention of the wider public, and this to satisfy his demented craving for a moment in the limelight."

The English newspapers printed every shred of rumor, hearsay, and speculation about the robbery; other stories were slanted to consider the robbery. Thus when Victoria made a visit to Paris in August, the press wondered in what way the robbery would affect her reception in that city. (It apparently made no difference at all.)

But the plain fact was that throughout the summer months no single new development occurred, and inevitably interest began to wane. People's imagination had been captured for four months. During that time, they had progressed from hostility toward the French, who had obviously stolen the gold in some sleazy, underhanded fashion, to suspicion of the English leaders of finance and industry, who were at best guilty of gross incompetence and at worst culpable of the crime itself, and eventually to a sort of admiration for the resourcefulness and daring of the English rogues who had plotted and carried out the escapade—however it was actually done.

But in the absence of fresh developments The Great Train Robbery became tedious, and eventually public opinion turned distinctly sour. Having wallowed in a delightful orgy of anti-

French sentiment, having deplored and applauded the villains themselves, having relished the foibles of bankers, railwaymen, diplomats, and police, the public was now ready to see its faith restored in the basic soundness of banks, railroads, government, and police. In short, they wanted the culprits caught, and quickly.

But the culprits were not caught. Officials mentioned "possible new developments in the case" with ever less conviction. In late September there was an anonymous story to the effect that Mr. Harranby of Scotland Yard had known of the impending crime but had failed to prevent it; Mr. Harranby vigorously denied these rumors, but there were a few scattered calls for his resignation. The banking firm of Huddleston & Bradford, which had enjoyed a mild increase in business during the summer months, now experienced a mild decline. Newspapers featuring stories of the robbery sold fewer copies.

By October, 1855, The Great Train Robbery was no longer of interest to anyone in England. It had come full circle, from a topic of universal and endless fascination to a confused and embarrassing incident that nearly everyone wished very much to forget.

PART V

ARREST

and

TRIAL

November, 1856 – August, 1857

CHAPTER 47

The Bug-Hunter's Chance

November 5th, known as Powder Plot Day or Guy Fawkes Day, had been a national holiday in England since 1605. But the celebration, observed the *News* in 1856, "has of late years been made subservient to the cause of charity as well as mere amusement. Here is a laudable instance. On Wednesday evening a grand display of fireworks took place on the grounds of the Merchant Seamen's Orphan Asylum, Bow-road, in aid of the funds of the institution. The grounds were illuminated somewhat after the fashion adopted at Vauxhall, and a band of music was engaged. In the rear of the premises was a gibbet, to which was suspended an effigy of the Pope; and around it were several barrels of tar, which at the proper time were consumed in a most formidable blaze. The exhibition was attended by a large concourse of people, and the result promised to be of considerable benefit to the funds of the charity."

Any combination of large crowds and distracting spectacles was, of course, also of considerable benefit to pickpockets, cut-purses, and dolly-mops, and the police at the orphan asylum that night were busy indeed. In the course of the evening, no fewer than thirteen "vagrants, vagabonds and petty villains" were apprehended by officers of the Metropolitan Force, including a female who was accused of robbing an intoxicated gentleman. This arrest was made by one Constable Johnson, and the manner of it was sufficiently idiosyncratic to merit some explanation.

The major features are clear enough. Constable Johnson,

a man of twenty-three, was walking the asylum grounds when, by the flaring light of the fireworks exploding overhead, he observed a female crouched over the prostrate form of a man. Fearing the gentleman might be ill, Constable Johnson went to offer help, but at his approach the girl took to her heels. Constable Johnson gave chase, apprehending the female a short distance away when she tripped on her skirts and tumbled to the ground.

Observing her at close hand to be "a female of lewd aspect and lascivious comportment," he at once surmised the true nature of her attentions to the gentleman; namely, that she was robbing him, in his intoxicated stupor, and that she was the lowest form of criminal, a "bug-hunter." Constable Johnson promptly arrested her.

The saucy minx put her hands on her hips and glared at him in open defiance. "There's not a pogue upon me," she declared, which words must surely have given Constable Johnson pause. He faced a serious dilemma.

In the Victorian view, proper male conduct demanded that all women, even women of the lowest sort, be treated with caution and consideration for the delicacy of their feminine nature. That nature, noted a contemporary policeman's manual of conduct, "with its sacred emotional wellsprings, its ennobling maternal richness, its exquisite sensitivity and profound fragility, i.e. all those qualities which comprise the very *essence of womanly character*, derive from the biological or physio-logic principles which determine all the differences between the sexes of male and female. Thus it must be appreciated that the *essence of womanly character* resides in every member of that sex, and must be duly respected by an Officer, and this despite the appearance, in certain vulgar personages, of the absence of said womanly character."

The belief in a biologically determined personality in both men and women was accepted to some extent by nearly everyone at all levels of Victorian society, and that belief was held in the face of all sorts of incongruities. A business-man could go off to work each day, leaving his "unreasoning" wife to run an enormous household, a businesslike task of formidable proportions; yet the husband never viewed his wife's activities in that way.

Of all the absurdities of the code, the most difficult was the predicament of the policeman. A woman's inherent fra-gility created obvious difficulties in the handling of female lawbreakers. Indeed, criminals took advantage of the situa-tion, often employing a female accomplice precisely because the police were so reluctant to arrest.

Constable Johnson, confronted by this dratted minx on the night of November 5th, was fully aware of his situation. The woman claimed to have no stolen goods on her person; and if this was true, she would never be convicted, despite his testimony that he had found her bug-hunting. Without a pocket watch or some other indisputably masculine article, the girl would go free.

Nor could he search her: the very idea that he might touch the woman's body was unthinkable to him. His only recourse was to escort her to the station, where a matron would be called to perform the search. But the hour was late; the matron would have to be roused from her bed, and the station was some blocks distant. In the course of being escorted through dark streets, the little tart would have many opportunities to rid herself of incriminating evidence.

Furthermore, if Constable Johnson brought her in, called for the matron, raised all manner of fuss and stir, and then it was discovered the girl was clean, he would look a proper fool and receive a stiff rebuke. He knew this; and so did the girl standing before him in a posture of brazen defiance.

Altogether it was a situation not worth the risk or the bother, and Constable Johnson would have liked to send her off with a scolding. But Johnson had recently been advised by his superiors that his arrest record left something to be desired; he had been told to be more vigilant in his pursuit of wrongdoing. And there was the strong implication that his job hung in the balance.

So Constable Johnson, in the intermittent, sputtering glow of the bursting fireworks, decided to take the bug-hunter in for a search—to the girl's open astonishment, and despite his own rather considerable reluctance.

Dalby, the station sergeant, was in a foul humor, for he was called upon to work on the night of the holiday, and he resented missing the festivities that he knew were taking place all around him.

He glared at Johnson and the woman at his side. The woman gave her name as Alice Nelson, and stated her age was "eighteen or thereabouts." Dalby sighed and rubbed his face sleepily as he filled in the forms. He sent Johnson off to collect the matron. He ordered the girl to sit in a corner. The station was deserted, and silent except for the distant pop and whistle of fireworks.

Dalby had a flask in his pocket, and at late hours he often took a daffy or two when there was no one about. But now this saucy little bit of no-good business was sitting there, and whatever else was the truth of her, she was keeping him from his nip; the idea irked him, and he frowned into space, feeling frustrated. Whenever he couldn't have a daffy, he wanted it especially much, or so it seemed.

After a space of time, the judy spoke up. "If you granny I've a pink or two beneath me duds, see for yourself, and now." Her tone was lascivious; the invitation was unmistakable, and to make it clearer, she began to scratch her limbs through the skirt, in languorous fashion.

"You'll be finding what you want, I reckon," she added. Dalby sighed.

The girl continued to scratch. "I know to please you," she said, "and you may count on it, as God's me witness."

"And earn the pox for my troubles," Dalby said. "I know your sort, dearie."

"Here, now," the girl protested, in a sudden shift from invitation to outrage. "You've no call to voker such-like. There's not a touch of pox upon me, and never been."

"Aye, aye, aye," Dalby said wearily, thinking again of his flask. "There never is, is there."

The little tart lapsed into silence. She ceased scratching herself, and soon enough sat up straight in her chair, adopting a proper manner. "Let's us strike a bargain," she said, "and I warrant it'll be one to your liking."

"Dearie, there's no bargain to be made," Dalby said, hardly paying attention. He knew this tedious routine, for he saw it played out, again and again, every night he worked at the station. Some little bit of goods would be tugged in on an officer's arm, all protests of innocence. Then she'd settle in and make an advance of favors, and if that was not taken up, she'd soon enough talk a bribe.

It was always the same.

"Set me to go," the girl said, "and you'll have a gold guinea."

Dalby sighed, and shook his head. If this creature had a gold guinea on her, it was sure proof she'd been bug-hunting, as young Johnson claimed.

"Well, then," the girl said, "you shall have ten." Her voice now had a frightened edge.

"Ten guineas?" Dalby asked. That at least was something new; he'd never been offered ten guineas before. They must be counterfeit, he thought.

"Ten is what I promise you, right enough."

Dalby hesitated. In his own eyes he was a man of principle, and he was a seasoned officer of the law. But his weekly wage was fifteen shillings, and sometimes it came none too promptly. Ten guineas was a substantial item and no mistake. He let his mind wander over the idea.

"Well, then," the girl said, taking his hesitation for something else, "it shall be a hundred! A hundred gold guineas!"

Dalby laughed. His mood was broken, and his daydreams abruptly ended. In her anxiety the girl was obviously weaving an ever wilder story. A hundred guineas! Absurd.

"You don't believe me?"

"Be still," he said. His thoughts returned to the flask in his pocket.

There was a short silence while the tart chewed her lip and frowned. Finally she said, "I know a thing or two."

Dalby stared at the ceiling. It was all so dreary and predictable. After the bribe failed, there came the offer of information about some crime or other. The progression was always the same. Out of boredom, as much as anything else, he said, "And what is this thing or two?"

"A ream sight of a flash pull, and no slang."

"And what may that be?"

"I know who did the train-robbery lay."

"Mother of God," Dalby said, "but you're a clever judy. Why, do you know that's the very thing we're all wanting to hear—and hear it we have, from every blasted muck-snipe, smatter-hauler, and bug-picker who comes our way. Every blasted one knows the tale to tell. I've heard a hundred blows with these very ears you see here." He gave her a wan smile.

In fact, Dalby was feeling something like pity for the girl. She was such a down-and-out case, a bug-hunter, the lowest form of common and sleazy crime, and hardly able to formulate a reasonable bribe. In truth, Dalby seldom was offered information about the train robbery any more. That was old news, and nobody cared. There were half a dozen more recent and captivating crimes to blow.

"It's no slang cover," the girl said. "I know the screwsman did the pull, and I can put you to him swift enough."

"Aye, aye, aye," Dalby said.

"I swear," the girl protested, looking ever more desperate. "I *swear*."

"Who's the bloke, then?"

"I'll not say."

"Aye, but I suppose," Dalby said, "that you'll find this gent for us if only we set you free for a bit of hunting him down, isn't that right?" Dalby shook his head and looked at the girl to see her expression of astonishment. They were always astonished, these low types, to hear a crusher fill in the details of their tale. Why did they always take a man of the force for a total flat and dumb fool?

But it was Dalby who was surprised, for the girl very calmly said, "No."

"No?" Dalby said.

"No," the girl replied. "I know exact where he's to be found."

"But you must lead us to him?" Dalby said.

"No," the girl said.

"No?" Dalby hesitated. "Well, then, where's he to be found?"

"Newgate Prison," the girl said.

Several moments passed before Dalby fully appreciated her words. "Newgate Prison?" he said.

The girl nodded.

"What's his name, then?"

The girl grinned.

Soon after, Dalby called for a runner to go to the Yard and notify Mr. Harranby's office directly, for here was a story so strange it very likely had some truth to it.

By dawn, the basic situation was clear to the authorities. The woman, Alice Nelson, was the mistress of one Robert Agar, recently arrested on a charge of forging five-pound notes. Agar had protested his innocence; he was now in Newgate Prison awaiting his trial in court.

The woman, deprived of Agar's income, had turned to various crimes to support herself, and was nabbed in the act of picking a bug. According to a later official report, she showed "a most overpowering apprehension of confinement," which probably meant she was claustrophobic. In any case, she turned nose on her lover, and told all that she knew, which was little enough—but enough for Mr. Harranby to send for Agar.

CHAPTER 48

Kangaroo-Hunting

"A thorough comprehension of the devious criminal mind," wrote Edward Harranby in his memoirs, "is vital to police interrogation." Harranby certainly had that comprehension, but he had to admit that the man seated before him, coughing and hacking, presented a particularly difficult case. They were in their second hour of questioning, but Robert Agar stuck to his story.

In interrogations, Harranby favored the introduction of abrupt new lines of inquiry to keep the villains off balance. But Agar seemed to handle the technique easily.

"Mr. Agar," Harranby said. "Who is John Simms?"

"Never heard of 'im."

"Who is Edward Pierce?"

"Never heard of 'im. I told you that." He coughed into a handkerchief offered him by Harranby's assistant, Sharp.

"Isn't this man Pierce a famous cracksman?"

"I wouldn't know."

"You wouldn't know." Harranby sighed. He was certain Agar was lying. His posture, his flicking downcast eyes, his hand gestures—everything suggested deceit. "Well, now, Mr. Agar. How long have you been forging?"

"I didn't do no soft," Agar said. "I swear it wasn't me. I was in the pub downstairs, having a daffy or two is all. I swear."

"You are innocent?"

"Aye, I am."

Harranby paused. "You're lying," he said.

"It's God's truth," Agar said.

"We'll see you in the stir for many years. Make no mistake about it."

"There's no blame upon me," Agar said, getting excited.

"Lies, all lies. You're a counterfeiter, pure and simple."

"I swear," Agar said. "I'd not do any soft. There's no sense to it—" Abruptly, he broke off.

There was a brief silence in the room, punctuated only by the ticking of a clock on the wall. Harranby had purchased the clock especially for its tick, which was steady, loud, and irritating to prisoners.

"Why is there no sense to it?" he asked softly.

"I'm honest is why," Agar said, staring at the floor.

"What honest work do you do?"

"Local work. Here and there."

That was a nonspecific excuse, but possible enough. In London at that time, there were nearly half a million unskilled laborers who worked at various odd jobs whenever the jobs were available.

"Where have you worked?"

"Well, let's see, now," Agar said, squinting. "I did a day for the gasworks at Millbank, loading. I did two days at Chenworth, hauling bricks. A week past I did some hours for Mr. Barnham, cleaning his cellar. I go where I can, you know."

"These employers would remember you?"

Agar smiled. "Maybe."

Here was another dead end for Harranby. Employers of casual labor often did not recall their workers, or recalled them incorrectly. Either way, it wouldn't mean much.

Harranby found himself staring at the man's hands. Agar's hands were clenched in his lap. Then Harranby noticed that the little fingernail on one hand was long. It had been bitten at, to conceal this fact, but it was still somewhat long.

A long fingernail might mean all sorts of things. Sailors wore a nail long for luck, particularly Greek sailors; then, too, certain clerks who used seals kept a nail long to pluck the seal from the hot wax. But for Agar . . .

"How long have you been a screwsman?" Harranby said.

"Eh?" Agar replied with an expression of elaborate innocence. "Screwsman?"

"Come, now," Harranby said. "You know what a screwsman is."

"I worked as a sawyer once. Spent a year in the north, working in a mill as a sawyer, I did."

Harranby was not distracted. "Did you make the keys for the safes?"

"Keys? What keys?"

Harranby sighed. "You've no future as an actor, Agar."

"I don't take your meaning, sir," Agar said. "What keys are you talking of?"

"The keys to the train robbery."

Here Agar laughed. "Cor," he said. "You think if I was in on that flash pull I'd be doing a bit of soft now? You think that? That's glocky, that is."

Harranby's face was expressionless, but he knew that Agar was right. It made no sense for a man who had participated in a twelve-thousand-pound theft to be stamping out five-pound notes a year later.

"There's no use in pretending," Harranby said. "We know that Simms has abandoned you. He doesn't care what happens to you—why are you protecting him?"

"Never heard of 'im," Agar said.

"Lead us to him, and you'll have a fine reward for your troubles."

"Never heard of 'im," Agar said again. "Can't you see that plain?"

Harranby paused and stared at Agar. The man was quite calm, except for his coughing attacks. He glanced at Sharp, in the corner. It was time for a different approach.

Harranby picked up a piece of paper from his desk, and put on his spectacles. "Now, then, Mr. Agar," he said. "This is a report on your past record. It's none too good."

"Past record?" Now his puzzlement was genuine. "I've no past record."

"Indeed you do," Harranby said, running his finger along the print on the paper. "Robert Agar . . . hmm . . . twenty-six years old . . . hmm . . . born Bethnal Green . . . hmm . . . Yes, here we are. Bridewell prison, six months, charge of vagrancy, in 1849—"

"That's *not true!*" Agar exploded.

"—and Coldbath, one year eight months, charge of robbery, in 1852—"

"Not true, I swear it, not true!"

Harranby glared at the prisoner over his glasses. "It's all here in the record, Mr. Agar. I think the judge will be interested to learn it. What do you suppose he will get, Mr. Sharp?"

"Fourteen years transportation, at least," Sharp said, in a thoughtful way.

"Umm, yes, fourteen years in Australia—that sounds about right."

"Australia," Agar said, in a hushed voice.

"Well, I should think," Harranby said calmly. "Boating's the thing in a case like this."

Agar was silent.

Harranby knew that although "transportation" was popularly portrayed as a much-feared punishment, the criminals themselves viewed banishment to Australia with equanimity or even pleasant expectation. Many villains suspected that

Australia was agreeable, and to "do the kangaroo hunts" was unquestionably preferable to a long stretch in an English prison.

Indeed, at this time Sydney, in New South Wales, was a thriving, handsome seaport of thirty thousand. In addition, it was a place where "personal history is at a discount, and good memories and inquisitive minds are particularly disliked. . . ." And if it had its brutal side—butchers were fond of plucking poultry while it was still alive—it was also pleasant, with gaslit streets, elegant mansions, bejeweled women, and social pretensions of its own. A man like Agar could view transportation as, at the very least, a mixed blessing.

But Agar was greatly agitated. Plainly, he did not want to leave England. Seeing this, Harranby was encouraged. He stood.

"That will be all for now," he said. "If in the next day or so you feel that you have something you wish to tell me, just inform the guards at Newgate."

Agar was ushered out of the room. Harranby sat back at his desk. Sharp came over.

"What were you reading?" he asked.

Harranby picked up the sheet of paper from his desk. "A notification from the Buildings Committee," he said, "to the effect that carriages are no longer to be parked in the court-yard."

After three days, Agar informed the Newgate guards that he would like another audience with Mr. Harranby. On November 13th, Agar told Harranby everything he knew about the robbery, in exchange for the promise of lenient treatment and the vague possibility that one of the institutions involved —the bank or the railway or even the government itself— might see fit to present him with a stipend from the still-outstanding offers of reward for information.

Agar did not know where the money was kept. He said that Pierce had been paying him a monthly stipend in paper currency. The criminals had previously agreed that they would divide the profits two years after the crime, in May of the following year, 1857.

Agar did, however, know the location of Pierce's house. On the night of November 13th, the forces of the Yard surrounded the mansion of Edward Pierce, or John Simms, and entered it with barkers at the ready. But the owner was not at home; the frightened servants explained that he had left town to attend the P.R. spectacle the following day in Manchester.

CHAPTER 49

The P.R.

Technically, boxing matches in England were illegal, but they were held throughout the nineteenth century, and drew an enormous, loyal following. The necessity to elude authorities meant that a big match might be shifted from town to town at the last minute, with vast crowds of pugilistic enthusiasts and sporting bloods following all over the countryside.

The match on November 19th between Smashing Tim Revels, the Fighting Quaker, and the challenger, Neddy Singleton, was moved from Liverpool to a small town called Eagle Welles, and eventually to Barrington, outside Manchester. The fight was attended by more than twenty thousand supporters, who found the spectacle unsatisfactory.

In those days, the P.R., or prize ring, had rules that would make the event almost unrecognizable to modern eyes. Fighting was done bare-fisted by the combatants, who were careful to regulate their blows in order to avoid injury to their own hands and wrists; a man who broke his knuckles or wrists early in a contest was almost certain to lose. Rounds were of variable duration, and the fights had no prearranged length. They often went fifty or even eighty rounds, thus lasting the better part of a day. The object of the sport was for each man slowly and methodically to injure his opponent with a succession of small cuts and welts; knockouts were not sought. On the contrary, the proper fighter literally battered his opponent into submission.

Neddy Singleton was hopelessly outclassed by Smashing Tim from the start. Early in the fight, Neddy adopted the ruse of dropping to one knee whenever he was struck, in order to halt the fight and allow him to catch his breath. The spectators hissed and booed this ungentlemanly trick, but nothing could be done to prevent it, especially as the referee —charged with giving the count of ten—called out the numbers with a slowness that demonstrated he'd been paid off smartly by Neddy's backers. The indignation of the fans was tempered, at least, by the recognition that this chicanery had the side effect of prolonging the bloody spectacle they had all come to witness.

With thousands of spectators standing about, including every manner of coarse and brutal ruffian, the men of the Yard were at some pains to operate unobtrusively. Agar, with a revolver at his spine, pointed out Pierce and the guard Burgess from a distance. The two men were then apprehended with great adroitness: a barker was pressed to each man's side, with a whispered suggestion that they come along quietly or take a bit of lead for their trouble.

Pierce greeted Agar amiably. "Turned nose, did you?" he asked with a smile.

Agar could not meet his eyes.

"Doesn't matter," Pierce said. "I've thought of this as well, you know."

"I had no choice," Agar blurted out.

"You'll lose your share," Pierce said calmly.

At the periphery of the P.R. crowd, Pierce was brought before Mr. Harranby of the Yard.

"Are you Edward Pierce, also known as John Simms?"

"I am," the man replied.

"You are under arrest on a charge of robbery," Mr. Harranby said.

To this Pierce replied, "You'll never hold me."

"I fancy that I will, sir," Mr. Harranby said.

By nightfall on November 19th, both Pierce and Burgess were, along with Agar, in Newgate Prison. Harranby quietly informed government officials of his success, but there was no announcement to the press, for Harranby wanted to apprehend the woman known as Miriam, and the cabby Barlow, both still at large. He also wanted to recover the money.

CHAPTER 50

Winkling Out

On November 22nd, Mr. Harranby interrogated Pierce for the first time. The diary of his assistant, Jonathan Sharp, records that "H. arrived in office early, most carefully attired and looking his best. Had cup of coffee instead of usual tea. Comments on how best to deal with Pierce, etc., etc. Said that he suspected nothing could be got from Pierce without softening up."

In fact, the interview was remarkably brief. At nine o'clock in the morning, Pierce was ushered into the office and asked to sit in a chair, isolated in the middle of the room. Harranby,

from behind his desk, directed his first question with cus-
tomary abruptness.

"Do you know the man called Barlow?"

"Yes," Pierce said.

"Where is he now?"

"I don't know."

"Where is the woman called Miriam?"

"I don't know."

"Where," said Mr. Harranby, "is the money?"

"I don't know."

"It seems that there is a good deal you don't know."

"Yes," Pierce said.

Harranby appraised him for a moment. There was a short
silence. "Perhaps," Harranby said, "a time in the Steel will
strengthen your powers of memory."

"I doubt it," Pierce said, with no sign of anxiety. Soon
after, he was taken from the room.

Alone with Sharp, Harranby said, "I shall break him, you
may be sure of that." The same day, Harranby arranged for
Pierce to be transferred from Newgate Prison to the House
of Correction at Coldbath Fields, also called the Bastille.
"The Steel" was not ordinarily a holding place for accused
criminals awaiting trial. But it was a frequent ruse for police
to send a man there if some information had to be "winkled
out" of him before the trial.

The Steel was the most dreaded of all English prisons.
In a visit in 1853, Henry Mayhew described its features.
Chief among them, of course, were the cockchafers, narrow
boxes in a row with "the appearance of the stalls in a public
urinal," where prisoners remained for fifteen-minute intervals, treading down a wheel of twenty-four steps. A warder
explained the virtues of the cockchafer in this way: "You see
the men can get no firm tread like, from the steps always
sinking away from under their feet and *that* makes it very
tiring. Again the compartments are small, and the air be-

comes very hot, so that the heat at the end of a quarter of an hour renders it difficult to breathe."

Even less pleasant was shot-drill, an exercise so rigorous that men over forty-five were usually exempted. In this, the prisoners formed a circle with three paces separating each. At a signal, each man picked up a twenty-four-pound cannon-ball, carried it to his neighbor's place, dropped it, and returned to his original position where another shot awaited him. The drill went on for an hour at a time.

Most feared of all was "the crank," a drum filled with sand and turned with a crank handle. It was usually reserved as a special punishment for unruly prisoners.

The daily regimen of Coldbath Fields was so debilitating that even after a short sentence of six months, many a man emerged "with the steel gone out of him"—his body damaged, nerves shot, and resolution so enfeebled that his ability to commit further crimes was severely impaired.

As a prisoner awaiting trial, Pierce could not be made to undergo the stepper, the shot-drill, or the crank; but he was obliged to follow the rules of prison conduct, and if he broke the rule of silence, for example, he might be punished by a time at the crank. Thus one may presume that the guards frequently accused him of speaking, and he was treated to "softening up."

On December 19th, after four weeks in the Steel, Pierce was again brought to Harranby's office. Harranby had told Sharp that "now we shall see a thing or two," but the second interrogation turned out to be as brief as the first:

"Where is the man Barlow?"

"I don't know."

"Where is the woman Miriam?"

"I don't know."

"Where is the money?"

"I don't know."

Mr. Harranby, coloring deeply, the veins standing out on

his forehead, dismissed Pierce with a voice filled with rage. As Pierce was taken away, he calmly wished Mr. Harranby a pleasant Christmas.

"The cheek of the man," Harranby later recorded, "was beyond all imagining."

Mr. Harranby during this period was under considerable pressure from several fronts. The bank of Huddleston & Bradford wanted its money back, and made its feelings known to Harranby through the offices of none other than the Prime Minister, Lord Palmerston himself. The inquiry from "Old Pam" was in itself embarrassing, for Harranby had to admit that he had put Pierce in Coldbath Fields, and the implications of that were none too gentlemanly.

Palmerston expressed the opinion that it was "a bit irregular," but Harranby consoled himself with the thought that any Prime Minister who dyed his whiskers was hardly in a position to berate others for dissembling.

Pierce remained in Coldbath until February 6th, when he was again brought before Harranby.

"Where is the man Barlow?"

"I don't know."

"Where is the woman Miriam?"

"I don't know."

"Where is the money?"

"In a crypt, in Saint John's Wood," Pierce said.

Harranby sat forward. "What was that?"

"It is stored," Pierce said blandly, "in a crypt in the name of John Simms, in the cemetery of Martin Lane, Saint John's Wood."

Harranby drummed his fingers on the desk. "Why have you not come forth with this information earlier?"

"I did not want to," Pierce said.

Harranby ordered Pierce taken away to Coldbath Fields once more.

On February 7th, the crypt was located, and the appropriate dispensations obtained to open it. Mr. Harranby, accompanied by a representative of the bank, Mr. Henry Fowler, opened the vault at noon that day. There was no coffin in the crypt—and neither was there any gold. Upon reexamination of the crypt door, it appeared that the lock had been recently forced.

Mr. Fowler was extremely angry at the discovery, and Mr. Harranby was extremely embarrassed. On February 8th, the following day, Pierce was returned to Harranby's office and told the news.

"Why," Pierce said, "the villains must have robbed me."

His voice and manner did not suggest any great distress, and Harranby said so.

"Barlow," Pierce said. "I always knew he was not to be trusted."

"So you believe it was Barlow who took the money?"

"Who else could it be?"

There was a short silence. Harranby listened to the ticking of his clock; for once, it irritated him more than his subject. Indeed, his subject appeared remarkably at ease.

"Do you not care," Harranby said, "that your confederates have turned on you in this fashion?"

"It's just my ill luck," Pierce said calmly. "And yours," he added, with a slight smile.

"By his collected manner and polished demeanour," Harranby wrote, "I presumed that he had fabricated still another tale to put us off the mark. But in further attempts to learn the truth I was frustrated, for on the first of March, 1857, the *Times* reporter learned of Pierce's capture, and he could no longer conveniently be held in custody."

According to Mr. Sharp, his chief received the newspaper story of Pierce's capture "with heated imprecations and ejaculations." Harranby demanded to know how the papers had been put on to the story. The *Times* refused to divulge its

source. A guard at Coldbath who was thought to have given
out the information was discharged, but nobody was ever
certain one way or the other. Indeed, it was even rumored
that the lead had come from Palmerston's office.

In any case, the trial of Burgess, Agar, and Pierce was set
to begin on July 12, 1857.

CHAPTER 51

The Trial of an Empire

The trial of the three train robbers was greeted by the public
with the same sensational interest it had earlier shown in
the crime itself. The prosecuting officials, mindful of the attention focused upon the event, took care to heighten the
drama inherent in the proceedings. Burgess, the most minor
of the players, was brought to the docket of Old Bailey first.
The fact that this man knew only parts of the whole story
only whetted the public appetite for further details.

Agar was interrogated next, providing still more information. But Agar, like Burgess, was a distinctly limited man,
and his testimony served only to focus attention on the personality of Pierce himself, whom the press referred to as "the
master criminal" and "the brilliant malignant force behind
the deed."

Pierce was still incarcerated in Coldbath Fields, and neither
the public nor the press had seen him. There was plenty of
freedom for eager reporters to conjure up wild and fanciful
accounts of the man's appearance, manner, and style of living.
Much of what was written during the first two weeks of
July, 1857, was obviously untrue: that Pierce lived with

three mistresses in the same house, and was "a human dynamo"; that he had been behind the great check swindle of 1852; that he was the illegitimate son of Napoleon I; that Pierce took cocaine and laudanum; that he had previously been married to a German countess and had murdered her in 1848, in Hamburg. There is not the least evidence that any of these stories is correct, but it is certainly true that the press whipped public interest to the point of frenzy.

Even Victoria herself was not immune to the fascination with "this *most bold* and *dastardly* rogue, whom we *should like* to perceive at first hand." She also expressed a desire to see his hanging; she was apparently not aware that in 1857 grand theft was no longer a capital offense in England.

For weeks, crowds had been gathering around Coldbath Fields, on the unlikely chance of getting a look at the master thief. And Pierce's house in Mayfair was broken into on three occasions by avid souvenir hunters. One "wellborn woman"—there is no further description—was apprehended while leaving the house with a man's handkerchief. Showing not the slightest embarrassment, she said that she merely wished to have a token of the man.

The *Times* complained that this fascination with a criminal was "unseemly, even decadent," and went so far as to suggest that the behavior of the public reflected "some fatal flaw in the character of the English mind."

Thus, it is one of the odd coincidences of history that by the time Pierce began his testimony, on May 29th, the public and the press had turned their attention elsewhere. For, quite unexpectedly, England was facing a new trial of national proportions: a shocking and bloody uprising in India.

The growing British Empire—some called it the Brutish Empire—had suffered two major setbacks in recent decades. The first was in Kabul, Afghanistan, in 1842, where 16,500 British soldiers, women, and children died in six days. The second setback was the Crimean War, now concluded, with

demands for army reform. That sentiment was so strong that
Lord Cardigan, previously a national hero, was in disrepute;
he was even accused (unfairly) of not being present for the
charge of the Light Brigade, and his marriage to the notorious
equestrienne Adeline Horsey de Horsey had further tarnished
his standing.

Now the Indian Mutiny arose as a third affront to English
world supremacy, and another blow to English self-confi-
dence. That the English were confident in India is evident
from the fact that they had only 34,000 European troops in
that country, commanding a quarter of a million native soldiers, called sepoys, who were not excessively loyal to their
English leaders.

Since the 1840s, England had been increasingly high-
handed in India. The new evangelical fervor of righteousness
at home had led to ruthless religious reform abroad; thuggee
and suttee had been stamped out, and the Indians were not
altogether pleased to see foreigners changing their ancient religious patterns.

When the English introduced the new Enfield rifle in
1857, the cartridges for the rifle came from the factory liber-
ally coated with grease. It was necessary to bite the cartridges
to release the powder. Among the sepoy regiments there was
a rumor that the grease was made from pigs and cows, and
thus these cartridges were a trick to defile the sepoys and
make them break caste.

English authorities acted quickly.

In January, 1857, it was ordered that factory-greased cartridges were to be issued only to European troops; the sepoys
could grease their own with vegetable oil. This sensible edict
came too late to halt the bad feeling, however. By March, the
first English officers were shot by sepoys in sporadic incidents. And in May a genuine uprising broke out.

The most famous episode of the Indian Mutiny occurred
at Cawnpore, a town of 150,000 on the banks of the Ganges.
From a modern perspective, the siege of Cawnpore seems a

kind of crystallization of all that was noble and foolish about Victorian England. A thousand British citizens, including three hundred women and children, were under fire for eighteen days. Living conditions "violated all the decencies and proprieties of life, and shocked the modesty of . . . womanly nature." Yet in the early days of the siege, life went on with extraordinary normalness. Soldiers drank champagne and dined on tinned herring. Children played around the guns. Several babies were born, and a wedding took place, despite the constant rain of rifle and artillery fire, day and night.

Later, everyone was rationed to a single meal a day, and soon they were eating horsemeat, "though some ladies could not reconcile themselves to this unaccustomed fare." The women gave up their undergarments for wadding for the guns: "The gentlewomen of Cawnpore gave up perhaps the most cherished components of their feminine attire to improve the ordnance. . . ."

The situation became increasingly desperate. There was no water, except from a well outside the encampment; soldiers trying to get water were shot in the attempt. The daytime temperatures reached 138 degrees Fahrenheit. Several men died of sunstroke. A dry well inside the compound was used as a grave for corpses.

On June 12th, one of the two buildings caught fire and burned to the ground. All medical supplies were destroyed. Yet the English still held out, beating back every attack.

On June 25th, the sepoys called a truce, and offered the English safe passage by ship to Allahabad, a city a hundred miles downstream. The English accepted.

The evacuation began at dawn on June 27th. The English moved onto forty riverboats, under the watchful eye of armed sepoys all around them. As soon as the last Englishman was aboard the boats, the native boatmen jumped into the water. The sepoys opened fire on the ships, still tied up to the shore. Soon most of the boats were aflame, and the river was littered with corpses and drowning bodies. Indian cavalrymen splashed through the shallows, cutting down survivors with sabers. Every man was killed.

The women and children were taken to a mud building
along the shore and held there in suffocating heat for some
days. Then on July 15th, several men, including a number of
butchers by trade, entered the house with sabers and knives
and slaughtered everyone present. The dismembered bodies,
including "some not altogether lifeless," were dumped into a
nearby well, and were said to have filled it.

The English at home, expressing their "muscular Christianity," screamed for bloody revenge. Even the *Times*, swept
along in the fury of the moment, demanded that "every tree
and gable-end in the place should have its burden in the
shape of a mutineer's carcass." Lord Palmerston announced
that the Indian rebels had acted as "demons sallying forth
from the lowest depths of hell."

At such a moment, the appearance of a criminal before the
docket of Old Bailey, for a crime committed two years past,
was of very minor interest. But there were some reports on
the inside pages of the dailies, and they are fascinating for
what they reveal about Edward Pierce.

He was brought before the bar for the first time on July
29th: "handsome, charming, composed, elegant and roguish."
He gave his testimony in an even, utterly calm tone of voice,
but his statements were inflammatory enough. He referred to
Mr. Fowler as "a syphilitic fool" and Mr. Trent as "an
elderly nincompoop." These comments led the prosecutor to
inquire of Pierce's views on Mr. Harranby, the man who had
apprehended him. "A puffed-up dandy with the brains of a
schoolboy," Pierce announced, drawing a gasp from the
court, for Mr. Harranby was in the gallery as an observer.
Mr. Harranby was seen to color deeply, and the veins stood
out on his forehead.

Even more astounding than Mr. Pierce's words was his general demeanor, for "he carried himself extremely well, and proudly, and gave no hint of contrition, nor any trace of moral remorse for his black deeds." Quite the opposite, he seemed to demonstrate an enthusiasm for his own cleverness as he recounted the various steps in the plan.

"He appears," noted the *Evening Standard*, "to take a degree of delight in his actions which is wholly inexplicable."

This delight extended to a detailed accounting of the foibles of other witnesses, who were themselves most reluctant to testify. Mr. Trent was fumbling and nervous, and greatly embarrassed ("with ample reason," snapped one outraged observer) at what he had to report, while Mr. Fowler recounted his own experiences in a voice so low that the prosecutor was continually obliged to ask him to speak up.

There were a few shocks in Pierce's testimony. One was the following exchange, which occurred on the third day of his appearance in court:

"Mr. Pierce, are you acquainted with the cabby known as Barlow?"

"I am."

"Can you tell us his whereabouts?"

"I cannot."

"Can you tell us when you last saw him?"

"Yes, I can."

"Please be so good to do so."

"I saw him last six days ago, when he visited me at Coldbath Fields."

(Here there was a buzzing of voices within the court, and the judge rapped for order.)

"Mr. Pierce, why have you not brought forth this information earlier?"

"I was not asked."

"What was the substance of your conversation with this man Barlow?"

"We discussed my escape."

"Then I take it, you intend with the aid of this man to make your escape?"

"I should prefer that it be a surprise," Pierce said calmly.

The consternation of the court was great, and the newspapers were plainly outraged: "A graceless, unscrupulous, hideous fiend of a villain," said the *Evening Standard*. There were demands that he receive the most severe possible sentence.

But Pierce's calm manner never changed. He continued to be casually outrageous. On August 1, Pierce said in passing of Mr. Henry Fowler that "he is as big a fool as Mr. Brudenell."

The prosecutor did not let the comment go by. Quickly he said, "Do you mean Lord Cardigan?"

"I mean Mr. James Brudenell."

"That is, in fact, Lord Cardigan, is it not?"

"You may refer to him however you wish, but he is no more than Mr. Brudenell to me."

"You defame a peer and the Inspector-General of the Cavalry."

"One cannot," Pierce said, with his usual calmness, "defame a fool."

"Sir: you are accused of a heinous crime, may I remind you of that."

"I have killed no one," Pierce replied, "but had I killed five hundred Englishmen through my own rank stupidity I should be hanged immediately."

This exchange was not widely reported in the newspapers, out of fear that Lord Cardigan would sue for libel. But there was another factor: Pierce was, by his testimony, hammering at the foundations of a social structure already perceived as under attack from many fronts. In short order, the master criminal ceased to be fascinating to anyone.

And in any case, Pierce's trial could not compete with tales of wild-eyed "niggers," as they were called, charging into a room full of women and children, raping and killing the females, skewering the screaming infants, and "disporting in a spectacle of blood-curdling heathen atavism."

CHAPTER 52

The End

Pierce concluded his testimony on August 2nd. At that time, the prosecutor, aware that the public was perplexed by the master criminal's cool demeanor and absence of guilt, turned to a final line of inquiry.

"Mr. Pierce," said the prosecutor, rising to his full height, "Mr. Pierce, I put it to you directly: did you never feel, at any time, some sense of impropriety, some recognition of misconduct, some comprehension of unlawful behavings, some moral misgivings, in the performance of these various criminal acts?"

"I do not comprehend the question," Pierce said.

The prosecutor was reported to have laughed softly. "Yes, I suspect you do not; it is written all over you."

At this point, His Lordship cleared his throat and delivered the following speech from the bench:

"Sir," said the judge, "it is a recognized truth of jurisprudence that laws are created by men, and that civilized men, in a tradition of more than two millennia, agree to abide by these laws for the common good of society. For it is only by the rule of law that any civilization holds itself above the promiscuous squalor of barbarism. This we know from all the history of the human race, and this we pass on in our educational processes to all our citizens.

"Now, on the matter of motivation, sir, I ask you: why did you conceive, plan, and execute this dastardly and shocking crime?"

Pierce shrugged. "I wanted the money," he said.

Following Pierce's testimony, he was handcuffed and escorted from the courtroom by two stout guards, both armed. As Pierce left the court, he passed Mr. Harranby.

"Good day, Mr. Pierce," Mr. Harranby said.

"Goodbye," Pierce replied.

Pierce was taken out the back of Old Bailey to the waiting police van, which would drive him to Coldbath Fields. A sizable crowd had gathered on the steps of the court. The guards pushed away the crowd, which shouted greetings and expressions of luck to Pierce. One scabrous old whore, slipping forward, managed to kiss the culprit full on the mouth, if only for a moment, before the police pushed her aside.

It is presumed that this whore was actually the actress Miss Miriam, and that in kissing Pierce she passed him the key to the handcuffs, but that is not known for certain. What is known is that when the two van guards, coshed into insensibility, were later discovered in a gutter near Bow Street, they could not reconstruct the precise details of Pierce's escape. The only thing they agreed upon was the appearance of the cabby—a tough brute of a man, they said, with an ugly white scar across his forehead.

The police van was later recovered in a field in Hampstead. Neither Pierce nor the cabby was ever apprehended. Journalistic accounts of the escape are vague, and all mention that the authorities showed reluctance to discuss it at length.

In September the British recaptured Cawnpore. They took no prisoners, and burned, hanged, and disemboweled their

victims. When they found the blood-soaked house where the
women and children had been slaughtered, they made the
natives lick the red floor before hanging them. They went on,
sweeping through India in what was called "the Devil's Wind"
—marching as much as sixty miles a day, burning whole
villages and murdering every inhabitant, tying mutineers to
the muzzles of cannons and blowing them to bits. The Indian
Mutiny was crushed before the end of the year.

In August, 1857, Burgess, the railway guard, pleaded the
stresses of his son's illness, claiming that it had so warped his
moral inclinations that he fell in with criminals. He was sentenced to only two years in Marshalsea Prison, where he died
of cholera that winter.

The screwsman Robert Agar was sentenced to transporta-
tion to Australia for his part in The Great Train Robbery.
Agar died a wealthy man in Sydney, New South Wales,
Australia, in 1902. His grandson Henry L. Agar was the
Lord Mayor of Sydney from 1938 to 1941.

Mr. Harranby died in 1879 while flogging a horse, which
kicked him in the skull. His assistant, Sharp, became head of
the Yard and died a great-grandfather in 1919. He was
reported to have said he was proud that none of his children
was a policeman.

Mr. Trent died of a chest ailment in 1857; his daughter
Elizabeth married Sir Percival Harlow in 1858, and had four
children by him. Mr. Trent's wife behaved scandalously following her husband's demise; she died of pneumonia in 1884,
having enjoyed, she said, "more lovers than this Bernhardt
woman."

Henry Fowler died of "unknown causes" in 1858.

The South Eastern Railway, tired of the inadequate arrangements of London Bridge Station, built two new terminals for its line: the famous vaulted arch of Cannon
Street in 1862, and Blackfriars Station soon after.

Pierce, Barlow, and the mysterious Miss Miriam were never

heard from again. In 1862, it was reported that they were living in Paris. In 1868, they were said to be residing in "splendid circumstances" in New York. Neither report has ever been confirmed.

The money from The Great Train Robbery was never recovered.